The DAMNeD HigHWaY

FEAR AND LOATHING IN ARKHAM

The DAMNeD HigHWaY

FEAR AND LOATHING IN ARKHAM

A Savage Journey into the Heart
of the American Nightmare, and Back Again

By
UNCLE LONO
(with Nick Mamatas and Brian Keene)

MILWAUKIE

A part of this book was first published as the short story "And Then, And Then, And Then" in *Innsmouth Free Press*, 2009.

Cover Design by **Tina Alessi**
Cover Illlustration by **Ian Miller**
Book Design by **Krystal Hennes**

Nick Mamatas would like to thank Olivia Flint, and Peter Vroutos for showing him Hunter S. Thompson as a kid.

Brian Keene would like to thank his sons, Mary SanGiovanni, and Jack Shue for making him read Hunter S. Thompson as a teen.

Both authors would like to thank Rachel Edidin, Jemiah Jefferson, everyone else at Dark Horse, and the members of "The Collective."

Published by Dark Horse Books
A Division of Dark Horse Comics, Inc.
10956 SE Main St., Milwaukie, OR 97222
DarkHorse.com

Library of Congress Cataloging-in-Publication Data

Mamatas, Nick.
The damned highway : fear and loathing in Arkham : a savage journey into the heart of the American nightmare, and back again / by Uncle Lono, with Nick Mamatas and Brian Keene. -- 1st Dark Horse Books ed.
p. cm.
ISBN 978-1-59582-685-5
1. Journalists--United States--Fiction. 2. Writer's block--Fiction. 3. Bus travel--Fiction. I. Keene, Brian. II. Title.
PS3613.A525D36 2011
813'.6--dc22

2011007786

First Dark Horse Books Edition: July 2011

Printed at Transcontinental Gagné, Louiseville, QC, Canada
1 3 5 7 9 10 8 6 4 2

For our fathers, Panagiotis Mamatas and Lloyd Keene, both of whom are the backbone of the American Dream, whether they like it or not.

ONE

The Long, Cold Winter of My Discontent . . . Heavy Weather . . .
Strange Rumblings and General Weirdness . . . The Death of the American Dream . . .
The Birth of the American Nightmare . . . Bad Apple Daze . . . We've Gotta Get Out
of This Place, If It's the Last Thing We Ever Do . . .

Winter in Woody Creek, Colorado. It is just after midnight on January 5, 1972, and this is when the fun begins. They call this the wee hours, but there is nothing small about the hours between midnight and dawn. These hours last forever, each one as long and endless as the black gulf between the stars. As I pound the keys, the ticking of the clock syncs with the world's heartbeat, and the rapid-fire staccato of my typewriter slows. Each breath is an eternity. These are not wee hours; these hours are larger than life.

They also call this the witching hour, and who knows? Perhaps they are right. All that I know for sure is that this is when I do my best work, under the cover of darkness. This is when I am strongest—when the whiskey and the mescaline and the pills course through my body, and my mind burns with a terrible righteousness and sense of indignation. This is alchemy. This is magic. When the going gets weird, the weird turn pro, and I am certainly both. Ask anyone. They know. They'll tell you that I am both weird and a pro. I am a professional writer and my role is that of the background observer. I am a doctor of journalism, and there is nothing more professional than that. And the night? The night has never been weirder.

The world has turned dangerous and strange, like some severely deformed child who should have been put down at birth in an act of mercy, but instead has been allowed to live and suffer for far too long. There is something prowling around outside my front door, and though I have heard it many times tonight, I don't know what it is. It can't be the peacocks because I killed them earlier in a moment of blind rage and gripping paranoia, but there is something out there, lurking in the night. It might be a deer or a coyote or a big bastard of a bear, but then again, maybe not, because the darkness has a way of changing things. Darkness is mother nature's LSD, and instead of a wild animal, the thing on my doorstep could be a cop or a politician or even an editor. Worse, it could be a fan. I hate fans as much as I hate editors. They fill my heart with fear and loathing. But never mind that, eh? I am armed with a typewriter and many guns, and I have cigarettes and whiskey, and a wide assortment of pharmaceutical enhancements that the peacocks didn't eat, and with these, I can handle almost anything.

Outside, the snow is falling in large, ponderous drifts. In between Bob Dylan and the Rolling Stones, the radio tells me that we might have another twelve inches on the ground by morning, and I believe this to be true. Here in my fortified compound, both the snow and the fan mail are piling up. The pile of fan mail is deeper. I must face its terrible power alone, because the roads are closed and the plows won't come this far tonight. The phones and television are out, and my only companions are the radio and my typewriter and the mad, wretched thoughts in my poisoned head. With the holidays over, I've sent my wife and son back to Washington, DC. They left this morning on the first flight out of Denver while I stayed behind to take care of business. Writing is a cruel and savage way to earn a living, and even when it provides for your family, you question the cost. If you lose your family in the process of providing for them, is it worth it? Only a fool would think so, but we are a nation of fools these days.

My family does not like Washington, and I don't like it, either. Washington, DC, is a bizarre and frightening scene, man. But with the election coming, that dope-addled, pig-fucking magazine editor has had the audacity to make me head of the national-affairs desk, and set my family and me up in an apartment in the nation's capital. Given my new position, Washington is a necessary evil.

In truth, I'm glad that my family is gone, because the walls here at the compound have been breached, despite their fortifications, and this place is no longer safe. As I said, our sanctuary is inundated with the bleating sheep cries of a thousand fan letters. Each time I open an envelope, ignorance and madness spill forth and flutter around the room like deranged bats. All because of that goddamned Las Vegas book.

Now the radio is playing something by a new British band called Black Sabbath. The music has a dark, ugly vibe, and there is something lurking beneath the bass and drums like a tumor ready to burst, spilling poison upon the land. This ain't the Summer of Love, and we are not wearing flowers in our hair. Black Sabbath is a far cry from "Mr. Tambourine Man" and Woodstock, and I don't dig this kind of sound. It doesn't speak to me, and there is nothing in it that I recognize, but that's okay, because I don't recognize anyone anymore, especially myself. I am constantly surrounded by strangers who call themselves my friends. Ho ho ho! Maybe they are. But with friends like these, who needs fucking enemies, right? Everywhere I go, I draw a crowd of raving, ravenous beasts—a pack of wild hyenas, all slavering for a piece of me. They call me a cult hero and a prophet and a spokesman for our generation. They say that I am violent and paranoid and weird, an ex–Hells Angel turned celebrated journalist and writer. They say that my influence is recognized by all politicians and celebrities, and that my work is marked by a glorification of life's dark side, including drugs and heavy personal risk. And who knows? Maybe this is true, but if I am the embodiment of the dark side of life, then why is it that I take no enjoyment from this Black Sabbath?

Is this how England will reclaim our little breakaway republic—by foisting Black Sabbath upon us? Some call the sound they make heavy metal, and perhaps that is appropriate. In any case, it's heavy music for some heavy weather.

But never mind all that, eh? I don't give a hoot in hell what people think or say about me. What do they know, anyway? The majority of Americans are stupid, bleating sheep. They always seem surprised when they learn that I have a wife and a child and a mother, as if I were some demonic, whiskey-swilling hell spawn sprung whole from the earth and incapable of loving something or nurturing it. When I get invited to speak at universities, I am never sure who it is that they expect to show up. Quite often, they act disappointed when they get me, rather than my alter ego from the Vegas book. And now we come to the nut of it, because Vegas was where it all changed. Las Vegas was the start of the great downward spiral. I first felt the fear and loathing in Chicago at the Democratic National Convention back in 1968, when the entire scene descended into violence and madness, spurred on not by the freaks or the media, but by the powers that be. I felt the fear and loathing there, but it took root after Vegas. I am afraid of the future.

Nixon is on the radio now, following that evil music, and the irony is bright and shiny and clear. His voice makes me want to cut my skin off with a broken beer bottle. There is something incredibly insectile about it, almost as if he weren't human. And who knows? Maybe he isn't. Maybe Nixon is just the brown stain left behind on Satan's mattress. It wouldn't surprise me, because Richard Milhous Nixon is an ignorant brute who represents nothing but the dark side of the American Dream. He is a big, dumb, repugnant beast who exudes greed, treachery, and contempt for our system from his diseased, swollen pores, and every breath he takes forms the basis for another poisonous lie. If he were a dog we'd have put him down by now for the safety of the community, shot him in the head and burned the flea-ridden corpse.

Did I say Nixon represented the dark side of the American Dream? Forget that; it was the whiskey talking. Forgive me. The drugs have kicked in and I know not what I type. Richard Nixon doesn't represent the dark side of the American Dream. Richard Nixon represents the American Nightmare. The American Dream is dead. I know this because I proved it was dead two years ago when I ran for sheriff of Aspen on the Freak Power ticket. There is no American Dream anymore—no guiding principle for generations of our countrymen. In the end, the American Dream was left raped and bleeding and lying face down in an alley, drowning in its own vomit and urine. That was how it ended, but the American Dream didn't die overnight. No, its death was slow and insidious, like a long, painful bout of intestinal cancer that starts out as just a little flatulence and terminates with you vomiting out your own bloody intestines through your mouth. There were a number of symptoms, but we didn't spot them in time. The downfall of our last, true American hero, Muhammad Ali, mixed with the treacherous doings in our nation's capital and the vacation paradise that is Vietnam and the savage anarchy of the Hells Angels and the riots and the sick depravity manifested in Las Vegas. All of this and more contributed to the death of the American Dream and gave birth to the American Nightmare.

The American Dream's headstone is a burned-out slab of concrete in Las Vegas. And yes, the corpse beneath is restive; under the flashing neon lights of its own grave it twitches and rolls and shimmies on prime-time television covered in Day-Glo body-paint catch phrases that were once revolutionary slogans but that now sell soap and mugwump Republicanism. Sock it to whom?

I am reminded of what a wise and powerful sage—myself—wrote not so long ago, of how the sixties were a wonderful time, when the energy of an entire generation came to a head and we were all riding the crest of a high and beautiful wave. The time was ripe for change, but in the end, like all ripe fruits, things spoiled on the vine and turned rotten. These are the bad-apple days, even though it's less than five years since that magical moment in time. Go up on a hill in Las Vegas in the afternoon when the sun boils in the sky like a great, bloated pimple, and look west, and you can see the high-water mark in the distance, that place where the wave finally broke and rolled back, revealing a horrible, tentacle-faced monstrosity called Richard M. Nixon. It's enough to drive anyone insane, unless they have access to good drugs. Maybe God, if such a thing exists, was merciful when He gave us the inability to sort all this conflicting shit out in our collective brains, because one thing is for sure—the good times are over. There will be no chickens in your pot this Christmas because the time of the Great Confusion is coming. This is the end, beautiful friends, the end. Rape and murder shall be the law of the land, and dogs will lie down with cats, and people will copulate in the streets like rabid, frenzied rabbits. The gutters shall run with blood, and mothers will kill their own children because it's what they've been told to do. Like lemmings, we shall flee into the false peace and safety of a new dark age. The stars are right and the Age of Aquarius is over. This is the age of R'lyeh.

What's that word? R'lyeh? Where the hell did that come from, and what does it mean? Never mind; it doesn't matter. Just a typo, induced by the drugs or the whiskey or good old-fashioned fatigue.

That thing is still out there, prowling through the snow and scratching at the windowpanes. I would go confront it, but I can't stand. Indeed, only my fingers seem to work, and I am afraid that if I stop typing, they will freeze up, too.

I am tired, and I need to get out of here and be free again. The fan mail is getting higher, and if I fall asleep, I could drown in it. The weasels are closing in with their beady red eyes and their sharp little teeth, and they prevent me from doing my job. I used to be able to stand in the back of the room and observe, but because of the Vegas book, I can't do that anymore. When I cover a press conference, I get asked more questions than the politicians. When I interview a celebrity, I sign more autographs than they do. A BBC film crew wants to shoot a documentary about me and stick a camera in my face and have me perform like a trained monkey. And then there's that fucking comic strip. That thing is published all over the world. My myth has taken over my reality, and with each passing day and each new word that I write, it's becoming more and more warped. I need to escape, but where would I go? I could hide in hotel rooms for the rest of my life, but what kind of existence is that? I've pushed my luck about as far as I can, and I'm operating on vapor trails and residue. How long, oh Lord, how long? I wish I could die soon. The doctors have given me six months to live, but they do that about every two years, so they are of absolutely no help.

I want to reinvent myself again—start over fresh in a place where nobody knows me. A place where my books aren't in print and the newspapers don't carry that comic strip. I want to rediscover myself and find new truths under the rocks. The last time I did that, I went in search of the American Dream. It occurs to me that maybe I should search for its counterpart, the American Nightmare. After all, this country is in a grim slide, and I see little hope for it to reverse course. Perhaps I should examine the cause. Obviously, Nixon is a part of that, but there must be more. I need to explore it. Find the nut of the thing. Feel it deep down in my journalistic testicles. But where would I go? I could go west, I suppose. Steal a car and drive through the vast, perilous wastelands of Los Angeles and Las Vegas and Henderson and San Francisco, but I've already taken that trip and it's not one that I wish to repeat any time soon. So I can't go west, young man, and I can't go to Washington, either. I can't face that crowd. Not now. Not in my current condition. There will be no peace in Washington, no chance at self-discovery. In Washington, the fans are everywhere and I am always in a crowd, even when I'm alone.

When I went in search of the American Dream, the only way to prepare for the trip was to get crazy with my attorney, screeching off across the desert in search of the story and running amok until we'd found it. But not this time. Fame and the smothering, claustrophobic power of my own legend will prevent me from doing that. No, for this journey, I must be clever and careful and cautious. This time, I have to go undercover, under the radar, slip beneath the wires, a shadow of a shadow. I must be like a ninja. And I have to go alone, too, with no assistant or attorney to aid me in my quest. That fat brown bastard is still pissed at me for what I said in the Vegas book, anyway. So no attorney, and no artist, either. That greedy Welshman will want money, and besides, this search would only frustrate him and quite possibly drive him mad. As decadent and depraved as the Kentucky Derby is, it is just a wet dream in comparison to what I expect to find this time, and I don't think he could handle it. He is a gentle soul, and this is a job for dark men.

So that's it. Never mind the snow or the roads or the thing lurking outside. I leave tonight, under the cover of darkness, alone and traveling light, armed only with my wits, my tape recorder, batteries, Moleskine notebook, pens, pencils, a gun, extra ammunition, a canister of mace, my Mojo Wire, two ripe grapefruit, some cocaine and marijuana, three tabs of blotter acid with colorful Jack Kirby characters emblazoned on them, four packs of cigarettes, a cigarette filter, and two pints of bourbon, all of which can fit into my brown leather kit bag. But that still leaves me with the problem of where to go and how to get there. A final destination is important, but the journey there is just as vital. The radio says the airport is shut down now because the runways are snowed in. That damned car out in the driveway won't make it very far—a few hundred miles at best. No planes and no automobiles. My only other option is the Greyhound station, so that's where I'll start. I'll buy a one-way ticket and take the ride, as long as the ride isn't to Los Angeles or New York or Washington or especially goddamned Vegas, because those are all places that I want to forget. They are a part of the old me, and I must forge a new me in someplace different. I can't use any of my pseudonyms, either. They are as well known now as I am. They have become a part of my legend. I will have to become somebody new. I must be born again. And there it is. Now, at last, we're getting close to the nut of the thing.

I have trouble zipping up my kit bag, bulging with my armament as it is. The bag is a heavy load but doesn't compare to the weight of my own mythos crushing down on me. I'm in a hurry now, and the walls seem to be closing in. They groan and quiver like old men, and I am not entirely certain that this is alcohol or drug induced.

I trip over the fan mail on my way out the door and suffer a thousand little paper cuts. The bastards have drawn blood, but I'll show them. I'm going to kill this life and start another. The name comes to me from out of nowhere, but I like the sound of it and decide to make it mine.

This time, I shall become Uncle Lono.

TWO

Uncle Lono Buys the Ticket and Takes the Ride . . . Road Dog for the Gods of Bad Karma . . .
I Read the News Today, Oh Boy . . . The Revenge of Jack Kirby . . .
A Shoggoth in Every Pot

I reach the bus terminal just before dawn, and after a long and harrowing drive down treacherous, snow-covered mountain roads, where each blind curve illuminated in my lone, functioning headlight promised death and dismemberment and the possibility of flaming wreckage, I am in no mood for nonsense. My eyes are watering from hours of desperate, snow-blind squinting, and it will be a wonder if I ever type again because my fingers carry the indentation of the goddamned steering wheel and are curved into crablike claws. I am tense and tired and have lost most of my high, and a terrible anger simmers beneath the surface of my skin, bubbling and percolating, desperate to come out, eager for release. When the parking-lot attendant tells me that it will cost me fifty cents a day to park my car, I stub my cigarette out in his whiskered face and tell him he can keep the junk heap, because I am abandoning it. Shrieking, he paws at his smoldering cheek, and I tell him that I accept his gratitude and thanks. Then I grab my kit bag and flee for the station before he can give chase.

"I know you," he screams. "I know who the fuck you are, you monster! You're that guy who writes for—"

"No," I shout, not bothering to turn around. "You do not know me. You have no idea who this is. I am something different, and none of you have met me before. I am a new kind of monster."

I run across the parking lot, and his cries echo behind me like those of a tortured, mewling kitten. The sound brings me joy, and I laugh. It feels good. Reborn and recharged, I have never been more dangerous than I am right now. I am Uncle Lono. You should run.

Inside, the bus station is almost deserted, populated only by winos and junkies and whores, and a sloe-eyed ticket agent behind the counter who stares at me as if I've just stepped out of a flying saucer. She has a wad of pink gum in her wide, gaping mouth, and she snaps it while she studies me. The noise fills my heart with hate, and I fear that I will soon grow violent if it doesn't cease. The bus station feels wrong. The overhead lights are too bright, and one of the bulbs flickers like a strobe. Flies buzz around it, worshiping this strange new fluorescent god. I quickly scan the big board, searching for a destination. Beneath the board is a map of the United States with a network of route lines drawn across it like sprawling tentacles. I could go to Wichita, Kansas, or Lincoln, Nebraska, or Sioux Falls, South Dakota, but all of those are still too close to Las Vegas, and I need to escape that dark proximity. I need someplace else. The drone of the flies grows louder. The air is hot and cloying. I study the map and the tentacle lines blur, congealing into a massive spider web. The woman behind the counter snaps her gum at me again, and I grind my teeth and try not to moan. Joni Mitchell sings on someone's radio, but her voice sounds strange.

I blink, and when I look at the map again, one destination stands out from the others—Arkham, Massachusetts. It appears that the bus will be traveling Interstate 70, because to get to Arkham, we will have to pass through the diseased, blackened heart of this country, where the dregs of society live and breed and elect people who send their children overseas to die in a foreign jungle for something the French should have handled long ago. It occurs to me for a moment that Vietnam has been causing all kinds of trouble for a while now, and perhaps I should go and see it for myself, but not now. That is a trip for another day and another me. Uncle Lono seeks the American Nightmare. I turn back to the map again. The route goes through Salina, Topeka, Kansas City, St. Louis, Terre Haute, Indianapolis, Dayton, Columbus, Wheeling, and Pittsburgh. Then we jump up to Interstate 90 toward Erie and Buffalo, and pass through Rochester, Syracuse, and Albany before finally arriving in Arkham. It is a bizarre, insane trip, like going from Philadelphia to Seattle by way of the moon and Mars, but I have taken bizarre, insane trips before. You buy the ticket, you take the ride, and if that ride is atop a hunk of lead fired from the barrel of a snub-nosed .38 and plowing straight into the heart of darkness, then you hold on tight and keep grinning, even as the bugs splatter against your teeth. Ho ho.

I approach the counter and smile, and the ticket agent stops popping her gum. There is a brief, crystalline moment of silence, and then other sounds seep through the terminal. Creedence Clearwater Revival plays softly over the PA system, and I pause to wonder where Joni Mitchell has gone. A toilet flushes in a nearby restroom, and a sleeping drunk snores incessantly. The ticket agent seems uneasy, perhaps frightened by the look in my eyes or the smile on my face. Her bottom lip quivers and she tugs at her earlobe. Enjoying the effect I'm having on her, I request a one-way ticket to Arkham. I pay cash, and she takes the bills cautiously, her expression suggesting that perhaps I've wiped my ass with them or sprayed the money with LSD. It is a good idea, and I make a mental note to try it later.

The woman is polite and laconic, but when I ask her for a receipt, I can sense her annoyance and disdain. In her eyes, I represent everything that is wrong with this country, and what she doesn't understand is that I see the same in her. I represent Freak Power, and she represents Sheep People. We are two sides of the same coin, mirror images in alternate realities, symptoms of the same disease. Still smiling, I thank her, expressing my sincere desire that God bless her, and then I suppress my laughter when she flinches. I stuff the receipt into my bag, knowing full well that my whore-hopping editor will decline reimbursement when I try to apply it to the magazine's expense account later on, but old habits die hard, and fuck him, anyway. Then I duck into the restroom, eat one of the tabs of Jack Kirby acid, and feel the alkaline linger on my tongue. It is like licking a battery, and not at all unpleasant. In fact, I relish the taste. I splash cold water on my face and walk back out into the terminal, where I take a seat next to a vagrant and wait for the trip to begin.

The derelict smells like the inside of a gorilla's stomach, and his skin has the sickly complexion of a hunk of Provolone cheese left out in the sun for too long. Gray stubble lines his cracked, ruddy cheeks and a multicolored collection of tattered rags masquerading as clothing hang from his skeletal frame. A worn valise sits on the floor between his feet and a folded newspaper lies in his lap.

"Taking a trip?" He smiles. Someone has stolen this poor soul's teeth.

"Something like that." I point at his newspaper. "Care if I take a peek? I'm a bit of a news junkie."

"Go ahead. I know what's gonna happen, anyway. It's not news to me."

Frowning, I flip the paper open and scan the headlines. The big story is the Irish Republican Army's continuing campaign of terror in Ulster. Here we are, five days into the new year, and there is already speculation that 1972's outrages will eclipse all others. Nineteen seventy-one saw the murder of Ulster Defence Regiment members in their homes, the assassination of a senator from Stormont, and over six thousand other terrorist incidents, including two hundred attacks on police stations, a thousand bombings, and the deaths of hundreds of civilians, including children.

"Ye Gods," I mutter. "Happy New Year."

"Reading about the Troubles?"

Nodding, I hand him the newspaper and reach for my cigarettes, wishing the acid would kick in. Where is Jack Kirby when we need him the most?

"It'll get worse," the vagrant says. "You just wait. The last Sunday of this month will be very bloody. There have been signs and portents."

I flick my lighter open and touch flame to cigarette. Then I inhale, snap the lighter shut, and blow smoke in my new companion's face. He frowns as I poke him in the chest.

"What are you jabbering about?"

The vagrant squirms, clearly agitated. "The Troubles. The end of this month, there's gonna be a massacre in Derry. The Brits will gun down twenty-six protesters. Cold-blooded fucking murder. They shoot 'em in the back. Run 'em down with tanks and trucks. Like I said, it's gonna be bloody. It needs to be. That's what he wants."

"What *who* wants? Stop raving like a lunatic and speak English, man! Obviously, you can read, so I must assume that you're literate. Learn how to string a goddamned sentence together and communicate clearly."

"I am. It's you who ain't listening, writer guy. Oh yeah, that's right. I know who you are, and I ain't impressed. You need to pay attention to what's coming. You need to get in touch with some starry wisdom, man. You dig? Starry fucking wisdom. Look. It ain't dead if it's only sleeping, and if you wait long enough, even death can bite the big one."

I dismiss his ramblings with a wave of my hand. "Wonderful. I'm trapped in this terrible place with a madman and a Nixon supporter who chews her gum too loud. This must be what hell is like."

"No," the bum says. "Hell ain't like this at all. I know, man. I've seen it. And I don't want to go back there again. Hell is cold and full of fungi."

"Well, of course it is. All the fun guys go to hell when they die."

He squints at me, eyebrows furrowing beneath the dirt and grime caking his face, and when he responds, his voice is barely a whisper. "And people think *I'm* crazy."

I take another drag off my cigarette and glance at my watch, wondering how long I have until the bus arrives, when—holy Jesus—the acid kicks in. I know this because a long, pale tentacle with a tapered, pink tip slithers out of the bum's valise and creeps toward me. The tendril is almost translucent, and veins throb beneath the doughy flesh.

"Holy Jesus . . ."

The vagrant grins with his horrible mouth. "Isn't it beautiful?"

"Isn't what beautiful? This bus station? No, it smells like a urinal and there are flies everywhere."

"Not this place. My pet. Isn't it beautiful? It's a Shoggoth."

"A what? You're rambling again."

"When he comes back, everyone will have their own Shoggoth."

"Sort of like a chicken in every pot and two cars in every garage?"

The vagrant appears confused. "What's that?"

"That was the American Dream."

"I don't know about that. I don't dream much. But *he* dreams. Deep beneath the ocean, *he dreams.*"

The bum leans over and strokes the tentacle. I drop my cigarette on the floor and stub it out beneath my heel. Then I lean back and close my eyes and wait for the bus to come. It occurs to me to ask the vagrant how it's possible that he sees the pink tentacle, too. This is my trip, after all. Jack Kirby kicked me in the head, *not* him. If the vagrant wants to trip, then let him buy his own acid, the swine. But my tongue is too thick to say these things, and then the tentacle is gently caressing my ankle. I should be repulsed or frightened, but I'm not. In truth, the sensation is nice. The tentacle's flesh is warm and smooth, and not at all slimy. Its touch makes me think of a woman I once knew in Puerto Rico. She touched me in just the same way. I still miss her sometimes.

The first time I tripped on acid was back when I was writing the Hells Angels book. Ken Kesey was having a big party at his place in La Honda. He was desperate to meet some of the Angels, so he reached out to me and invited us all down for the weekend. About fifty of us came rolling in on our bikes, and the Angels began to mingle with Kesey's friends. Then he offered them acid, and I decided I'd better join in, if only to bear witness to the bizarre scene to come. The bikers were already loaded on cheap wine and bennies when we arrived, and now they had LSD in their systems. I expected a weekend of great and terrible violence and bloodshed, but other than the gangbang, the entire experience was actually peaceful and nice, much like the current trip with the friendly tentacle.

"My friend likes you," the derelict informs me.

"That's good. I like your friend, too."

We stay like that until the bus arrives.

THREE

Aluminum Shit Tubes Four Hundred Miles Long . . . The Bilious Man-Boobery of Dogbane
Fiends . . . Twenty-Ounce Margaritas Lined with the Blood of the Industrial Proletariat . . .
Pardon Me, Waiter, but There Is a Three-Lobed Burning Eye in My Starfish . . .
The Power of Names and Cuff Links . . . The Ibogaine Effect Redux

I haven't actually spent much time on buses. In Colorado, there are very few, of course. Mass transit is like the varicose veins of the aging East, tortuous and dilated, pushing oxygen-starved ham and eggers to the outskirts in the evenings, only to suck them back into the diseased heart of the city at dawn. Out West, the wanderer is king. Whether it's the Great White Freaks in their jam-packed Falcons or VW microbuses getting off on the thin air of Colorado, or fourteen-year-old farm girls who were born with stick shifts in one hand, everyone drives everywhere.

In the cities of the East, I'd learned the easy way that buses were for the Bad Craziness. They're the worst of both worlds to begin with—you're stuck in a tube full of lunatics, just like the subway, and also stuck in traffic at the same time, just like a taxicab. One time in New York City, when I was rushing uptown to the *New York Times*, I made the near-fatal error of taking the bus instead of just hailing a cab and expensing it. Walking would have been better. She sat down next to me, a girl who looked like she had come right off another bus, a Greyhound perhaps, hailing from some dying New England mill town. She was blond, with hair so light that it was nearly colorless, and thin like a tree in autumn.

She didn't return my smile, but instead looked down at her hands and played with her fingernails. When the bus lurched into the streets, it started.

"I'll fuck for horse," she said.

"What?"

"I'll fuck for horse," she said, this time a little louder, but she wasn't talking to me. She was talking to anyone who'd listen.

"Get a grip on yourself," I told her, but I don't think she understood me. I am afflicted with a Southern accent, and some people say I'm given to mumbling. The girl stared at me for a moment and then turned away.

A little louder came the third time: "I'll fuck for horse."

I thought about rummaging through my leather kit bag and pulling out my tape recorder, but I had a head full of acid then, too, though not the quality of Jack Kirby, and my fingers felt like tiny sausages.

"I'll *fuck* for *horse*."

By the time we were three blocks uptown, everyone in the bus could hear her, though many of her fellow commuting citizens tried not to. "I. Will. FUCK. For. HORSE." Her affect never changed; she could have been reading from a phone book, but she cranked up the volume with every iteration, stating a fact as plain and obvious as the times of the tides, or the black, ichor-drenched heart of President Nixon. This girl, this sweet young thing who was probably not even three years removed from Girl Scouts and 4-H ribbons and maybe a summer job at the movie house—a theater that would never even show a restricted film—was ready to spread for anyone who could bring her some heroin. Not only that, she had obviously already burned through every connection she had, the phalanxes of eager would-be boyfriends and pimps who'd make sure she'd get fucked for horse three times a day, and fucked for pay seven additional times just to keep their own lights on and their own drug supplies flowing, had been chased out of the wretched alleyways of the Lower East Side and the needle-rich parks of Greenwich Village and found herself on a city bus, offering to fornicate with any of the elderly ladies who might just happen to have some black tar nestled in with their Entenmann's crumb cake and Hotel Bar unsalted butter.

Heroin is a useless drug, and I don't endorse it. I don't endorse any drugs, actually, though there are many who say I do. That's one of the problems with being me. People read magazine articles about me, and they believe them. Half the things attributed to me are things I never actually said—or don't remember saying. And when it comes to drugs, all I've said is that they have always worked for me. But horse is not my bag.

By the time the bus pulled up at Union Square, the girl had found a taker. She didn't make eye contact with me when she stood up to allow his big canned ham of a hand to clamp down on her shoulder and lead her off the bus, but he did. He wasn't a young guy, but instead looked like pretty much any regional assistant manager of a savings and loan might. He could have been a Rotarian, or an Odd Fellow, or one of the Knights of Columbus, or the guy who has a dolly in his garage just in case someone on the block needs help installing their new combination washer-dryer. His eyes glittered, and he smiled a tight little smile over his teeth. If I'd had my .44 magnum—I left it in the hotel safe, along with some loose bills, half a gram of cocaine, and a Moleskine—I would have put him out of my misery right then and there.

But never mind that, eh? Now here I am again on a Greyhound bus, the sort of bus young girls take to reinvent themselves as junk-addled whores in Manhattan or Los Angeles. And I am going the wrong way—into the wilds of the New England hills, instead of screaming away from them. But that is where the trip's taking me in this search for the American Nightmare. It's enough to almost make me long for the bum I met at the terminal back in Denver, if only so I'd have some conversation. There are few people on the bus: a driver who looks like he ate his own weight in pancakes this morning, a Hispanic girl hugging herself and staring out into the faux star field of the parking lot and its flickering lamps, a skinny little guy with his hair slicked back with pomade and a flannel shirt, the sleeves rolled up to his elbows, and a few random and shadowy shapes sitting in that extended last row by the chemical-smelling lavatory.

It occurs to me that we all have something in common, my fellow passengers and I. This is 1972. There is the youth vote now, thanks to the lowering of the voting age to eighteen, and the black vote, all the more important now that the hoses have been turned off and the police dogs corked fang by fang, and then there are the rest of us—the freak vote. Seventy-two promises to be a tight election, and the candidates are more or less identical—for all the blood on his hands, Richard Nixon isn't all that different than Gene McCarthy or Ted Kennedy. All of them are swine, and if you believe differently, then you're just a natural fool. Maybe 20 percent is the typical standard variation amongst mainstream politicians in bloodlust, in savvy, in the extent to which they hie to George Meany instead of General Motors. Enough to build a ziggurat of bodies from dead gooks, instead of a taller pyramid on which to plant their four-year throne and Five-Year Plans. When elections are tight, every vote counts, even the votes that end up chained shut in a ballot box drifting sullenly to the bottom of Lake Michigan.

Or on a bus driving down the ribbon of highway grown frayed and stained from soot and an industrial century of wind and fire. You get used to it quickly, taking the bus, if you've never had the chance to experience Automotive Consciousness. In the car, the world is a Panavision film splayed out ten inches from your nose. You control the vertical; you control the horizontal. The earth itself rumbles under your feet, and you eat up the miles so long as OPEC keeps the IV drip of black-tar gold running. To be without a motor vehicle at this late date means to be less than American, less than human. On the Greyhound, you're no more human than the bags in the undercarriage. Freight, humble and meek and smelling like last week's sweat. Greyhound never picks up enough speed for me; in my mind's eye I can see herds of the sleek gray whippets in V formations on either side of the bus, pacing it and then tearing ahead, howling deep into the night. Instead, we putter along from Podunk to Buttfunk, regurgitating passengers by the Dunkin' Donuts, by the gas station. Sometimes in front of the bus station, when the burg has sufficient tax base to rate two vending machines, a ladies' toilet (the men's are always broken), and a dirty pay phone.

All the towns we've passed are Potemkin villages of the worst sort. At least the clapboard and façades in Russia were designed to follow that great ruler and equestrienne, Catherine the Great. The church steeples and quaint little main streets, the burger joints and roller rinks, the satanic mills positioned right over brown rivers—they exist to fool the inhabitants. "Hootie hoo, you are too real Americans! There is your church; there is your steeple. Step out of line and we'll kill all the people!" And they vote for it. Every four years, the stupid sheep vote for it. And every fourteen miles the bus wheezes like a dying elephant and spills us out into one of them.

When the bus lurches to a stop again, I'm in St. Louis, Missouri, and I wonder how that happened. At the pace this bus has been moving, we should still be somewhere in Colorado. What happened to Salina, Topeka, and Kansas City? Have I slept through most of the trip, or have I had a bad reaction to the drugs? Could this be Jack Kirby's fault? A quick glance at my Moleskine notebook confirms that I've been jotting down observations, and although much of it is gibberish, I divine enough to know that we did indeed stop in those cities. Apparently, at one point, I wrote, "Kansas City is made of meat," with no further frame of reference as to what that might mean. Why did I do this? I don't know. People are very strange. I check my kit bag and notice that both of my grapefruits are gone, as are both of my pints of bourbon. These facts seem to confirm that I have indeed been on the bus a while.

I need a drink, and there's a bar in a strip mall across the four-lane highway from the concrete slab they call the local bus depot. There's little traffic, so it's easy enough to pick my way across the first two lanes of the four laner and hop the crash barrier. The second two lanes are a Kafkaesque nightmare of squealing pig greed. Nobody stops. Instead, they speed up. A pickup truck veers right and sends up a wave of blackish mud and slush. From inside the truck, I hear Merle Haggard singing the praises of being from Muskogee. A woman screams from the passenger's side of an ass-beaten sedan, "You're poor!" and waves a fist from the end of an arm that looks more like a canned ham than a limb. I raise my fist and extend my middle finger in that time-honored salute. Finally, I just dive into the middle of the street, hands up and whirling, shouting, "Ho, ho! Man needs a drink here! Lemme pass, you swine!" and the night is filled with burning brake pads and honking horns and cries of bewildered rage. The sound is like a symphony, and it fills my heart with joy.

I don't catch the bar's name. Back where I'm from, that means it is either a place for fairies or criminals (or both; nobody is angrier and more efficient than a homosexual Mafia assassin, and I have known a few). Here, it means something else. There's no pool table, no jukebox, no pictures on the wall, and no dartboard. Instead, there is just a long black bar that looks like it's grown out from the Earth Herself, like a wave of obsidian that erupted from the asphalt of the strip mall and then at its apex just stopped. Elbow height. The place is near deserted as well, at least up front. I don't even catch the bartender at first; then I see her—a wide-eyed midget of a woman, an hourglass of a gal squashed flat except for a tower of bangs and high hair.

"Bourbon," she says and is already pouring one.

"That's a good call," I say. "Old Crow, even."

"It's a gift," she says. "That I can tell a man's predilection for this or that liquor, that is. The beverage itself, that'll be two dollars, friend." Her voice isn't as Minnie Mousie high as I would have guessed it would be. It's deep, like her diaphragm is naturally low to the ground and thus her timbre is as well. I put down a fin, and she knows that I want another. She smiles. So do I.

"Good girl," I say when the second glass appears. I glance down at it and feel a rush of wind on my forehead. I look up to a machete, a real Haitian baby splitter. It's a serious blade meant for serious business. The bartender is holding it with two hands, like someone might on the cover of one of those Robert E. Howard novels you can buy at the drugstore. Her face is twisted with hate.

"What did you call me, you goddamned son-of-a-bitch pedophile?" Pedophile comes out slow and deep, like tar spread along the road. I take a sip of my second Old Crow, even though I want to slam it back, hit the lip against the bar, and then grind it in her face. I want to do this so badly that for a moment I think I actually have. Maybe it's the remnants of the blotter acid or maybe it's just wish fulfillment. But I don't, because she's a lady. I can see it in her cheeks and eyes. Only ladies get that angry, only women who have not since the cradle let a man get the better of them can even generate that sort of simmering supernova of ape rage, without a hair out of place, without lips bared.

"Sorry, ma'am," I say, keeping my voice steady. "I was just overcome by the quality of service here." The blade quivers like it's going to drop. "You see, I've been on a bus for two days. At least, I think it's been two days. I'm not really sure, because things have gotten weird lately, including time. Strangeness happens to me a lot. But never mind that. I'm a reporter. A journalist. I need my medicine or else I start spouting all sorts of bizarre nonsense. Copyeditors hate me. So does everybody else. The ombudsman has a red phone on his desk just for me. When I do freelance writing work, I have to file my stories in pencil so that the editor can erase every fourth word before the gi—women in the typing pool get to it. They'd all quit or be rendered infertile and insane otherwise. So you've got to believe me, ma'am, when I tell you that I am so terribly, terribly sorry. And I am certainly no girl lover or boy lover, ma'am. In fact, just the other day I helped corner one of those rampaging mongoloids for the police. That was back home, back in Colorado. My dogs could smell the lustful desperation on him, and so could I. We can't have that nonsense infecting where we live, now can we? We must take care of our own backyards. The police thanked me, but it was the least I could do. We found him outside the soda shop, rubbing his hands and listening to sinister Negro music on a transistor radio. God only knows what he would have done had we let him live. Selah."

I take another sip and let the Old Crow burn my wisdom teeth. The woman blinks. The machete lowers and vanishes behind her back.

"Reporter, eh?"

"Yes'm." That knife can come out again in a flash. My cranium has never felt so much like a melon in my life. "I don't enjoy it. I'm not one of *those* types. I write when I must. It's a wretched profession, but someone has to do it, and I haven't had another job in quite a long time. But believe me when I tell you that you pay weird dues for earning a living this way."

"So, if you're a reporter, then you must be here for the meeting in the back."

"The meeting," I say with a nod. Now I slam down my glass. "In the back. Yes. That's right. I just needed some medicine. It primes my muse, you see."

The lights flicker.

"You'd better head on back," she says, her eyes glancing toward the ceiling. "It's starting."

She pours me two doubles, and I accept them both. The glasses are damp and cold in my palms. Double fisting the drinks, I get up and head toward the back room. It's a dark bar, all right. Even if there were any light coming from outside, it wouldn't reach here. The lights above are dim and yellow, as if the darkness were an active thing, blanketing and smothering the glow of the filaments. In this place, light is the enemy. It is as unwanted and undesired as a Black Panther member at the local VFW meeting. There are no dartboards, no promotional mirrors for Budweiser, no pinups. There is nothing. Nothing but the dark and an eye floater or two worth of lights, and the smell of rancid beer and dead cigarettes. The back door is thick, made of the same obsidian-type substance as the bar itself, and there's no handle, but it looks like it has a decent swing to it even though I can't make out any hinges. I back into the door and push it open with my posterior, and turn to face the meeting, Old Crow to my lips so I can have a few seconds to spare before having to talk myself the rest of the way in.

And then—ho ho—I swear to sweet baby Jesus almighty that it's Senator Eagleton, spread-eagle on across the slab, wrists and ankles cuffed tight to the corners. Electrodes cover his face and chest, the wires reaching up into a jury-rigged light fixture. He can't see me, obviously, but I can see him, and what I see fills me with loathing. Understand, I've seen a lot of bad craziness in my time. When I was riding with the Hells Angels, I witnessed a gangbang take place at a Merry Pranksters party. I caught the whole thing on my tape recorder and wrote about it later on in my book. Then I lent the tapes to Tom Wolfe and he wrote about it, as well. That particular depraved scene stuck with me for a long time, and I thought it had numbed me to the perversions of weirdoes and sexual reprobates—until now.

Unlike the bar, the room is illuminated, bright even, from glowing lichen on the cavelike walls. The barmaid was right. The meeting has started and I am just in time. There are three men, all in fezzes and with the pasty faces of overstuffed Rotarians, sitting on a low bench on the far side of the room. One of them has his hand on a hefty switch with brass fittings—think James Whale and the smell of ozone—and a smile.

"Give him another one, Sherman," the fellow next to him says.

Sherman throws the switch, and Eagleton twitches like a spastic frog. Blood spills from his mouth. The bastards didn't even give him a rubber-ball gag on which to choke. The light in here doesn't flicker when the switch is thrown; the lichen on the walls seems to pulse and its luminescence grows brighter with every flail and sputter-cough of blood from the senator's mouth. Sherman reverses the switch and then stands. The room smells like bacon. My stomach grumbles, and I wonder how long it's been since I've eaten.

"Hello," Sherman says, turning toward me. "I'm afraid this is a private function. What can we do for you, son?"

My mouth is dry. I am a doctor of many things. Among them, I am a doctor of whiskey. Believe me when I tell you that Old Crow is utterly useless in situations like this. But I don't let them see my fear. "Is this the meeting of . . ."

"The Committee to Re-elect the President, St. Louis branch?" Sherman says. "Yes, sir. Every Tuesday night, after pinochle. And you are?"

"Drinking." As if to prove my point, I raise one of my glasses and take another sip of Old Crow. *And searching for the American Nightmare*—a task which at this moment seems rather too easily accomplished. Pretty much, I just have to step into any business establishment and make myself available.

"Indeed." He raises one hand to scratch his forehead, and I catch a glimpse of his cuff links. Solid gold, by the look of them, and emblazoned with a peculiar eldritch symbol—a rough star with an even cruder eye in its center. Just looking at them makes me nauseous, and I valiantly fight the urge to vomit because I don't want to waste my bourbon. Instead, I smile through gritted teeth and nod at him.

"Those are some nice cuff links," I say. "I don't have any myself, but I'd love to know where I could get some?"

"I'm afraid you have to be a member to obtain these."

"I see."

The other two men walk over to join us now, leaving Senator Eagleton to twitch and spasm all by himself. I glance in his direction and am disturbed to see that Eagleton is sporting a massive erection. For a moment, I am reminded of the vagrant and the tentacle back at the bus station in Colorado. Was that really two days ago? Eagleton's prick bobs and weaves, as if beckoning. There is an oddly shaped mole on the tip. How many whores have had to slide their mouths over that mole? Did they do it for horse? Probably not. The type of prostitutes a man like Eagleton could afford probably prefer cocaine.

When I turn back to Sherman and his friends, all three of them are gazing at me with suspicion. Things could turn weird and ugly real quick, and I'm not sure how to proceed. My first instinct is to react with great and terrible violence, but I've got the impression that I've stumbled into something big here, and wreaking havoc among them won't get me any answers, no matter how much fun it might be. Stalling for time, I drain one of my glasses, not gulping it, but not sipping either. When I'm finished, I smack my lips together and go, "Ahhhhh." Then I stick out my hand. "It's a pleasure to meet you, Sherman."

He looks at my hand as if I'm offering him an infected weasel, but then he takes it. His grip is firm, but his palm is clammy and wet. I'm not sure if it's the condensation from my glass or if Sherman just has sweaty hands. I turn to his companions and offer my hand to them, as well.

"And what are your names, gentlemen?"

One of the men, a squat, fat guy with a face like a toad, shakes my hand. His grip is not as firm as Sherman's, but it is just as wet. It feels like I'm holding an eel. He pumps my hand once, twice, three times, and then stops, holding it in midair. I brace my feet, in case he tries to pull me toward him.

"That's very rude," he says, licking his upper lip. "You should never ask a person what their name is. Names have power. If you know someone's name, then you have control over them."

I nod. "This is very true. But how else can introductions be made?"

"Instead of asking a person for their name, ask them what they prefer to be called."

"I see. And what do you prefer to be called?"

"I'm Livingston." He releases my hand, and I resist the urge to wipe my palm on my pants. Instead, I turn to the third man. "And you, sir? What do you prefer to be called?"

"You may call me Koehler."

"Well, it's very nice to meet you, gentlemen. And I believe I already know the fellow strapped to the slab."

"You've made his acquaintance?" Sherman asks.

"Not formally. But I watch the news. I'm something of a political junkie."

"So you know us." Koehler leans forward and stares at me intently. His eyes don't blink. "But you haven't given us your name yet, son."

I raise my glass and take another sip of Old Crow. The ice cubes clink against the rim.

"I prefer to be called Uncle Lono. I also answer to Dr. Lono."

Koehler asks, "What are you a doctor of?"

I respond simply, "Why is it that nobody asks me to name my nephews, or show off a snapshot of my pretty young niece?"

On the slab, Senator Eagleton moans and whimpers. Sherman and Livingston glance in his direction. Koehler's attention remains focused on me, perhaps now in a pedophiliac fugue state from my mention of a notional niece, maybe a blond with long, mosquito-scabbed legs flowing from the cuffs of her short-shorts. I decide then that he's the one I'll have to watch. Sherman walks over to the slab and tests Eagleton's bonds.

"Well," Koehler says, "as you can see, this is a private meeting. I'm afraid I'll have to insist that you tell us the purpose of your visit."

"It's like I told Sherman. I'm here for the meeting. I'm sorry if I interrupted all the fun. The bartender told me just to come right back."

"Did she? Something tells me you're not an initiate."

"Should I have knocked first?"

I'm aware that Sherman has circled around behind me, but I don't want to take my attention off the other two long enough to see what he is doing. His footsteps shuffle across the floor, and I'm fairly certain he's moving toward the door. My eyes flick down to my watch. The bus will be leaving any minute now, and I'm faced with a terrible decision. I can flee this scene and let the Greyhound carry me away, but doing so will mean abandoning this story, and believe me, there's a story here. I feel it deep down in my journalistic nuts. I can abandon the bus and stick around, scratching these guys and seeing what develops—but doing so might prove hazardous to my health.

"Uncle Lono." Koehler says it slowly, drawing out each syllable. "That's an interesting name. Lono was a Polynesian fertility god, of course. Descended from the skies on a rainbow and married Laka, I believe. Or maybe he was the god of music. It's hard to keep track of these minor deities. They pale in comparison to the one, true god."

"Amen." I try to hold my drink still so the clinking ice won't draw attention to the fact that my hands are shaking.

"Are you aware of the connection between Lono and Captain Cook?"

"Can't say that I am."

"Pity. You should look into it sometime. You might find it . . . illuminating. Still, it's an interesting name. I would imagine that it's not your real one, but then again, I would guess you have many names. Duke, perhaps?"

And just like that, my uneasiness and revulsion are eradicated by a white-hot flash of anger. I had taken great care in crafting this new pseudonym. I needed it for this journey. It should have worked. I was willing to bet that none of these three men had read either of my books, nor did they look the type to read the magazines my articles appeared in. There was no way they should have known me, and yet, they did. The malicious grin that spread across Koehler's face as he noticed my reaction certainly proved that he at least suspected who I was, and all because of that goddamned cartoon. That comic strip follows me wherever I go, regardless of what country or city I'm in. It doesn't matter if the people in that town think books are just something to be burned—if their local newspaper carries that cartoon, then sooner or later, they recognize me. It's very weird. When you're in high school and thinking about what you want to be when you grow up, you might decide on a fireman or an investment banker or a farmer or an attorney, but no one, to the best of my knowledge, decides that they want to be a fucking cartoon character. If they do, they should be shot in the head immediately, because such a desire would make all their other motivations suspect. There's no frame of reference for what to do or how to react when you've been turned into a comic-strip character. They don't teach it at college. No one has written any self-help books about it, although it occurs to me that I might have to one day.

I step to the side and Koehler moves with me, while Livingston shuffles forward, trying to flank me. The whiskey swirls in my gut.

"I don't know what you're talking about," I say. "Duke? I've been confused with many people over the years, but John Wayne isn't one of them."

Koehler's smile evaporates. He presses his lips together so hard that they turn white. His nostrils flare and I can see thick, black hairs lining their interior.

"Enough of this charade. We know who you are and what you do for a living. I'm not sure what brought you here. Perhaps it was fate or circumstance, or perhaps you received a tip. Regardless, you won't be writing about it."

"Oh, yeah? And why not?"

"Because you won't be leaving."

"You're wrong there, friend. I have a bus to catch."

Chuckling, Koehler steps forward, his fat hands raised as if to wring my neck. "I'm afraid not, Mr.—"

And that's when I toss my drink in his face, buying myself an extra second to act, and mourning the waste of perfectly good

Kentucky bourbon. Tough times call for tough measures, but I have never been one to abuse alcohol in that manner. Koehler reels backward, gasping and clawing at his eyes, and I take the opportunity to charge him. Head lowered, I slam into his gut. The air rushes from his lungs, smelling sour and curdled, and Koehler falls to the floor. Shouting, Livingston charges me, but I am already ahead of him. As he lunges, I sidestep, putting a table between us. "You bastard," Koehler cries, writhing on the floor. "You fucking bastard! My eyes."

"Damn your eyes," I shout. "What about my whiskey?"

Livingston weaves around the table and I move with him, coming back around again to Koehler, who is struggling to stand. His eyes are red, and whiskey drips from his nose. I swing my leather kit bag, smashing him in the face. Something breaks. I hope it's his nose rather than my tape recorder. Then I run for the door. Sherman blocks my way.

"Get him," Koehler screams.

I hear Livingston's footsteps pounding toward me as Sherman crosses his arms over his chest and smiles. Then I notice that the door is locked.

"Gentlemen," I cry, holding up my hands. "I'm telling you, this is all a terrible mistake. I don't know who you think I am or what I do for a living, but you've got it all wrong. If you'll just give me one second, I can prove it to you."

Sherman's smile wavers. "How?"

"My identification is in my bag. Here, let me show it to you." I stick my hand in the bag.

Sherman is clearly startled. "Don't you fucking move."

"Relax. I'm not some gun-toting lunatic." I pull out the can of mace and flip the top off with my thumb. "I am a different kind of lunatic."

I blast him in the face before he can react, and then, holding my breath and squinting, I spin around and mace Livingston and Koehler, as well. Koehler, already red eyed, tumbles over again, and Livingston sinks to his knees, sputtering a string of profanity that would make a sailor blush. But I am not a sailor, and I outmojo him with my own inventive string of cursing.

"You pig-fucking, whore-hopping, jizz-stained little bastards better lie the fuck down right now. Move so much as a single god-damned finger, and I'll spray this stuff up your ass."

Just to make sure they understand my point, I spray another blast at Sherman and then kick him in the testicles for added incentive. Wailing, he curls into a ball and cradles his nuts with one hand while wiping at his eyes with the other. Long strings of mucous drip from his nose.

"I've taken up enough of your time, and it's obvious that the senator needs your attention more than I do. Have a good evening. See you in the papers."

First I run to Senator Eagleton. As a journalist, I shouldn't interfere. As someone about to be pummeled to death, I should just leave. As a human being, I should be thrilled to see a real-live United States senator stretched out before me, injured and helpless, his brain full of guacamole. But I am a merciful god above all else, so I do the only thing I can—push the two tabs of Kirby acid I have with me between his lips. Eagleton's aura instantly explodes in a coruscating nimbus of pure power and freakish black dots. He grins like a typewriter. Then I dash past Sherman, unlock the door, and run out into the bar. The bartender looks at me in alarm and starts to say something, but again I flip her the finger, barrel past her, and plunge out into the night. It isn't until I'm outside that I breathe again, and my lungs are on fire. The mace residue stings my cheeks, but I know better than to wipe at it. A horn blows, and then I hurry to the bus. I'm the last one to get on.

"Thought you might not be joining us," the driver says as the doors hiss shut behind me.

"I thought so, too, but then I realized how much I'd miss your company."

"You're an odd one, Lono."

"You have no idea."

I wonder for a moment how it is that the driver knows my new name. Did I reveal it while in Jack Kirby's trip? It is possible, I suppose, but anything is possible. Hitler's remnant Nazis could still live in Argentina and bus-station bums could have tentacle appendages and United States senators could get electroshock treatments in the back rooms of backwater bars. The world is a strange place, and it grows stranger every day. If one is attuned, one often gets the sense that some new rough beast, giant and bulbous and smelling of madness, surges to the surface rather than shambling toward Bethlehem to be born. In such a world, I can be forgiven for not remembering whether or not I gave the driver my new pseudonym.

The engine revs and the gears groan as we slowly start to roll forward. I take my seat, ignoring the suspicious glances from the other passengers. The Hispanic girl shrinks in her seat as I walk by, and I can't really blame her.

We pull away and too late I realize that I've made a bad mistake. I shouldn't have told the Committee to Re-elect the President about the bus. They already know my true identity. Now they know where I'm going, as well. Making up my mind to get off at the next stop, I lean back in my seat, pull out my Moleskine, and begin to write.

There is no such thing as America, no such child born in a mansion on a hill. There aren't even two—not a white America and a Negro one, or an America of wealth and privilege held aloft by an America of the poor and twitchy. And even the dark wisdom of Richard Milhous Nixon, with his understanding of the great chasm between North and South, has an incomplete picture of this great experiment. Great, but not grand. Audacious, not enlightened. America is a Frankenstein's monster, stitched together from the corpses of the damned. The slaves of the Middle Passage, the raped and ruined red man, wave after wave of half-wit imbecile Scots-Irish not too different than the cats I've met so recently, swarthy Mediterranean inbreds, the insectoid masses of Asia, an electrified conglomeration lurching and howling in the frigid night. And in the abnormal brain of his monster, one so recently liberated from the brainpan of a criminal lunatic, there sits a single figure, a homunculus behind a bank of levers and switches, who dominates and controls us all. Nixon believes himself to be this entity, but he is not. Every candidate from the diabolical George Wallace of Alabama—he who perspires tear gas doesn't so much call Brazil nuts nigger toes as he actually chews on the feet of little black babies—to the surprisingly effective but ultimately delusional Patsy Mink wants their turn behind the console. But that is not a throne meant for a human posterior.

And speaking of posteriors, I met an old man in New York once in saner times, when tribes worshiped their totems of Democrat or Republican with an unwavering loyalty. When brats died to confront the swastika, and didn't even think to raise a peep for a part of the great franchise when they got back home. When the youth of America was as placid as a brace of well-dressed Negroes. He was an immigrant who came here as the free-range catamite of a Greek steamship, who painted the Brooklyn and Verrazano Bridges, and then sent back to his native island for a wife. Up to Massachusetts to find his version of the American Dream—a home, a fishing boat, and a little business of his own. The man was unused to the sheets of black ice that coated the region six months out of the year.

He broke his hip the hard way, against the thousand-ton anchorage of a suspension bridge, and now he slung hash at a luncheonette, huffing like a steamship as he moved from one end of the counter to the other, from the ever-rotating display of pies to the coffee machine—and why were they kept at opposite ends of the room? "The Jews," he said by way of answer. "They arrange things to make us Greeks suffer." He was good company, and as we shared pulls from my flask he told me a story of his native tribe: Once the parts of the human body had an argument over which was the most important. "It is I," said the eye, "for without me the world would be unknown to us." "No, it is I," said the hand. "I manipulate the world and make it so that we can live, and eat, and prosper." "You're all wrong," said the brain. "I am the most important. I interpret the input of the eye, and I direct the hand. I am the most important part of the body."

Then said the asshole, "Actually, it's me. I'm the most important part of the body. None of you would work or even dare move without me." Shocked, the hand reached down and slapped the ass hard for its impertinence. And then the asshole shut down. The days crawled by. The hands clenched and twitched from the pain of the backlog of shit. The eyes watered and squeezed shut, trying without result to evacuate the body of its increasingly fetid waste through the trivial power of blinking. And the brain found itself choked by pain and anxiety, driven to distraction and finally unable to even think. Not one equation, not a single strategy to gather food or gain the sexual attention of another body, nothing at all except for one statement that seared the spine—we surrender!

And then the asshole gave way. And it accepted the surrender of the body, or most of it anyway. To the hand it said, gloating, "And because you struck me, from now on, you are the part of the body in charge of wiping me clean!"

This is what we were reduced to, he and I. Him, in a food-service establishment, telling stories of talking assholes puckering and unpuckering in a mockery of human speech, and me, stirring through my chowder and wondering if I'd seen something in the chopped meat and veg that no man should ever see.

After Kent State, after Watts, after Innsmouth, I cannot help but wonder if the old man had it right. The brain cannot be tamed; it cannot be accommodated. It can, however, be usurped. Will the Americans who live out here, in flyover territory, in Greyhound land, in the asshole of the country, be the ones to rise up? Will there be Freak Power?

When I'm finished, I am cool and calm and collected again. Tired, though. Very tired. Writing often has that effect on me. I do my best work at night, sequestered in my kitchen and surrounded by a cacophony of television and music and copious amounts of alcohol and caffeine. The bus offers none of these amenities, but nevertheless, I am happy with the outcome. My muse is a Kentucky racehorse, sleek and slick and powerful, and at last, I am getting a grip on things. I see now how this journey should unfold. I understand where the search for the American Nightmare must truly begin. Until this point, I've only been sniffing around the ages, wandering haphazardly and waiting for the story to find me. But that is not how journalism works. Instead, I must find the story.

I've written before about the Ibogaine Effect, just a month ago, in fact. The story was a simple one—candidate Edmund Muskie had been acting a bit strangely, and rumors were that his handlers had summoned a doctor from the Brazilian rain forest to bring forth "some kind of strange drug" for the candidate. Ibogaine, from the plant *Tabernanthe iboga*, had been a part and parcel of the CIA's pharmacopoeia since the 1950s. The Frogs used it as a diet pill, all the better to oink away on rich desserts and buckets of red wine. Just the thing Muskie needed, really, even if his candidacy could have done without the scurrilous and utterly untrue rumors. The source of those rumors was, of course, myself. I created the rumor and then reported on the rumor. The Effect was that the rumor was quickly accepted as a fact and made the daily papers. That evening, news anchors in forty markets simply read off from the articles. In the bar at which I was drinking with the rest of the pool, my esteemed colleagues dutifully transcribed the material into their notebooks and then marched as one to a bank of pay phones to make the next morning's bulldog editions. It will be interesting to see how that impacts his campaign through the rest of the year.

Ibogaine is said to encourage introspection, to allow one to determine one's place in and path across the universe. The brave Pygmies were the first to harness the active elements of the plant, and they use it to pick their way across the otherwise-trackless jungle. To the Pygmy every puff of wind through the vines is a street sign, every leaf a traffic signal. My hope was, really, that a few of the more ambitious reporters would put down their bourbons, even for a moment, and try some Ibogaine themselves. It would only take one to dip his head into the Great Known—no *un* typed here, no *un* meant—and come out the other side ready to deliver a burning bushel of fragrant truth. But the little nerds just copied their notes from the blackboard and collected their A-double-pluses from their employers and the marks. Me, I got a good eight and a half minutes of fame, and a mission. I am untouchable now; even Nixon can't pull the strings like I can.

The media were too easy. I could do it to them again at any time. Even the marks that finally wised up would have to report something—*Deranged Lunatic Insists Mind Parasites Control Election Outcome*. One could prefix the words *deranged lunatic insists* to any headline, and only increase its accuracy. It's practically implied, and the reading public would hardly read the little phrase as a disclaimer these days. Success comes easy at a time like this; to really accomplish something I'd have to cut through the underbrush of ink and wires, to get to the real center of Americanus Assholius.

It occurs to me that Innsmouth is close to our final destination in Arkham. Yes, Innsmouth, home of the most violent and weirdest race riot of recent memory. Not an inner city, not don't-call-me-nigger-whitey rage, and oh so close to those dark New England woods where Muskie first went mad with wild tears, in New Hampshire, if not in Maine. That is where the American Nightmare truly started. That is the dark source. And that is where I'll start my own campaign, a campaign to save the world.

FOUR

Weird Memories . . . A Final Judgment on All Mankind, Hastily Rendered . . . John Lennon Is AWOL . . . We Don't Have Negroes, but We Do Have "Cannocks" . . . Something Fishy around Here . . . Bob Dylan Was Right in "Ballad of a Thin Man" . . . Fun Guys Go to Hell, Revisited; or, I Dose Heavily with a Fungi from Yuggoth . . . Tentacle Sex with a Z-Grade Vixen

Riding this bus has me thinking of other bus trips I have taken. Political buses are the worst. Anyone can follow a campaign, month to month, whistle stop to whistle stop. But if campaigns are wars, and they are, the real story is in the aftermath, when strange things grow from the scorched earth left in the wake of the candidates' passage. It is time to plant a seed. Luckily, my bus has a bathroom, and it is a very long trip, so I position myself toward the back, where the smell is the rankest, and make conversation where I càn. What I discover isn't very shocking in its presence, but its intensity unnerves even me.

"What do you think of McGovern?" I'd ask the barrel-shaped man next to me, a Joe Lunchbox type that supposedly makes up the base of the Democratic Party electorate in the Midwest. "He's the Democrat, right?" the guy might say. "Ipso facto, he's a cocksucker." Then, as his eyes suddenly turn beady, he adds, "Are *you* a cocksucker too?" I ask about the other Democratic hopefuls, but he can only remember "that nigger lady." Hubert Humphrey, Ed Muskie, none of these fellows even ring a bell. I long for stronger drink.

And it's the same along the whole trip across the ironed-over territory of middle America. "Is it an election year?" one old woman responds. She clutches my arm with her taloned fingers as if I've just casually mentioned that the Schutzstaffel would be boarding the bus in a few minutes to measure noses and brows with ice-cold calipers for signs of Yid contamination of the local germ plasm.

Nixon is on everyone's lips. Nixon has a secret plan to end the war, so he says, and the people I've met actually believe it. Nixon had a secret plan to end the Negro menace, and that was understood to have been said only between the lines, said with secret words filled with secret meaning, and the people I've met actually believe that as well. Worshipful, trembling lips, eyes swimming with blood and honor: "Nixon will do it. He will, he will. We believe in him. Nixon will bring change. Nixon offers hope." Hope and change are what the people want. The last few years have been tough—war, assassinations, unrest, bell-bottoms, the demon weed, and colleges full of unrepentant Marxists—but Nixon is finally going to set things aright. History is on the man's side. Lizard-brained LBJ scuttled back under his rock in disgrace, didn't he, "after trying to buy off the coloreds," as one precocious nine-year-old named Annalee puts it. Her curls are mathematically perfect and her voice soulless. She is going with her grandpa to Ohio "to start a new life." Grandpa sleeps heavily near the front of the carriage. As he snores, his dentures rattle in his mouth. LBJ is gone, vanished into the ether. Haven't all other obstacles to Nixon's ascension been *handled* so easily? Even a blood-soaked mobster like Joe Kennedy couldn't protect his kids, and then Martin Luther King was shot too, the Vietcong were just violent enough to keep their names in the papers, hemlines went absolutely crazy, everyone was tuning in and turning on, and angels wept. Nineteen seventy-two is just a bump on the carpet. Nixon will smooth that bump. Clean sweep, it will be a clean sweep. A fifty-state victory, and even the mongrel Puerto Ricans will agitate for statehood to make it an even fifty-one. *An even fifty-one!* That's what the heifer of a waitress says as she slams down a slice of blueberry pie, prefrozen but warmed on the spot, in front of me at one of the rest stops. Whatever New Math she learned, it doesn't make much sense . . . Was her geometry even Euclidian? Was there even such a thing as non-Euclidian geometry? As I eat the pie, juice leaking from it like dark purple ichor, I have visions of cities full of abandoned buildings with angles like something from a bad mescaline high. But never mind that. Hasn't Muskie already been seen broken and crying, weeping like an ugly woman? The many-fingered hand of Nixon is surely behind it all. That's what I'm told over and over again, and this is not something the housewives and bums and button-down young men I met on this bus trip view with any sort of suspicion at all. Not dread but glee. They are feverish and eager, their palms and loins wet with anticipation. All save one.

I meet my first Cannock at that same rest stop. He's made me somehow, in the manner of his secretive yet perceptive people. "Uncle," he calls me, "glad to see you here. I dig your work, especially your stuff for *Scanlan's* and *Rolling Stone*." There is no fooling him, I see, so I decide to confide.

"Keep it down," I say. "I am undercover and behind enemy lines. Call me Lono."

"That's cool. You were Lono before, though you didn't know it, and will be again." He was drinking tea in his coffee and licked his lips wildly. "It's all pretty interesting, what's been going on, eh?"

I know what I need to do now: nod and occasionally grunt in a manner the Cannock will perceive as interesting and affirming. That's three-eighths of the journalist's trade right there—know that the crazies want to talk, and they especially want to talk to a reporter, and they especially want to talk to a doctor of journalism and fellow brain-damaged geek, for which I qualify in spades.

"They say," he murmurs, glancing around to make sure no one is eavesdropping on our little tête-à-tête, and then plunging ahead as if he doesn't care, "that this election is going to be different. No more ward bosses, no more precinct-by-precinct street fighting, not even a single busload of old fogies being driven back into the inner cities where they were last registered. It's going to be about the young people, about issues, about the *Movement*!" He bellows with laughter at his own claim, slaps the Formica with a pancake hand. I notice that there are six fingers on his hand. "More like *bowel* movement, if you ask me, which I know you didn't."

"Listen, Mac," I say. "Get a grip on yourself. What's this all about?" Mentally, I weigh the saltshaker, the napkin dispenser, and the big glass silo of what is surely a solid hunk of sugar. My own coffee is only tepid—it would barely blind him if I flung it in his face. Unarmed and defenseless, I am a naked babe before this lunatic. I think about reaching into my kit bag for a weapon, but don't want to make any sudden moves. The silo comforts me; I pick it up and try to shake some sugar into my cup, but only a few wayward grains fall from the container. Mac doesn't notice.

"What they don't know," he continues, "what fancy dancers like you don't realize, is how deep the grassroots grow for the right. Muskie knows, but we took care of him already, eh?"

"We? You don't mean . . . Canadians, do you? Those rat bastards."

"Close, close, oh so close. You know the letter—of course you do. People like you feed on tears, but people like me, I'm the very father of tears."

"Well, you did just say *eh*—I know a . . . Canuck . . . when one's right in front of me." I grasp the silo of sugar for dear life. There is nothing more disconcerting than being trapped in a rest stop with a crazed Canadian. Especially a French one.

"Not *Canuck*," he says, still giggly. Everything is funny to this man. Perhaps he isn't Canadian after all. "*Can-knock*," he says. Then he knocks on the Formica counter, and even answers, "Who is it?" in a creepy falsetto. Then laughs again. But in a flash I know what he means: that infamous letter by Paul Morrison of Deerfield Beach, Florida, which claimed that Muskie had laughed when Mr. Morrison asked him about the plight of the American Negro. Hailing from distant Maine, where there are few blacks, how could Muskie understand the needs of the Afro-American? Well, some nameless aide said, "Not blacks, but we have Cannocks." Every copy desk in

America helpfully corrected the seeming misspelling to *Canucks*. Another blasphemous lie. The epistolary machinations of the Cannocks, hitherto a secret race of humanoid known only to the most discerning travelers of the New England backwoods, had simultaneously revealed their existence to the public at large and derailed the Muskie campaign, leaving the candidate a gasping, salt-spattered wreck and the Democratic machine a pile of steaming slag and the Cannocks themselves ready to launch a new offensive.

I put my sugar down. I notice that Mac has managed to crack the countertop with his most casual slap—the impression of his six-fingered hand left behind like the footprint of some long-forgotten specimen of megafauna. I'll have to talk my way out of this one.

"You know Morrison? I'd love to talk to him. Get an exclusive; maybe measure the lead content in his blood. I hear his penmanship is utterly awful."

Mac laughs and makes as if to pat me on the back, but he sees me cringe and at the last moment just points at me instead. "Aaah!" he says. "Aaa-ha!" He sounds like an attic door. "Looking for a scoop, are you? Undercover, indeed! But you can't get one from me, not about me, anyway." He points to himself with his meaty thumb. God, his mutant hands are huge—like someone took a cookie cutter to a baked ham. "I'm a member of the silent majority." A chatty little bastard, nevertheless, he is, though I choose—wisely—not to mention this.

"Listen, boss, I am a professional writer. What's this all about? I have little time for one of Nixon's stooges. I can talk to the old man himself, any time I wish to," I say, and I believe it.

"You think we're insane, but we're not. It's that gang on the other side, the Democrats. You and all those long-haired intellectuals are thinking of voting for them, and you don't even know who you're voting for yet—"

"That's the democratic process. We've come a long way since ward heelers and the animated dead shambling toward the ballot box."

"So you think!" Mac says, his voice shrill again. "So you think! But you've read the *Berkeley Barb*, you've checked out the *East Village Other*. The Reds have it right, but backward. They think both major parties are the tool of capital—industrial capital for the Democrats, and finance capital, well, that's supposed to be us."

Mac waves his hot-dog fingers at the diner. I notice for the first time that it has cleared out. Fear squeezes my heart. My bus is gone. Even the vending machines are unplugged. My sandwich has turned stale and green. For God's sake, how long have I been sitting here talking to this madman? I wish for a moment that the rest stop had a jukebox and that the jukebox had Bob Dylan's "Ballad of a Thin Man"—one of my all-time favorites—because something is happening here, but I don't know what it is, do I, Dr. Lono?

"But," he continues, "you already know we serve another Master. You were very adept at figuring that out. What you don't get, my friend, is who the Democrats serve."

"Oh yeah, who'd that be?"

"Moloch!" Mac shouts. I think he's about to break into a recitation of "Howl"—had the world shifted so far to the left that even that angry old poem was being repurposed for the Nixon campaign? But no, Mac has something more Biblical in mind. "You have lifted up the shrine of Moloch and the star of your god Rephan, the idols you made to worship," he says. "It's all in the Good Book, and I don't mean *The Naked and the Dead*. You know the Nam was always Kennedy's war, and that rat bastard from Texas who had him killed—"

"Whoa, whoa, LBJ killed—"

Mac waves my words away. I find myself unable to speak. Juju, bad juju, swims in the air. "For whom do children die in fire? For Moloch. And you shall not let any of your seed pass through Moloch; neither shall you profane the name of your God: I am the Lord."

"Wait, wait, who is the Lord in your equation? You're not making sense, man. And what's this about LBJ? He had Kennedy killed?"

Mac leans forward. "And had sex with the bullet wound while the corpse was still fresh."

I find my voice. It's a proud American voice. "That's obscene. Granted, I've known Kentuckians and Puerto Ricans who would do such a thing, but—"

Mac shrugs. "He needed some way to occupy himself onboard Air Force One while they were sitting around at Love Field Airport in Dallas."

The sugar shaker is still in reach if I need it. I debate reaching for my Moleskine. It's in the kit bag, along with my other weapons, but I'm afraid that if I did, Mac would lunge forward and suck the eyeballs out of my head. Instead, I repeat everything back to him, trying hard to get it down in my own mind. "So Kennedy started the Vietnam War as a child sacrifice to the hungry goat god of the Phoenicians, and you Republicans are just a bunch of happy Quakers looking to reclaim America for the Secret Race of six-fingered Cannocks. Is that what I should lead with, then? Write it up and tell the world?"

"It ain't what you think," Mac says. "This ain't what you think at all. This is no scoop, Lono. This is a warning. Stay out of our business, chum, and we won't have to cork you. The old man likes you; he's been following your career since the back pages of *El Sportivo*. He's a fan."

"If he's a fan, then he should know that I don't cotton to threats. Not from anyone, least of all some brain-damaged mutant half-wit from the foothills of New England."

Mac leans in close. "Well, sir," he says in a whisper, a whisper of paper sliding against paper, "if it'll make you feel better, you can put a bullet in my head. Reach into your bag and pull out your gun. I know you must have one in there. You've been glancing at it since we started speaking. Go ahead. Kill me. Work your aggressions out and whatnot. It's all fine and dandy with me. A new world awaits, for thee as well as me. *Ia, ia Cthulhu fhtagn*, ain't that what all the kids are saying? Well, who're you going to believe, me or them?"

"Maybe I'll just sit over here and wait for the next bus," I say.

"Here." He slides a brown paper bag across the table. "Maybe these will keep you company while you wait."

I pick up the bag and peek inside. There are three dried mushrooms, milk-white, porous things run through with tiny black spots. I am not adverse to the psychoactive effects of psilocybin and psilocin, but these are the strangest mushrooms I've ever seen. They appear unwholesome.

"What are these?" I sniff the mouth of the bag.

"Come now, Lono. Your reputation precedes you. Surely, you've done shrooms before."

"I'm being set up, aren't I? For whom do you really work, you swine?"

"I've already told you. Consider this a parting gift. One last gentle kiss before the beating to come. These fungi come all the way from Yuggoth."

"Where?" I've traveled all around the world, but I've never heard of this place. It's a strange name, Yuggoth. Could be Asian or Slavic or Hebrew, and yet, it sounds like none of them, nor any other language I can think of.

"Yuggoth. It's where the best shrooms come from. I read in your interview with *Playboy* that you like mushrooms."

"I do," I say, seeing no reason to deny it. "Mescaline and mushrooms are a genuine high. They're clean and interior, as all psychedelics are. Things like speed just give you a motor high. They don't clean out your brain pipes the way some good psychedelics do."

"Well, then, enjoy these with our compliments."

"They don't look right. How do I know they aren't poisonous, you swine?"

"You don't. But really, do we ever?"

He has a point, but I'm not about to admit that to him.

"So, what's it going to be, Lono? Are you going to beat me to death? Kill me with your bare hands? Or are you going to take the ride?"

"I already bought the ticket."

Somewhere, someone flicks a switch and the lights go off. I presume my coffee and sandwich are now free. Laughing yet again, Mac grabs the sugar silo and clonks himself over his own head with it. A babyish tap, but his left temple opens right up in the brightest NTSC red, just like a Saturday-morning wrestler. Head wounds bleed a lot, but I've never seen anything like what pours from his. He smiles at me under his new mask of crimson, flashing teeth that seem just a bit too large, and I decide I'll find a hotel. I grab the bag of mushrooms almost as an afterthought, and then beat feet right out of there. Mac doesn't follow me, but his hooting, piping laughter does.

"Moloch!" he shouts after me. *Moloch!*

If you think I am out of options or weaponry, then you don't know me very well at all. I have some technology with me, the sort of thing that will change the world one day. The Mojo Wire! From any phone jack I can plug it in and feed it finished copy, one sheet at a time, and facsimile sheets will spit forth from the wire's opposite number in the editorial office of whoever is paying my bar tab at the moment. If only everyone had one of these things, whole nations would collapse into the sort of mutualist anarchic Utopia only a Russian prince could dream of. Imagine a Mojo Wire in every home, and the masses accessing it from anywhere! That would be rich, eh? But for now, the tool belongs to me. Or it is lent to me occasionally by my editor, to keep me off his home telephone at three a.m. But this gem of a machine, only twenty-three pounds and sturdy enough to survive the Big One, if the Big One were a sufficient number of miles away, needs two things—a phone jack and an electrical receptacle. Neither is anywhere nearby, and the rest stop is no help, not with Mac stomping around on the other side of the dark glass, raving and flailing his arms as he finishes his exegesis without me. But I am in Middle America, damn it, walking on the sandy shoulder of a major highway. By law and common decency—the American Dream!—there will be a neon oasis sooner rather than later. Gas, Food, and Lodging, a veritable Disneyland compared to the awful Knott's Berry Farm of that last rest stop. Buses go by here, for the love of God!

I walk for what seems like minutes and see a faded billboard looming over the highway. WAR IS OVER, it reads, IF YOU WANT IT. I remember reading in the news that John Lennon and Yoko Ono commissioned a dozen or so such billboards several months back to promote his new single, which was unavoidable on the airwaves only a month before. Lennon could have been a warrior, but instead, he's become just another American, if by proxy. A Royalist turned Peacenik turned Royalist again. That's what this political climate does to people. Lennon stood for something once. Now his idea of a progressive decade is a camelhair jacket in every closet and a Gucci on every foot. Or maybe that's Tom Wolfe. I can't remember. I haven't heard from Tom since I gave him my tapes of the gangbang at the Merry Pranksters' party, that notorious weekend when Kesey and his people introduced acid to the Hells Angels. I wonder where Tom is now? New York, I guess, along with Lennon. I feel a surge of anger. He should be here with me. Where are the other warriors for truth? Where are Kesey and Hoffman and Ayers and the rest of the Happy Fun-Time Club? Someone should be here with me, on this dark and desolate stretch of damned highway. At this moment, I decide I was wrong to go on this journey alone. I even wish for my goddamned attorney, before remembering that the Brown Buffalo is probably dead and fish bait. At least, that's the rumor, and we have a saying in this business about rumors. But who am I kidding? The truth is, he's been living on borrowed time since Vegas. He saw the same things there I saw. One does not boldly go into Bat Country and expect to come through unscathed. Vegas took a terrible toll on his psyche and spirit. He was a walking corpse after that. His death is merely a hastened eventuality. I miss him, sometimes. At any rate, I owe him too much money—the retainer has long since been consumed by coke and grapefruits—even if he is alive.

A few minutes later, I come across a local knockoff of one of the big chain motels. Call it Super 7 if you like, because that's what they did. There's no concierge, no bellowing demands for three dozen grapefruit, no lounge with live light jazz and whores who spackle the wrinkles from their faces with foundation makeup, not even a color television. But it's cheap and takes credit cards. The night manager doesn't even blink at a man walking up the highway alone with a large kit bag and asking for a room. Hell, he doesn't blink at all. It's almost as though he's long forgotten how. Maybe I'm not the first to miss my bus out here in the wastelands. He barely acknowledges me as I check in, preferring to communicate to me in a series of grunts and wheezes. A Lucky Strike dangles from his mouth, dropping ashes onto the counter. Another burns in an ashtray behind him. His fingernails are stained yellow.

"And who are you going to vote for in the upcoming election—Democrat or Republican?" I ask.

He looks at me as if I were a brain-damaged geek. "Nixon, of course. Why? Who are you going to vote for?"

"It doesn't matter," I say. "What matters is the process itself."

"Well, of course it matters! Don't tell me you're one of those *doesn't matter who's in office, they're all gonna screw ya* type of people. Because that's not what I fought for during the war."

"Which war? Korea?"

The manager nods, and as he does, he sucks his gut in and stands a little taller.

"Thanks for your service, friend. I keep thinking I should go see Vietnam. The place is causing so much trouble; I ought to have a look at it. Haven't been there yet, though."

The manager sneers at me, the derision practically oozing from his pores. "I could have guessed you never served."

"Oh, but I serve my country in other ways. What part of Korea were you in during the war?"

His proud expression falters. "I was stationed in Germany the whole time. Sign here."

Sign I do, chuckling as I scribble my name on the receipt. It feels good to be writing. It always does. Almost as good as it felt to bait the inept little manager who proudly fought to protect this country from the Moloch-worshiping heathen Democrats by sitting on a base in Germany and peeling potatoes while his friends went off to die.

I have a lot to write this night, and on the tiny desk in the dank little motel room, that's exactly what I'll do. First I take a shower, letting the oily, strange-smelling motel water sluice away the road dirt my body collected during the bus trip. Then I light up a cigarette, find some ice from the machine down the hall, and pour myself a tumbler glass of whiskey. I like to drink when I write. That's when my writing is at its most pure in essence, when the truth comes barreling out like machine-gun fire, and typos abound, word counts be damned. Taking a big swig from the glass, I consider the brown paper bag lying on the bed. I pull out one of the mushrooms. It's cool to the touch, but not slimy, as its appearance would seem to indicate.

"Yuggoth, eh?" I announce to the empty motel room. "What the hell . . . Buy the ticket, take the ride."

Shrugging, I toss it into my mouth and chew slowly. It tastes just like any other shroom—basically, like a moist paper bag—so I swallow, and then get down to business.

I write about how despite all the demographical changes supposedly sweeping this great country—the Black Vote, the Women's Vote, the Youth Vote, the Antiwar Vote, the Labor Vote—none of it is going to matter. Nixon made his deal with devils unknown; the Democrats have the minority vote, but the Republicans are counting on hidden and secret races revealing themselves on Election Day. The Democrats are in bed with Moloch, that ancient god of one-sided trades and unfair deals. The Phoenicians were an industrious bunch for their time, trading across the Mediterranean on their triremes, but there was a price; oh, there was a price. Moloch, their great, fiery god, craved the succulent meat of children, and oh boy did those sandy buggers pay up with baby flesh. Never mind the pound. Those bastards paid by the ton. Anything to keep the lucre rolling in and the ships rolling out. That's what an insane mutant I met at a highway rest stop told me anyway, and while I have plenty of reasons not to believe a word of it, I can't think of a single thing that should stop me from reporting it as iron fact.

There is the ring of truth to it after all. The Great Society was born in the blood pools of Indochina as much as it was in the White House. Few whites could truly bear the thought of opening their wallets to help the Negro, but it was the evening bloodletting in every living room that let the white man believe that his mojo was still rising. Sure, the blacks could date their daughters and even run for office, provided the campaigns were sufficiently quixotic and starved for funds, but at least we were killing tons of gooks. A man could stand up. But now, with the war gone the wrong way and a social worker on every corner, what might the white man, with his diseased physiognomy and blank stare, believe in? Nixon has long transcended the need to even pretend to care about Jesus Christ—a hippie if anyone's ever seen one, and a suspected Jew besides, just like Noam Chomsky—and he has found another Lord to serve. He's laughing as the Democrats jockey for position; by week's end he might call a press conference at the National Cathedral. "Take a look at this, you homely bastards," he'll growl, then drop trou and take a dump into the Holy Host. "Line up and take what's coming to you!" By Tuesday, he'll be twenty points ahead in the Gallup Poll. Moloch is the faith of a cringing slave, of a man who worships the whip and the pike. But what Nixon has goes beyond commerce, beyond capitalism, beyond Christianity, beyond anything at all. The stars are aligning in his favor, and there is little the Democrats can do about it.

The motel room grows sullen and oppressive and too quiet. I wonder if and when the mushroom will kick in. There's a small transistor radio on the scratched bureau, and I turn it on for company.

I spin the dial, searching for Jefferson Airplane or the Grateful Dead or Bob Dylan or anything else that will soothe my soul and feed my muse, but all I find is that angry, new shit, Black Sabbath and Alice Cooper and the like. Dark music to be played after dark in dark times. I keep scanning and come across the news. Someone is interviewing Mamie Van Doren about her active role as a member of the president's reelection campaign. Incidentally, that's the same group I ran into before, the ones who had Senator Eagleton spread-eagled across a slab in the back room of a two-nit bar, wrists and ankles cuffed tight to the corners, electrodes attached to his balls. This is how those people like to play. Trust me. I'm a journalist. Apparently, Mamie Van Doren was granted a personal tour of the White House, conducted by Henry Kissinger himself. The reporter asks her if anything occurred at the end of the tour. The actress giggles and then says, "No comment. He took me back to my hotel. We were accompanied by several of his security men. One can't be too careful, you know. He was a complete gentleman. He said he'll call me when he gets back from Moscow. He has a lot of girlfriends, but that's okay, because I have a lot of boyfriends."

I smash my fist down on the radio so hard that the plastic casing cracks. That makes me even angrier, so I sweep it to the floor and stomp it beneath my feet until I feel better. Then I scavenge through the debris, searching in an act of postmodern divination. And there it is, a tiny piece of broken plastic that reads MADE IN TAIWAN. Because more and more, that is our country's slogan. We used to make things here, but that seems to be sliding away. I envision a time, decades from now, when America's only notable export will be our entertainment. Everyone in America will be involved in the movies somehow, because that will be the only type of job left for us, once our manufacturing and service centers have shipped overseas. Durable goods will be made in Taiwan, and B-movie actresses like Mamie Van Doren will go from movies and television to politics, and then maybe back to movies and television once they're done in Washington. How long, oh Lord, how long? We live in a country where Mamie Van Doren, star of such classic fare as *High School Confidential* and *Sex Kittens Go to College*, is getting personally guided tours of our seat of power by good old Henry the K. And why not, eh? Everyone knows Van Doren models herself after Marilyn Monroe. This third-rate blond bombshell was even engaged to a baseball player. Monroe snagged the great Joe DiMaggio, so Van Doren hitched herself to that sore-armed, left-handed pitcher Bo "Bad Boy" Belinsky.

But never mind that. I have no patience for America's greatest pastime, unless I'm betting on the game. I've always been more of a football fan myself. But so is Nixon. In fact, as far as I know, that's the only time Nixon ever told the truth about anything. I interviewed him in the back of his limo and all we talked about was football. He knew the name of a second-string Oakland flanker who only played seven plays in one Superbowl and was never used again. Indeed, here's the rub. Nixon not only knew the player's name; he knew where the son of a bitch had gone to college. Nixon takes his football very seriously. He openly talks about politics and international diplomacy as if they were a series of plays. He doesn't want to be president. He wants to be coach. He thinks in terms of end sweeps and touchdowns and mousetrap blocks. Football is Nixon's game, and it's my game too. It's a sport for ugly brutes and vicious bastards, and there is nothing uglier or more vicious or more brutish than Richard M. Nixon. Oh, I get along fine with some of the folks around him. Ray Price and Nick Ruwe seem like good people, and Pat Buchanan can hold his own with me and a bottle of whiskey. Indeed, I've always seen Pat as sort of a wild-eyed Davy Crockett for the Nixon team, and if that's so, then I wonder what Nixon's Alamo will be? I only hope I am there to see it. But it doesn't matter how many good people he surrounds himself with. Nixon himself is evil, a congenital liar who would let the Devil himself fuck his own mother if it meant a rise in the polls. For my entire adult life, Nixon has been a national bogey-man of sorts. There have been other evil men. Lyndon Johnson,

King Herod, and Adolf Hitler come to mind. But they are mere punters compared to old Tricky Dick. Sooner or later, he will fail and fall, and I hope I am there to give the final push.

Ye gods, now I'm rambling. Where am I and, more importantly, where was I? Oh, yes. Van Doren and Kissinger and Nixon. We will reach a point in this country, perhaps only a decade from now, when our politicians and our celebrities will be indistinguishable. Trust me on this, for I am wise. I have medicine. And Mamie Van Doren is a great example of this malady. Not only did she date a baseball player just like Marilyn Monroe, but when Monroe fucked Kennedy, Van Doren apparently decided to do the same. Why else would she volunteer to serve on the Committee to Re-elect the President (and sweet Jesus, how is it just now occurring to me that the acronym for that is CREEP)? I feel a stirring in my loins when I imagine Monroe spread-eagled on Kennedy's desk in the Oval Office, but I feel no such lust that night in the motel room, as mushroom-induced visions of Nixon and Kissinger and Van Doren and the rest of the Happy-Fun Club frolicking naked and rolling around with each other in some subterranean bunker beneath the White House invade my brain. The things I bear witness to . . . I must testify, for confession is good for the soul, and what I experience leaves my soul feeling dirty and raped.

Everyone knows there are underground tunnels beneath Washington, but do we really know what goes on there? I see Kissinger, lathered with some sort of noxious grease, wiry body hair glistening like a mountain ape hosed down with vegetable oil, as he slides his remarkably fat prick into Van Doren's backside, while some vague and indefinable form in the shadows does the same to him. I concentrate on Kissinger's suitor, trying to see it better, but it remains shadowed, which is odd, since the entire orgy is brightly lit. I have a sense it is not human. Indeed, unless human silhouettes are suddenly shaped like eight-foot-tall cactuses with tentacles, there is nothing human about it at all. It's one of these whipping tendrils that the creature thrusts into Kissinger's rump, and all the while he moans and writhes with Van Doren doing the same beneath him, and everyone else in the room joins in the terrifyingly perverse festivities, fucking with a frenzy their kind usually reserve for killing brown people or gooks or long-haired hippie types. I recognize most of them. None of them is aware of my presence, lost as they are in their throes of passion, and for that, I am glad. One doesn't watch the Speaker of the House fornicate with his twin daughters and live to tell about it too long. Not these days, and not in this town. I walk among them, stepping over copulating bodies like they are cordwood. I bear witness to sodomy and bestiality and masochism and incest and things that are impossible to describe. Those creatures lurk in the background, thrusting forth with their long tentacles, filling every orifice, regardless of function or gender. It is very loud, a cacophony of grunts and squeals and screams and sighs, and only some of them are human. The air stinks of sex and ammonia and fish, like worms on a sidewalk after a warm summer rain. And there in the midst of it all sits Nixon, looking squeamish and uncomfortable and about to vomit. This is a man who does not look like he's having fun. Ho ho! He looks like he's constipated and depressed and absolutely miserable. I've often heard rumors from other reporters that Nixon keeps an Asian mistress on a houseboat in San Francisco, but I've never believed it. In truth, Richard Nixon always struck me as asexual more than anything else. His overall demeanor at the spectacle surrounding him seems to verify this, his presence notwithstanding.

"Mr. President," I say, wading through naked bodies to reach his side. "We meet again."

"You!" Here is a reaction, an emotion other than revulsion. Surprise. Shock. Anger. Here is a man who is not happy to see me. I am about to ask him more when the bunker vanishes and I find myself back in the dingy motel room, fingers hovering over the keyboard. I still don't know what country Yuggoth is in, but their psychedelic mushrooms are incredible.

At around three a.m., there is pounding on the door. I'm unarmed and in nothing but boxer shorts and thick black socks. The Mojo

Wire squeals and shivers as it eats my last page ever so slowly. I quickly get the sense that the knocking has been going on for hours, as the hinges of the door have been beaten halfway free of the doorjamb. But I am a serious writer and at serious work, and their interruptions be damned. It's easy enough to match the timing of the banging with my own exhalations, and at the right moment I open the door and in flies, then tumbles, the hotel manager, a fire extinguisher-cum-battering ram leaving his hands and flying right out the window with a musical crash.

I plant a foot on his neck, realizing as I do so that there is a hole in the toe of my stocking. "What's this all about, junior? Speak quickly and truly, and I may let you live."

"Y-you dirty son of a bitch," he sputters. "The phones, what the hell are you doing to my phone system? Nobody can make any calls. The other guests are complaining. Even the pay phone is just howling like an amateur-night microphone." Then his eyes, wide and froggy as ever, spot the Mojo Wire. "And what the hell is that! Are you one of those Red Chinese spies? I should have known."

"Yes," I tell him. "I'm a Red Chinese spy. You've found me out, you bastard. I'm here to track down President Nixon and give him a special herbal remedy that he mistakenly left behind in Peking. It's very important—without it Trish may go mad-dog crazy on her Secret Service detail. We don't want that now, do we?"

He's excited. "Yes! Please, may I see it? Will you be delivering it to the man in person? Will you? Oh, boy! Won't you tell Mr. Nixon that I love him? Please!"

"Yes, yes, I'll do all that. Get a grip on yourself, man. Now let me see . . ." It's a gamble, but I'm pretty sure this cat has never seen real-life marijuana, and I'm sure I have a reefer somewhere. I consider giving him some of the mushrooms, but I want to experiment with them more later. Such medicine would only be wasted on a rube like this. He stays prostrate on the ground where he landed, almost worshipful, as I dig through my sweaty bags. I find a bit of hash wadded up in the bottom of my knapsack, and then he is on me. He slams against my back, slides an arm under my chin, and starts choking me like a judo expert. I throw myself backwards. He howls, "Lies, lies! You goddamn son of a bitch, you think I don't know who you are? I know damn well who you are! You're that guy who rode with the Hells Angels! You're the one in the comic strip. You're what's wrong with this country. You think I won't be rewarded for bringing Nixon your fucking stone heart!" as we roll around. He's a little guy, this Korean War–vet motel manager, a real Renfield, but scrappy as hell. I manage to dig my chin into the guy's forearm and get a little breathing room, but then he sinks his teeth into my ear. I reach out and yank the power cord of the Mojo Wire hard as I turn onto my belly. The corner of it must have got him right in the temple, because he goes limp. I bite my tongue as my own head slams into the floor, and then my mouth fills, not with my blood, but with something blacker and sticky. Ichor. It takes a minute or so for me to crawl out from under him. He's alive, twitching even, and bleeding. It was his blood that gushed into my mouth, but it wasn't blood at all.

"Sweet Jesus in a jumped-up sidecar." Muttering, I fumble a cigarette from a crumpled pack and light up, catching my breath. It's a good thing the credit card I used to check in wasn't mine. I don't know how much of the story I managed to file via the Mojo Wire, but I know I have to leave—and quickly. I am better off putting on a shirt and walking right back out onto the highway. Nothing good can come of sticking around, of trying to explain myself to the authorities, or paying the bill. I snuff the cigarette, wash the manager's ichor from my mouth, pack up quick, put the hash in my little bowl, and hit the parking lot, toking up good, wishing I had some Ibogaine, some something else, anything better to take the edge off this evening of revelations and assault. I am a marked man now, and the long tentacles of the Republican establishment are uncoiling my way. Twice now, in my journey to find the American Nightmare, I've rubbed shoulders with them. They will not be pleased. But the Democrats . . . Moloch? I am already a journalist; I may as well throw myself into the fiery maw of Moloch, if only to avoid the suspense of a future assignment. I turned pro a long time ago, but the world grew weirder than I ever knew it could be.

As I walk by it, the pay phone rings a plaintive ring, and I pick it up.

"Hello, Super 7 pay phone. Lono speaking."

It's my editor, and he has another assignment for me. Luck and happenstance are mine again. A plane ticket is waiting, he says. My per diem, in cash, is at the airport's Western Union and currency exchange. I have thirty minutes to get to the plane. My assignment is to travel to Arkham, Massachusetts, and cover some problem with the Democratic Party's rogue county committee. A rental car, paid for by my editor, will be waiting in Arkham. I'm instructed not to wreck it, but I barely hear the reprimand because my mind is making connections and swimming in synchronicity. Arkham, it just so happens, is very close to Innsmouth and a town called Dunwich. I don't give a damn about the latter. It's the former that interests me. Suddenly somebody is paying for this little journey into America's dark and twisted heart. Luck and happenstance, my friends. Happenstance and luck. Lines within ley lines. Synchronicity and such. Ho ho, hey hey. I'd started out going to Arkham. Then I had set my sites on Innsmouth. It looked like those plans might have been stymied when I missed my bus, but now here I am, on the road again and on someone else's dime, and continuing onward to the same destination.

Looking back, it occurs to me now that I should have just killed myself then. Things would have been far easier that way.

FIVE

The Third Eye ... Keep on Truckin' ... The Ballad of the Human Guinea Pig ...
The Good Doctor Meets the Professor and the Starry Wisdom Wacko ... The Nutcracker ...
Please Wait Until the Captain Has Turned Off the No-Smoking Sign ...
No Sleep till Innsmouth ...

With only thirty minutes to get to the airport, I don't dawdle or even wash my hands, especially because I do not want to be there when the weirdo motel manager recovers his senses. Sticking around for such an eventuality would only lead to more great and terrible violence or a visit from the police, or both, and I am in no mood for such nonsense. I have a job to do, damn it, and a plane to catch. The hash has leveled me out some, but I still feel edgy and wired. I want to eat another shroom, but experience has taught me that those things are dangerous. I can't afford to get sucked into another vivid nightmare, only to wake up in a gutter somewhere along the side of the road and nowhere near the airport. Not now. Besides, the previous one has left a nasty aftertaste in my mouth, as if I've bitten into a gorilla's stomach. My tongue feels like it has hair on it, and the insides of my cheeks are dry. My head throbs slightly, right in the center, and I wonder if the hallucinogen has somehow affected my pineal gland.

A strange thing, the pineal gland. Oh, the human body has many strange things inside our workings, most of them nothing more than leftover tissue that evolution has made obsolete; the appendix, tonsils, and adenoids serve no useful purpose anymore, yet still we have them. The pineal gland is a different sort of organ. It's in charge of our waking and sleeping patterns, makes melatonin, and helps our bodies adjust to the changing seasons, but some people believe that it serves another, more metaphysical purpose. Some people believe that the pineal gland is where the human soul resides, and who knows? Maybe they are right. That old Frog philosopher René Descartes believed it to be so, but he also believed that the external world didn't exist, and he also had a hard-on for God, so he is not to be trusted. Never trust a man who works from his bed, especially if that man is French. I have worked from many strange places, including beaches and my kitchen, but I have never written in bed. But never mind that. Many other cultures give special significance to the pineal gland, as well, believing it to be a third eye, of sorts, and that if one learns to utilize it properly, one could then see into the future and all sorts of other things. *Was that what happened to me*, I wonder as I prepare to leave. Did the shrooms Mac gave me somehow stimulate my pineal gland, allowing me to see what was actually occurring at that exact moment in the subterranean dungeons beneath the White House? If so, I'll need to obtain more of them, because what few caps I have in the bag won't last very long at all.

I leave the motel, kit bag in tow, and begin hitchhiking in the darkness. It's cold outside, and the dampness seeps right through my shoes and clothes. Within minutes, they are numb. Traffic is non-existent, so I start walking, keeping one arm cocked and my thumb outstretched. Like everything else in this country, hitchhiking has turned into a dangerous and foolhardy thing to do. There are a lot of sickos in America these days, and not all of them reside in Washington or Hollywood. You have to be crazy to hitch a ride from a total stranger, and when it comes to being crazy, I am just the man for the job. The only thing I need is a passing car, but that sudden burst of luck and happenstance has apparently already faded, because transport is not forthcoming. The kit bag weighs heavy on my back, and the throbbing in my head is growing worse. The numbness spreads to my arms and legs. I fear that my ears and nose might blacken from frostbite and fall off to be eaten by rats.

But then, just as I am about to despair, headlights appear on the horizon, filling my heart with hope—only to have those hopes dashed a moment later when the car speeds by without even slowing. I retract my thumb and extend my middle finger, flashing that universally understood hand gesture, and trudge along, muttering curses beneath my breath. Another car appears, slowing as it approaches me. I hold up my thumb hopefully, smiling the smile I use when I want to convince people that I'm not a madman but just a simple country boy from Louisville, Kentucky, who goes to church and pays his taxes on time and always votes for the correct party, and there's nothing to worry about with me, you can trust me because I am not like the others. The car's brake lights flash, and the driver rolls to a stop about ten yards ahead of me.

"Hot damn!" Grinning, I run for the car, my kit bag swaying back and forth, whapping me in the rump again and again. It is too dark to see inside the vehicle, but I don't care. Charles Manson, or hell, G. Gordon Liddy, could be driving the fucking thing, and I would still accept the lift. As I reach for the door, the car speeds away. I hear the driver laughing inside, cackling like a rabid hyena.

"You pig-sucking bastard!" I shake my fist at the receding tail-lights. The driver honks his horn in a final farewell. "I hope you slide into a station wagon with a family of six inside it around the next bend and go to prison for manslaughter and get raped so much that you contract ass cancer and shit out your own bloody bowels on a daily basis until you die!" I take a deep breath, preparing to launch another string of obscene threats, when I hear a rumbling sound. A tractor-trailer is approaching, looming over the hill like some great mythical beast. I stick out my thumb again, all too aware that the clock is ticking and I am no closer to the airport. Providence shines down upon me then, as the eighteen-wheeler slows to a stop. The air brakes whoosh loudly and the suspension groans. Gravel crunches beneath the hulk. I approach with trepidation, wondering if this bastard will take off at the last moment too, but the truck remains in place. Grateful, I reach up, open the door, and climb aboard. The cab is dimly lit, and I have to let my eyes adjust, but nothing seems off kilter. The driver is young, probably in his late twenties or early thirties, dressed in blue jeans and a T-shirt emblazoned with R. Crumb's Mr. Natural and the Day-Glo block-letter slogan *Keep on Truckin'* overtop the character. Greasy, limp, brown locks stick out from beneath the brim of a green John Deere ball cap. Merle Haggard plays softly on the truck's radio, singing about what it is like to be an Okie from Muskogee, and from what I can gather, it doesn't sound like a whole lot of fun, unless your idea of a good time is a good old-fashioned tent revival with members of the Hitler Youth Party. My eyes drift back down to the trucker's T-shirt. That damn Mr. Natural image is everywhere these days. I wonder for a second if Crumb based Mr. Natural on a real person, and if so, how the poor bastard feels seeing his caricature emblazoned on T-shirts, stickers, and acid tabs. Probably not. I stand alone in that fraternity of one.

"You gonna gawk all night, fella," the driver asks, impatient, "or are you gonna sit down? I've got a tight schedule to keep and I aim to beat it." His accent is odd, unplaceable, as if I'm hearing him underwater. Like so many things these days. The shrooms, could it be?

"Sorry." With a nod I sit down next to him and pull the door shut, then sink into the puke-green Naugahyde vinyl seat. "I've got a schedule to keep as well, friend. I was just momentarily admiring the decor. This is my first time in one of these big rigs. Thanks for the ride."

The trucker nods back and then grabs the gearshift like it's his own manhood and rolls back onto the highway. The engine rumbles as he quickly shifts gears, and then we're picking up speed.

"Say," I say, "this thing really moves. I would have thought it would be slower, given the size. And it seems to handle well, too."

"She'll run like a raped ape once I give her full throttle, on account of that four-stroke diesel and the turbocharger and aftercooler."

"I'm impressed."

He glances sideways at me. "You don't strike me as much of a motor head, if you don't mind my saying so."

"Oh, I dabble. I dabble. I like fast things. Cars. Motorcycles. Women. Secret planets. Never had the opportunity to drive something like this, though. I may have to try it some day. Do you enjoy it?"

"There ain't anywhere else in the world I'd rather be." He takes one hand off the steering wheel and offers it to me. "My name's Smitty. Nice to meet you."

"Lono," I say, and I shake his hand. His palm is callused and his fingers are thick and strong, like mine, the hands of a workingman, a kindred spirit perhaps, though his musical choice leaves something to be desired. I would much prefer Blind Boy Fuller's "Truckin' My Blues Away" to Merle Haggard wailing about how the kids in Muskogee don't wear their hair long and shaggy, and still respect the college dean. "Good to meet you, as well, friend."

"Where you heading, Lono?"

"The airport, and hopefully soon. I've got a very important plane to catch and it leaves in less than half an hour."

"Well, then I reckon you're in luck. That's where I'm heading, too. Gotta pick up a load of stuff what come in air freight and then haul it back home."

"And where's that? Home?"

"St. Louis, technically. Or at least that's where my apartment is. Not that I stay there much. In truth, if anything is really home, it's this here cab we're sitting in. I spend more of my time on the road than anywhere else."

"And you like that, do you?"

"Wouldn't have it any other way. Something about the open road that's always appealed to me."

"I know that feeling well. Must be hard on your loved ones, though." I glance at his finger. There is no wedding band or even the ghostly shadow of where one has been. This tells me he's not married. A professional journalist always pays attention to the little details, and I am nothing if not a professional journalist. And he has five fingers. Thank God, five fingers and not six, like Mac.

"Nah," Smitty replies, pausing long enough to shake a Marlboro from a pack. He offers me one and I accept, partaking in this new dark age's version of breaking bread. I offer my lighter and he thanks me. After we've both lit up, he continues, exhaling a puff of smoke. "Ain't never been married. Hell, I don't even have a steady girlfriend. Oh, don't get me wrong. I ain't no queer or nothing like that. I've got girls I see sometimes along the various routes. Just never seemed to settle down with one. Last steady girlfriend I had was in college."

"And what happened to her?"

The trucker's mood noticeably sours. "We both dropped out. She headed out to Berkeley while I was in Vietnam. Haven't heard from her since."

"Berkeley? I used to live there."

"Ain't never been myself. Doesn't much sound like my kind of place."

"It's not my kind of place anymore, either. It's changing, and not for the better."

"Reckon the same could be said of the rest of the country."

"You may very well be right, Smitty. So, Vietnam, eh?"

"Yep." He says it reluctantly, and his tone is pensive, as if he's expecting to be beaten.

"When did you serve?"

"Couple years ago. Sixty-eight into sixty-nine. First Cavalry."

"Airborne, eh? You've got bigger balls than I do, friend. I've never understood the impulse that compels men to jump out of a perfectly good airplane."

Smitty chuckles. "Helicopter, actually, but in truth, I wasn't all that fond of it, either. Most of our guys were so fucked up half the time, I doubt they even thought about it much. But believe me, looking back on it, I'd have rather stayed in college than parachuting out of a low-flying chopper and into a tree. Fucking gooks used to cut us up before we'd even hit the ground and rolled. Sorry. I reckon I shouldn't use that term."

"No need to apologize. We live in an era when Hamilton Jordan can run around calling Arabs sand niggers, and nobody seems to mind much. I guess you can get away with calling the North Vietnamese gooks."

Smitty shakes his head, seeming genuinely regretful. "No, it ain't right. I've been meaning to stop. It just slips out sometimes. Old habits die hard, I guess."

"You're telling me, friend. I am a creature of old habits, and almost all of them are bad, or so my doctors and my attorney have said. But my attorney is most likely dead, and I've been ducking my doctor's calls because I owe that bastard money, so never mind them, eh?"

"You're a strange one, Lono. No offense."

"None taken."

"What do you do for a living?"

I listen carefully to his tone, seeking any sign that he suspects my true identity, and am cautiously overjoyed when I determine that he doesn't. Could this be the one person in America who hasn't read my work or seen me on television or laughed over that goddamned newspaper comic strip? A moment later, he confirms my suspicions.

"I'm a writer."

"Oh, yeah? What do you write?"

"Magazine articles. Books. Whatever they'll pay me for."

"I don't read much. No time for it out here on the road. Comics, occasionally, but that's about all."

"Comics as in the newspaper funnies?" I tense up, once again expecting him to put two and two together and realize who I am.

"No, I don't read that shit. I mean comic books."

Grinning, I relax, roll down the window, and flick my cigarette butt out into the dark. The horizon is that blue-black color that arrives just before dawn. I glance at my watch and wonder how close we are to the airport. Cold air whips my face. I roll the window up again and say, "I had an adventure with Jack Kirby just a few days ago."

"The guy who draws for Marvel? I don't read that stuff. Too much melodrama. I like the underground comix."

Merle Haggard fades away, and the song segues into a duet between Hank Williams and Patsy Cline. I tap along in time with the music. It's not so bad.

"You are not an easily definable man, Mr. Smitty. Indeed, you remind me, in some ways, of myself. I like the cut of your jib."

"Thanks . . . I think?"

"I'm being sincere. Are you a political junkie?"

"Not so much, no. I mean, I can't remember the last time I voted. It's all just the same thing since Kennedy died. Know what I mean? Ever since he was shot it just seems like America is going downhill faster and faster, and nobody cares as long as they still have money, a roof over their heads, a Ford or a Chevy in the driveway, and a piece of ass to keep them warm at night."

"A chicken in every pot," I whisper. "The American Dream. Not a burned-out slab of concrete in Las Vegas, but the real deal. The real American Dream. The guiding principle that made this country great."

"Yeah, but I don't reckon Kennedy would have fixed things either. I don't think they would have let him. This country is going to hell in a fucking handbasket, and I don't think either side has our best interests at heart anymore. They all answer to someone else."

"Indeed, they serve dark masters. Different masters, as I'm discovering, but malignant all the same."

"What's that?"

"Nothing," I say, waving my hand in dismissal. "Ramblings of a diseased mind. I have been up working all night and am low on medicine. How close are we to the airport?"

"Not far now. About another ten minutes. Which terminal are you flying out of?"

I tell him, and perhaps it is the tone of my voice or the look in my eye, but he leans harder on the accelerator and the big rig's speed increases. Trees rush by in the darkness. The tires thrum.

"Need for speed, eh?" I ask with a wink.

Misunderstanding me, Smitty shakes his head. "No, I don't mess with that stuff. Some of the other drivers do. They pop those black beauties and shit like that, but not me."

"You don't use anything at all?"

"I got high a few times in the Nam. To be honest, I liked it. It's natural, ya know? Not like this chemical shit people are snorting and shooting and swallowing. Weed comes from the earth. But I don't do it much anymore. It always makes me hungry and sleepy, and ain't neither one of those things good for a long-haul truck driver."

"Indeed. How about shrooms?"

"Mushrooms? I've heard about them, but I ain't never took one. Saw a thing on TV once. Cronkite was talking about them and peyote. Some folks want to use them in religious ceremonies and such. I can't say as I see the harm in it, but I've never had them. Only mushrooms I eat is on my pizza." He laughs at this, and I chuckle along with him, even as my great and terrible mind is seized with an idea. I need to find out if what I'd seen while under the shrooms' influence was a real, transcendental experience or simply yet another nonsensical, drug-fueled hallucination, and what better way to find out than to test Mac's stash on someone else? And a pigeon like my new friend Smitty is an absolutely perfect test subject. Here is a man who very rarely uses drugs, let alone powerful hallucinogens. He has a belief structure that he seems firm and steadfast in, and a relaxed demeanor. He is a solitary man who probably spends much of his day in a forced-laconic silence broken only by his occasional interactions with truck-stop patrons, waitresses, fuel-station attendants, and the flotsam and jetsam of America's highways—hitchhikers like myself. If Smitty sees the same things I saw, if he reports Nixon squirming in shame and embarrassment while some writhing green-black tendril shoots a jet of semen over Kissinger's face, then I'll know the trip was real. If he doesn't . . . well, the high is still an enjoyable one, and I'll take the rest of the mushrooms eventually. Perhaps I'll try to write while under their influence. There could be a new book in it.

The only risk in dosing Smitty is that I can't do it while he's behind the wheel. Oh, I could, I suppose, but I need to make that flight. I can't risk him missing our turn or wrecking the big rig. My only option is to wait until we arrive at the airport, and hope the psilocybin kicks in before I have to leave. Of course, before I can do any of that, I have to convince the trucker to be my guinea pig, so I start laying down some heavy patter. I tell him all about how natural it is, and the long tradition of medicinal and shamanic uses for mushrooms, and how it will give him an extra boost of energy for the long drive back home, and that there are no side effects or danger. No indeed. Mushrooms are a mild drug, milder than weed. Everybody knows that, don't they? I trot out my best lies and my patented smile, the kind I use when I need to rob a bank or get into someone's bed or secure an interview that no one else can get, and of course, it works, for my powers are great and varied and wondrous. "It'll cut two-tenths out of every mile," I tell him. An eyebrow jerks. "Girls like it. It's like a first hug from a topless woman who likes a shy man." By the time we pull up to a loading dock near the terminal, my new friend is ready to try it.

"Why not?" He turns toward me, his expression eager. "Ain't nobody gonna be able to load me up for another hour anyway. Damn union workers don't come in till later."

"Well then, this will be a great way to pass the time."

"And you're sure I'll be able to drive later?"

"Oh, absolutely. Have I ever lied to you, my friend?"

"Well, I don't really—"

"Never mind that! You can trust me. I am not like the others."

I sweep my kit bag off the seat and rummage through it, producing the brown paper bag. I pull out a shroom and hand it to Smitty, who accepts it gingerly. He seems unsure.

"Aren't you gonna take one, too?"

"I already have. I took one earlier before I started hitchhiking. I'm still under its effects right now. And I'm fine. We had a nice, civilized conversation about John Fitzgerald Kennedy and underground comix, and I didn't mention bats or lizard people once."

"Is that the kind of thing you normally do?"

"Only when I'm in Bat Country."

He visibly relaxes, shoulders slumping and face growing less taut. "Well, you seem okay. Don't guess it will turn me into an axe murderer or anything."

"Of course not." I glance at my watch. "Let's go. Down the hatch. Airborne!"

"All the way!" He takes a tentative bite and scowls. "Ewww. It's bitter."

"Chew the whole thing and swallow. Try not to taste it. Just let it hit the back of your throat, rather than your tongue. There you go. That's the way."

While he does as I've instructed, I search through my kit bag some more and produce my tape recorder. I test it, making sure the batteries are fresh. I once lost a great interview with Grace Slick because I was so stoned that I forgot to put batteries in the damn tape recorder. Satisfied that this won't be the case now, I place the machine on the seat between us and press record.

"What's that for?" Smitty eyes the tape recorder like it's a skinned raccoon.

"Professional tool of the trade. Nothing to worry about. How do you feel?"

Smitty leans back in the seat and closes his eyes. "I feel . . . I dunno. It doesn't really feel like anything. Are you sure these things can—" And then, before he can say anything else, his body begins to spasm.

"Hot damn," I shout. "Now we're getting somewhere. This is science!"

"I'm proud to be a stogie from Tuskegeee," Smitty shrieks in a high singsong voice. "A place where even balls can have a square!" He flops on the seat, arms and legs jittering, head lolling back and forth so hard that for a moment I fear he might snap his neck. Frothy saliva bubbles appear on his lips, and when he moans, it is a deep, mournful sound—the kind that breaks your heart, if you happen to have one. But I have no time for tugging heartstrings or sad sentiment. I am a man with a mission.

"What do you see, Smitty? Quick! Tell me everything. Where are you? Do you see President Nixon?"

"No. Oh, God. Oh, goddamn. They're shooting up the high school. All dressed in black . . . They . . . Where'd they get guns like that? Hell, they've got better rifles than what we had over in the Nam. And they . . . oh, I can't watch. I don't want to be here. The blood . . . that poor girl's head. It's just like fucking Nam . . . It's like being back in the jungle . . . I've got to go! They'll find me. Better hide behind one of these tables."

"Where are you, man? Beneath the White House? Talk to me, damn you."

"No . . . not the White House. I'm . . . I'm in a . . . in a high-school cafeteria, I think. Or maybe . . . no . . . no, it's changed. It's all changing. The world turned . . . changed colors for a second . . . I think I'm in New York City now. Yeah! That's it. New York City. God, I always wanted to see this place! It's really something. Look at those buildings."

"What's happening in New York?"

"Nothing and everything. People are rushing around. I guess on their way to work. Oh, look! Look, Lono. There's the Twin Towers, all bright and shiny. Damn if that ain't something to see."

I check my watch again and decide it would be best to just let him ramble, rather than trying to guide him through the vision. Obviously, he isn't seeing what I saw, but his hallucinations are interesting nevertheless. I can easily record it all now, until it is time for me to go, and then play it back later and try to make sense of it.

"It's such a pretty day, too. Ya know, I always figured the sky over New York would be all polluted and cloudy, but it's not . . . It's very blue. And warm. And . . . holy shit. Look at that! It's a fucking airplane. I reckon he's flying too low. He ought to . . . Oh my God. He . . . goddamn . . . the fire. Oh, Lord, I can't look. Two of them. How could there be two of them? That ain't no accident . . . And the people are jumping . . . and . . . and . . . where did they go? Where did the skyscrapers go? There was all that dust and smoke and now they're . . . oh, wait a minute. I see . . . they're not there because I'm not there anymore. Hey, mister, it's . . . your father or someone. Oh man, a gun. The words on a typewriter—no, just one . . . counselor."

"What the hell are you talking about, Smitty? Something happened to the World Trade Center?"

"No, I'm in New Orleans . . . Hell, I know this place. Done so many runs to New Orleans and back. But it looks . . . different, somehow. More . . . I dunno. The sky is . . . Boy, this storm is really bad. I reckon it's gonna . . . oh, hell no! Oh, Christ. Jesus fucking Christ! The wind . . . the wind! Sounds like a goddamned freight train. The water keeps getting higher and it's full of . . . there's oil and . . . bodies . . . The stadium. And they're in the streets . . . all those people . . . and . . . here come the cops. They'll help, right? The police always help . . . they . . . why is he drawing his gun? What does he think . . . Fuck! The cops are shooting them . . . wait, something's happening again . . . where am I? I don't . . . urrrggghhh . . . maybe India? There's a lot of Indian people on the beach . . . not the *Woo-Woo* kind . . . the kind with the dots . . . they . . . Oh, Jesus, oh sweet Jesus . . . fuck . . . FUCK . . . fuckfuckfuckfuck . . .

the goddamned ocean . . . the goddamned ocean rose up and at-
tacked . . . I swear to God the ocean just declared war . . . it can't
. . . water everywhere . . . here it comes . . ."

A particularly strong spasm rocks Smitty. His entire body shud-
ders as if he's touched a live wire, which he probably has. His teeth
chatter like nuts cracking. The cab suddenly smells like piss. I
glance down and see a spreading stain on the crotch of his jeans.
I check my watch. It's almost time to board.

"Listen," Smitty wheezes. "This is important. South forty-
seven . . . nine . . . West . . . one twenty-six . . . forty-three . . ."

I realize that he's giving me coordinates. Latitude and longi-
tude. But where do they go? What do they lead to?

"He's coming! Oh, he's coming, Lono . . . They said he would!
This has all . . . this has all been written. *Ph'nglui mglw'nafh Cthulhu
R'lyeh wgah'nagl fhtagn* . . . In his house at R'lyeh dead Cthulhu
waits dreaming . . . That's not dead . . . which can eternal lie, and
with strange eons even death may die! Don't you see? He wasn't
dead. All this time, he wasn't fucking dead. Only sleeping . . .
Gods never die . . . He's . . . He's coming back. Great Cthulhu is
coming back . . . R'lyeh is rising, you see? The Mayans . . . they
knew, man. They fucking knew!"

R'lyeh. The word runs around in my head, looking for something to connect to. I've heard it before, but I can't remember
where. I turn my attention back to Smitty. His eyes have rolled up
into his head, and he's bitten his bottom lip. Blood runs down his
chin.

"I reckon all these things are like ripples," he says. "The shooting, the towers . . . the water. It's like he's sending shock waves across
the world as he gets closer and closer . . . Wait . . . R'lyeh is there
now, like an island . . . Except that it's a city. It's a huge fucking city
from the . . . bottom of the ocean . . . It was down there in the Pacific
. . . and now it's . . . and . . . All dripping and covered with slime
and seaweed . . . The pillars . . . oh, the pillars, Lono . . . And now
there's . . . I ain't . . . I can't . . . A mountain walks! A mountain

walks . . . I don't understand, Lono. It's big, whatever it is. Like them pictures of . . . It's . . . oh my God, his face! *IT'S HIS FACE! Ia ia, Cthulhu fhtagn . . .*"

"Sorry, Smitty, but I have to run. Got a plane to catch and other places to be. I wanted to stop at the duty-free store. I mean, I know I have a domestic ticket and so can't quite buy anything there legitimately, but I usually find that a smile works wonders over the course of any sort of transaction. Thanks for the lift."

"He has a squid where his face should be! How can he have a fucking squid for a head? Lono? Are you there? His face is . . . *moving.*"

"Get a grip on yourself! Courage, man."

He begins to weep, and in between the sobs, he babbles about a black goat with a thousand young and something called a Shoggoth. The phrase strikes a chord with me, just as the word R'lyeh did. Didn't the vagrant in the bus station where I began this journey mention that word, *Shoggoth,* as well? I think it's possible, but then again, I haven't always been in control of my faculties during this trip. As I consider this, Smitty's sentences turn into more of that weird, inhuman gibberish. It sounds like somebody sneezing backward during an epileptic seizure.

I grab the tape recorder and stuff it in my bag. Then I hop out of the cab and slam the door, cutting off the rest of his plaintive cries. He'll be all right. This is what I tell myself so that I can safely abscond with a clear conscience. An hour from now, one of the union dockworkers will come in and find him there, sitting in his idling truck and drooling all over himself and bleeding and babbling about oceans attacking people and squid-headed demigods. Business as usual for the late shift, probably. Your average union member deals with strangeness like that every day, and if they can't, then they shouldn't pay their dues.

Moloch. Cthulhu. Ancient religions and weird cults and politics as usual. Just what the hell have I gotten mixed up in? None of it makes any goddamned sense, and trying to sort it out as I run across the tarmac only gives me a headache. I need sleep and whis-key. Both await me on the plane. All I have to do is reach it.

It started raining while I was in the truck with Smitty, and I get soaked as I race across the tarmac, heading for the terminal. I burst inside, breathless and dripping and most likely looking like a rabid dog in heat judging by the expression of the people around me. I didn't expect the terminal to be this crowded so early in the morn-ing. Who knew this many people out here in the middle of nowhere had other places to be? Perhaps they're fleeing, or maybe they're on their own personal quests, as well. If so, I wish them luck, and hope that they'll appreciate my efforts toward saving the world should those efforts lead to my untimely demise. I feel an unsettling cer-tainty that said demise will be happening sooner rather than later, but then again, I've felt that way most days. It is true that I have gone through life expecting that demise to happen at any time. As a teen, back in Kentucky, I never expected to reach my twenties. A psy-chiatrist might say that's because my father died of myasthenia gravis when I was fourteen. Poor bastard. One day, he was fine. The next, his eyelids began drooping and he had trouble talking and swallow-ing. Eventually, he couldn't even breathe on his own as, one by one, his muscles grew weak and betrayed him. He was only fifty-eight years old at the time, not a spring chicken by any means, but still in good health, strapping and robust and full of life—until suddenly when he wasn't. Late at night, when the whiskey and caffeine and drugs and tobacco are coursing through my system working their special form of alchemy, I think about that. I certainly inherited my father's patriotism, but I suppose his untimely passing is where my nihilistic fatalism came from. In my twenties, I never thought I'd make it to thirty. I was sure that my time in the air force would finish me, or that the editor of that newspaper in Jersey Shore, Pennsylvania, whose car I crashed into his home (while his daughter was sitting next to me) would shoot me dead. And Puerto Rico . . . ye Gods, how did I ever survive that gig as a stringer? And yet, I did. I survived unscathed and crossed over into my thirties. The

Hells Angels. Las Vegas. I should be dead a hundred times over, just like my attorney the Brown Buffalo, but I'm not dead yet, and I don't have time to fuck around with the complete water heads staring at me like I am a madman.

"Move aside," I shout. "I am here on official business and you are impeding my progress. I have a plane to catch and a world to save, and so help me God, if you people don't make a hole, this morning will end with great and terrible violence. I own many guns."

The crowd parts like the Red Sea, more from bemusement and the sheer impulse to obey (and aren't those often the same) than from fear, and I rush to the ticket counter, leaving wet tracks in my wake. I give the woman my name, my real name rather than my current adopted moniker, lowering my voice so that no one else overhears it, and she lets me know that I have barely made it in time, but that's okay, because she will call ahead and let them know to wait. Then she compliments me on the Vegas book and asks if I will sign an autograph for her. I scribble my name on the back of a receipt, add a little doodle that would make Ralph weep in pity at my digital retardation, and then head for the gate. Behind me, people stare and mutter amongst themselves, and I hear a fat, sweltering businessman ask the woman at the counter, "Who was that guy?" My cover is blown, and that's not good for business. I walk faster, hoping to melt into the crowd on the causeway, only to find my escape impeded by some nut in a brown robe. I step to the side and the geek steps with me, blocking me a second time. I dart left and so does he. I move right, and he does the same, smiling beatifically, his eyes blinking rapidly behind the huge lenses of his fingerprint-smudged eyeglasses.

"Excuse me, junior," I snap at him. "I don't have time to dance."

"Have you seen the Yellow Sign?" His voice is breathless and small, and filled with rapturous wonder, as if doing the two-step with me here in this airport is the best thing that has happened to him all day, and who knows, perhaps it is. I am anything if not a good dancer.

I take a closer look at my new friend. The only thing even remotely remarkable about this brain-damaged pinhead is the pendant hanging around his neck on a pewter chain. It's a gem in the shape of a trapezohedron that shines when the overhead lights hit it just right. Other than that adornment, the geek is uninteresting. His head is shaved clean right down to the scalp. Nothing wrong with that style, of course. I sported the same look back when I ran for sheriff of Aspen a few years ago, but on this guy, it looks strange. His skull is misshapen, and covered with strange knobs and indentations and a mole that bears an uncanny resemblance to either Jesus or Che Guevara. The brown robe hides what I suspect is a skinny frame. I estimate him to weigh one hundred and forty pounds, maybe soaking wet, and he is much shorter than me—just the sort of fellow one can run right over. He didn't even come in a trio like those Hare Krishnas do at the better airports. There's no threat here, unless the weirdo has a gun or a knife hidden inside the folds of his attire. Still, he's in my way, and I'm done with the dance. I reach out, find his balls beneath the robe, and give them a friendly squeeze hello.

"Now listen to me, you gap-toothed skunk fucker. I do not have time to play with you today. I don't know what your bag is or what you are about, and I don't really care, because right now, you are in my way. If you don't get out of my way, I will rip your balls off and stuff them in your mouth, after which I'll cut off your head and stump fuck your neck. I have never passed up an opportunity to relieve my fevered loins, and your spurting, headless corpse is just as good a receptacle as any. Do you dig? Nod once for yes and twice for no."

"I—"

"That's not a nod." My fist tightens in time with my smile. His testicles feel like two pralines in my hand. I wish I had the time to stop at the bar, get some bourbon for the flight up, for the head trip down, maybe grab a handful of nuts for my pocket, but these will have to do. Tears run out from behind his thick, smudged lenses. "Now try again, shit weasel."

He nods once, but then opens his mouth to speak. I squeeze harder, eliciting a squeak of pain and fright. Just then, someone taps me on the shoulder.

"We'll miss our flight."

Still holding the geek's balls, I turn at the intrusion and find myself staring at a middle-aged man in a gray tweed sports coat and sharply creased slacks. His salt-and-pepper beard is neatly trimmed, and his glasses, unlike those of my new dance partner, are immaculate. Almost lensless.

"What's that?"

"The six fifteen to Arkham," he says. "You're on it too, yes?"

"Who are you, and who do you work for?" My eyes narrow with suspicion. Was he CIA? FBI? DEA? Irish mobster? A rival editor?

"Professor Madison Haringa of Miskatonic University. We're on the same flight."

"How do you know that?"

"I was two people behind you in line at the ticket counter, and I'd recognize you anywhere. I'm an admirer of your work." I start to protest, but he cuts me off. "I also had the sense that perhaps you are . . . undercover, shall we say? If so, then please don't worry. Your secret is safe with me. What shall I call you instead?"

"Lono. Uncle Lono."

"Ah, very good. We should go. They won't hold the plane for long, I imagine."

I turn back to the geek. "What about you, smiley? If I let you go, are you going to behave yourself?"

He nods vigorously, the pendant swaying back and forth as he does, catching the light and shining brilliantly. It's very striking, and for a moment, my eyes center on it. "What the hell are you, anyway? A Moonie?"

"Close," the professor says. "In that he's a member of a cult. But your friend is no follower of Reverend Moon. Unless I'm mistaken, and I don't think I am, he is a devotee of the Church of Starry Wisdom."

"The what?" I let go of the geek, who collapses to his knees, moaning and cradling his balls in his hands. As we walk away, he bends over and vomits all over the tiles. *That's me in six hours,* I decide. I need another drink. Or twelve.

"The Church of Starry Wisdom," the professor continues as we hurry down the concourse, "also known as the Starry Wisdom Cult. They've been active since the mid-1800s, albeit not so publicly as they are now. All of these groups really went public with the Age of Aquarius."

"And how do you know this? Are you an expert on freak religions? What kind of religion even refers to itself as a cult?"

"No, I'm not an expert on freak religions, but I *am* an expert on ancient languages. I specialize in ancient grimoires. We have a remarkable library on campus. You should visit it sometime. We are the envy of occult researchers worldwide. So many rare volumes. *The Book of Eibon.* The *Daemonolatreia.* Abdul Alhazred's *Necronomicon.* Two different translations of Ludvig Prinn's *De Vermis Mysteriis.* We even have an original edition of Friedrich von Junzt's *Unaussprechlichen Kulten.*"

"Unspeakable cults," I translate. I mean, it's easy enough to do so. I could have made up *Unaussprechlichen Kulten.* Or how about *El Booko Loco de la Cultas Unspeakabalo,* in comedy Spanish, while I'm at it?

The professor nods. "Very good, Mr. Lono. I'm impressed." He's not really, but he's still friendly enough. It must be rough for a multidegreed scholar like him, specializing in writing about books nobody wants to read. "You've heard of these volumes?"

"I get around. I can order a whiskey in about twenty different languages."

"Indeed. I've read some of your dispatches. In truth, I'm surprised you haven't been to Vietnam yet."

"I keep meaning to. The place has been causing enough trouble that I suppose I'll have to look in on it sooner or later. But not right now. I have another assignment."

"I see."

"So this Starry Wisdom Cult . . . they're in this book?"

"*Unaussprechlichen Kulten*? No. The Church of Starry Wisdom didn't come along until 1844, when Professor Enoch Bowen founded it in Providence, Rhode Island. Bowen was an Egyptologist and archaeologist. He was an occultist, as well. He had a small fortune, and upon his return to the United States, he purchased the former Free-Will Church that sits atop Federal Hill and started the cult. They worshiped a deity they referred to as the Haunter of the Dark, who was most likely one of the thousands of guises of a malign god known as Nyarlathotep. The Haunter of the Dark gave them limitless knowledge, revealing the mysteries of the cosmos in exchange for human sacrifice. Of course, like any other religion, the cult had their share of sacred relics, the most prominent of which was known as the Shining Trapezohedron."

"Which is what Laughing Boy back there had around his neck." Even as I speak, I realize my error. This Haringa character isn't going to shut up—he speaks in term papers and gestures in footnotes. "*Was known* as Shining Trapezohedron, but now you see, Mr. Lono, it's called by a new generation of cultists the City that Shines upon the Hill, because . . ."

We continue our conversation, or Haringa does it for me, as we board the airplane. Outside, the sun has finally risen. It looks like it is going to be a beautiful day. I am very tired.

"The cult grew quite popular over time, despite the fact that it was denounced by the other local churches and scorned by many prominent local citizens and the local government. Eventually, they ran afoul of everyone from the authorities to Rhode Island's Sicilian crime families and by 1877, they publicly disbanded."

"But if they disbanded, then who was the guy in the airport?"

"Oh, they were run out of Providence, but the sect had already spread to other locales, and it flourished. San Francisco, Yorkshire, Chicago, Toronto, and even my beloved Arkham had church members."

"Church members? Church members are people who behave like pagans all week long—cheating on their spouses and their taxes, and maybe beating their kids around on Thursday night—and then go to church on Sunday to wash it all away. These Starry Wisdom wackos sound a little more . . . interestingly counterculture than that. Extreme. I'm a bit surprised the cat back there even retained enough scrotum to squeeze. Even as I reached out for him, I thought, *I hope this guy isn't one of those piano-wire eunuchs.*"

"They were back then," he says. "Extreme, I mean, not that other nasty business with the wire. But nowadays, Starry Wisdom is just another so-called"—and here Haringa raises his hands and flicks his fingers as though putting quotation marks around his exhalations, the sort of habit that normally earns a body a nose full of my forehead—"*New Age* religion. They congregate in airports and other public places, mostly selling trinkets like the one that fellow had around his neck, or trying to get people to sign up for their newsletter, *The Yellow Sign*. They did away with human sacrifice in the twenties."

We take our seats and the stewardess brings us our drinks, as though she knew what we were going to order. I have two double Wild Turkeys, a bottle of Heineken, and a fresh-squeezed grapefruit juice. Professor Haringa has a martini as dry as the stewardess can make it, which, Haringa declares after a whiff, "is not very." Soon enough, the airplane rockets down the tarmac, and then we're in the air. I've never minded flying, but I don't care for taking off and landing, and I find I do better with a drink in my hand. Luckily, I have two hands and two drinks. I make quick work of them both. Then I chase them down with the beer and the juice. Finally, I lean back in my seat and close my eyes. I plan on sleeping until we've landed in Arkham. After that, I'll pick up the rental car and make my way to Innsmouth. I consider asking the professor for his perceptions of the Innsmouth race riots, but he is already snoring. Apparently, he's tired, too. Shrugging, I decide to join him.

SIX

Witch-Cursed and Legend-Haunted . . . It's a Two-Newspaper Town, but Ain't Nothing
Worth Reading . . . This Is Radio Dunwich . . . Perky Coeds and Puppy Love . . . Strange
Rumblings at Miskatonic University . . . Spaghetti Dinners with the Nixon Youth . . .
Moloch! . . . Race Riots Delivered to Your Door, Courtesy of the Teamsters Themselves . . .
Never Trust an Intellectual, Even If He Has a Nixon Bumper Sticker Emblazoned on His
Soul . . . Speak Softly, but Drive a Big Truck . . .

Arkham has two newspapers, which is pretty amazing given that there can't be more than fifty thousand people living in the town, which is only forty minutes outside of Boston, itself the home of the mighty *Boston Globe*. Not to mention the fact that everyone in the town seems walleyed and illiterate, a legion of drooling hatchlings all fired up just in time for election season! How long, oh Lord, how long? For a pair of dimes, I get copies of both the *Arkham Advertiser* and the *Arkham Gazette*. I buy one of each from the newsstand in the airport, and then I pick up my rental car.

The travel writer Howard Phillips, who wrote extensively about the New England area back in the 1930s, once described Arkham as an "ancient, moldering, and subtly fearsome town" that was "witch-cursed, legend-haunted" and whose "huddled, sagging gambrel roofs and crumbling Georgian balustrades brood out over the centuries beside the darkly muttering Miskatonic River." Sort of purple and wordy, but you get the gist, eh? If there's an American Nightmare anywhere in this Norman Rockwell region, it's here. I was curious to see if that description still held water forty years later, but after about twenty minutes of skimming the pages of the paper and sipping some river-water coffee—an inexplicable local delicacy—I decide that I've about had my fill of both the town and its newspapers.

I still don't know what's going on, other than that two opposing deities, Moloch and Cthulhu, seem hell bent on getting their political spawn elected. With this in mind, it's pretty easy to figure out that the *Gazette* is the local Cthulhu rag, and the *Advertiser*'s editorial board is Team Moloch through and through. Arkham is a twisted little burg, half desiccated mill town, half college town, with a black river cutting right through the city and leading to Boston Harbor. Even the greatest moonshine-addled John Bircher knows that Massachusetts will go to the Democrats in November, so what could the story possibly be in this poisonous, inbred little pit of a town? Eagleton out, and who . . . in? Or was it a black op by the Republicans—Eagleton appeared in my vision just as he had appeared before me in what I'm having increasing trouble calling real life. Eagleton strapped spread-eagled, taking electroshock to his groin and nipples . . . Was he the key to Democratic victory somehow, or would he be a pawn in a Byzantine plan to throw the election to Nixon? Eagleton's a Catholic, like Kennedy was, and a Harvard man, but he's also a whimpering midwestern simpleton. And if he wasn't before, the Kirby acid should have done something to him. And the connection to Arkham . . .

It's all in the newspapers. It always is. You can divine things from newspapers the same way you can from tea leaves or star patterns or a bloody pile of chicken guts. You just have to know what you're looking for. Reporters know how to read the hidden column inches, the grafs cut from the bottom and hidden from the gaping eyes of the upright, clueless citizen. The placement of ads, the pseudonyms used on the letters page, the increasing contamination of "op-ed" pages, almost all of which are written directly by Dick Nixon himself, that pathetic, pig-raping Quaker, always with an eye toward fairness and balance and the whole story, so long as the whole story is all about himself and his dark plans for America.

The *Gazette* is a broadsheet, the *Advertiser* a tabloid—neither of them breaks the brains of its readers in the vocabulary department, but the former paper at least licks a sixth-grade reading level. My old friend Professor Haringa will probably be very pleased to sit on the commode reading the Saturday edition, a tune-up match for his manful tussling with the Sunday *New York Times* at brunch the next day. The *Gazette*'s front page is a mix of Boston news and denunciations of the campus hippies and freaks, while the *Advertiser* leads with unemployment statistics and photos of dead boys in their dress blues. Nam has chewed up and spit out a full English of Arkham boys from the lower orders this past week: kids named Maciej, Pilonovsky, Serrano, and even a Negro named Washington.

But one curious thing catches my attention. It is the sort of thing that makes the hair on my arms tingle and gets my curiosity jiggling deep down in my journalistic loins. The papers have something in common—horoscopes with signs of the sort I've never seen before. Symbols are printed next to the signs in black and white. They are strange, eldritch things. Apparently, my sign is the Hound, and today's horoscope, which went to press just about the time I was squeezing Smiley's balls back in the airport, reads as follows:

Gazette: Today the stars are right to discover that you are a part of something greater than yourself. Do away with the narcissism of the modern age and embrace your role in the universe.

Advertiser: Hungry hounds today would do well to eat out; treat yourself to a spaghetti dinner or even some midnight pancakes tonight.

Hey, hey! A spaghetti dinner, just the sort of thing the Essex County Democratic Party Committee would throw in order to shore up the troops on the ground. And, lo verily, I spy an ad inviting "all and sundry" to just such a dinner. I should have packed a bib. Six p.m. at the village fire station. I've plenty of time to burn until then and not a lot of town to burn it in, so I decide to follow up on the only other lead I have—Miskatonic University. Professor Haringa gave me his card when we parted at the airport, and college campuses are still college campuses, after Austin, after Columbia, and even after Kent State. Perhaps more so now.

Miskatonic University was one of the also-rans for children of the wealthy too inbred and silly for the Ivy League, and its original curriculum was simple—law, clerical studies, and the classics of Greek and Latin. How to be bourgeois in four easy lessons, the first being simply the practical expression of that timeless recipe for success—selecting and then being born to wealthy, white, Protestant parents. Lacking the cachet, and the business college, of Harvard or Princeton, Miskatonic University's twentieth century was shaping up to be as dark as the rest of the town, Unspeakable Cults or no. But when the sixties swept through America, and when on a warm summer day in August several years ago, a former marine named Charles Whitman killed his wife and mother and then mounted that tower at UT–Austin and fired his opening salvo in the war against history by killing sixteen people and wounding over thirty more, Miskatonic was unmoved. Down in Morningside Heights, blocks from simmering Negro Harlem, the sons and daughters of privilege took to the barricades and threatened Aristotle, Spinoza, and Hume with expulsion, to be replaced by Marx, Lenin, and Mao. Miskatonic finally let up on its collar-length-hair rules in the same year. And when members of the Ohio National Guard opened fire into a crowd of student demonstrators, when campus quadrangles across the country went mad with the fever of revolution and dissent, Miskatonic, or at least one Professor Madison Haringa, who had certainly achieved tenure just at that very moment, found himself more interested in another shape: the trapezohedron—both the symbol of the Starry Wisdom Cult and, flattened as if by a rolling pin, the outline of the Miskatonic University campus.

I know this because I have been paying attention. I am not some talking head, some corporate toady filing empty bylines approved by the party of choice. No, I am something different. I am a writer, and a practitioner of ancient Gonzo wisdom.

My old friend, Professor Madison Haringa, is a member of the Starry Wisdom Cult; of that I have no doubt. My instincts are finely honed after years on the Freak Power beat; that he had found me was too much of a coincidence to be a coincidence; that he was so forthcoming with his invitation that my arrival would be the last thing he expected, that he was so loose with esoteric information that there must be another 777 layers of occult truth in the stacks of the special-collections room. Oh, he is good. He is crafty. But I am better. On the airplane he drank and then immediately napped, just like a faculty advisor would. On the streets of Arkham, in this rough proletarian district, any bald-headed Smiley would be torn to shreds by a mass by burly hardhats in the throes of a homosexual panic. Those geeks have to be holed up in a dormitory somewhere, contemplating the mysteries of the cosmos and praying that their finals will be graded on a curve.

I tear out the horoscopes and stuff them into my pocket. Then I toss both papers in a nearby trash can, and finally, after sucking my cigarette down to the filter, throw the still-smoldering butt into the receptacle, as well. The cigarette tasted better than that useless cup of coffee did. I stand up, wincing at the stench wafting off the river. A moment later, wisps of smoke begin billowing out of the trash can. As I walk away, there's a good old-fashioned bonfire going, fed by the official periodicals of Team Moloch and Team Cthulhu, and the air begins to smell like burning garbage. The odor is much preferable to that of the river. I return to my rental car and drive away with the windows down, despite the freezing temperatures. The cold air washes me clean.

Renewed, I roll up the windows and turn on the heater and the radio. As warm air flows over my ankles and hands and defrosts my windshield, I scan the dial, sampling the local flavors. There are lots of stations out of Boston, playing everything you'd expect—soul and rock to country and western. I spin the dial faster, eliciting a bizarre, high-speed mix of Frank Sinatra, Sly and the Family Stone, Led Zeppelin, Trini Lopez, Neil Diamond, Mac Davis, and Vivaldi, along with hog and farm reports, stock updates, and news. I find an interesting local call-in show at 580 on the AM dial, a station identified as broadcasting from nearby Dunwich, yet another decrepit town whose populace are poor, inbred, uneducated, and very superstitious. The announcer, who identifies himself as Ned Derleth, takes call after call from locals offering items for sale—refrigerators, cars, clothing, unwanted toys, fresh produce. If it can be fetched down from the attic and turned into a buck, they're offering it on the radio. Ned's voice is a deep and sonorous baritone. The accents of the callers set my teeth on edge, but I listen, unable to change the dial. My heart bleeds for these people. The desperation in their voices, the emptiness of their lives . . . It's all too much. A young woman who says her name is "Roberta Price from down near Kingsport" tells Ned that her infant daughter has passed away—crib death—and she's looking to sell the child's clothes, crib, and high chair. She gives her phone number, and Ned takes the next call. A farmer named Gilman is selling four tires. Ned has the man give his phone number so that interested buyers can reach him, but then Gilman launches into a bizarre and rambling monologue about a dream he had the night before. Ned politely cuts him off and moves on to the next caller. It's a man named Whateley, and he's looking for his Uncle Wilbur. I get the impression that old Uncle Wilbur must be the town drunk, and is currently sleeping it off up at some place called Sentinel Hill. Anyone who has seen Wilbur is asked to call. After a commercial for Tremblay's Chevrolet (with locations in Dunwich, Innsmouth, and Arkham, the jingle says) the show returns, but I am gone, unable to take any more. I turn the radio off and listen to the wind instead. It howls off the river like some mythical wendigo, intent on running me off the road and ripping the roof from the rental car. Gritting my teeth, I light another cigarette and struggle against the wintry gale. The car responds well, and I decide that I like it.

Not my usual type of vehicle—not sporty or fast enough—but dependable and sturdy, all the same.

I drive through a cluster of desultory strip centers, mostly vacant, their dusty windows dotted with signs advertising COMMERCIAL SPACE FOR RENT. Then I make my way through street after street filled with those "huddled, sagging, gambrel-roofed, crumbling Georgian balustrades" that Phillips wrote of. The travel writer was correct. The houses do brood over the centuries here. They have nothing to look forward to, and looking back on their past—at least the past of the last few decades—is an exercise in both futility and madness. And speaking of madness, there's the Arkham Sanitarium. A quick look seems to confer that the architect who designed it was most likely inspired by the Danvers State Insane Asylum. Not much else to tell. It is as decrepit and huddled as the rest of Arkham's buildings. I see something out of the corner of my eye, some *thing* on the doorstep of the sanitarium, but then the traffic light changes and I am moving again. When I glance back, the thing on the doorstep, whatever it was, is gone. Unnerved by the experience, but unable to articulate why, I focus on the bucolic businesses and buildings that surround me—a gas station, Forringer's Foreign Currency and Coins, a grocery store, the local VFW and American Legion halls, a sporting-goods store, Pickman's Motel, a hardware store, a Ruritan Club, the Arkham Historical Society, a used bookstore, the Future Farmers of America, a haberdashery, a bar called the Barrens, another tavern simply called Joshi's Place, and an assortment of other merchants and social clubs. All are just what you'd expect in any town the size of Arkham, albeit quieter or more desultory. There are a number of small offices, belonging mostly to lawyers, dentists, doctors, and accountants, and a few abandoned factories and mills, their chain-link fences rusted and their once-towering chimney stacks leaning like non-Euclidian Towers of Pisa. For some reason, the image makes me think of Smitty's fevered mushroom hallucinations, and his ramblings about R'lyeh, the submerged city rising from the

Pacific Ocean at some point in this planet's future. I drive on, because there is nothing else for me to do.

The one thing that is noticeably absent in Arkham is places of worship. There are no churches, or at least I encounter none. Arkham has a distinct lack of Methodists, Lutherans, Catholics, Episcopalians, Presbyterians, Mormons, Jews, Muslims, Seventh-Day Adventists, Baptists, Christian Scientists, or any other mainstream religious group. It's not just that there are no churches. That in and of itself is strange. But perhaps more alarming is that I see no traditional religious symbolism of any kind—there are no crosses or Jesus fish or Stars of David or crescent moons. Not even a shrine to Holy Mother Mary in anyone's front yard.

What Arkham lacks in churches, it makes up for in asphalt and traffic lights. There are more roads in Arkham than you'd think; it was once a bustling little city of its own, Boston notwithstanding, but now, in 1972, Arkham looks distinctly as though a neutron-bomb test had been conducted—the buildings stand, but they're mostly empty of people. This is confirmed with each passing block. Miskatonic University is only a partial exception; I drive right onto campus, past the wrought-iron gates that look like they're being strangled by dead, withered ivy, and onto one of the vertices of the Blaylock Trapezium. There is no campus security guard to greet me, but there is a memorial garden, snowed under now, with a bronze plaque commemorating it in the names of Henry Armitage, Francis Morgan, and Warren Rice. I slow down to read the plaque in its entirety. Apparently, the three are former faculty members, now deceased. Armitage, the sign tells me, was the head librarian and passed away in 1946. Rice was a professor of classical languages who died in 1957. Morgan is listed as a professor of medicine, comparative anatomy, and archaeology who lived until 1966. Obviously, he or she was the golden boy . . . or girl. The memorial doesn't tell me why they are being honored, or what they did to deserve such a remembrance. I wonder if Haringa knew any of them, and if they were messed up in the same garbage as he is.

Like the rest of the place, the memorial garden is still. There is no laughter, no voices, no traffic of any kind. Birds do not sing here, and something tells me that even if it were springtime, the insects would avoid this place. Indeed, the entire campus is almost desperate in its emptiness, and my journalistic instincts tell me it has nothing to do with the winter temperatures. I'm tempted to leave my keys in the ignition, if only to see if the Republican rumors are true, that I'll return to my rental to find it inhabited by a hundred naked college hippies smoking and humping in honor of the full moon. I don't, though. I haven't gotten this far in life by being stupid. I stuff my kit bag under the seat, but I take my keys, and my press pass, and the last little bit of fungi from Yuggoth I have, and then I go to find someone, anyone, who might talk to me. This will be fun. I can see tomorrow's headlines before my eyes:

Arkham Gazette: UNRULY MAN CLAIMING JOURNALISTIC BACK-GROUND EJECTED FROM MISKATONIC DIVINITY SCHOOL SEMINAR.

Arkham Advertiser: TEXTILE MILL CLOSES, FOUR HUNDRED JOBS TO END BY FRIDAY.

"This school is like a shadow out of time," Betsy Ferrar tells me over coffee. She's a twenty-year-old coed, and a legacy. Her grand-mother was in the first Miskatonic University class to admit wom-en, and her mother also attended. Betsy claims to have been con-ceived in the Ollman dorms. "Seriously. Do you know what they serve in the cafeteria on Mondays? Corned beef hash, because pot roast is on Sundays and the hash is made from leftovers. I mean, can you imagine that? Do you think you could walk into a restau-rant anywhere in Boston and order a corned beef hash off the menu? We don't even have Coca-Cola machines on campus. It's like we're living in the fifties." When I remind her that the fifties weren't really that long ago, she waves me off. Betsy is that enthu-siastic, and that outraged over everything. The Equal Rights Amendment, Nixon in China, how CBS put *The Waltons* on against both *The Mod Squad* and *The Flip Wilson Show* this season "to keep the black man down," she says. She's a proud, rabid Democrat, having scandalized the Ferrar family, and an "endangered species" here at Miskatonic. "I have to go down to Boston proper and date BU men," she explains to me.

But this is not why I am talking with Betsy Ferrar. I do not give a damn about the lack of soft-drink machines in the dorms or how she has to make the trek all the way to Boston just to rut with the Great God Pan of BU men so that she can give birth to more greedy, spoiled little brats like herself. No, I am interested in other things. Betsy Ferrar knows all about the Starry Wisdom Cult, and about my new friend Professor Madison Haringa, who teaches a mandatory course on religion and civilization. I show her the horoscopes in the local papers, and she seems amazed that I've never heard of the peculiar Arkham zodiac. "I'm a Plateau. May. We don't match, I'm sorry to say. That's too bad, because you're sort of cute. You remind me of one of my dad's friends." She doesn't want to tell me much about Starry Wisdom right now, though the only reason I sprung for coffee was to hear from an intelligent, busty, local girl, but she does have Photostatted notes from Haringa's class, which she offers to me. She promises to come back after class— "Introduction to Neoclassical Economics. More like Introduction to the Unseen Hand of Fascism!"—with some friends who are really tuned in to campus goings-on, and leaves me in the empty campus coffeehouse. There isn't even a barista behind the counter. I get up and pace. Then I light a cigarette. The smoke seems to hang in the air. The jukebox is unplugged, dark. A yellowed flier on the wall advertises a free concert by Erich Zann. I've never heard of him. The grainy black-and-white photo, apparently of Zann, shows a third-rate Donovan, and I imagine that's probably what Zann plays—cheap covers of things like "Hurdy Gurdy Man." I touch the paper with my index finger. It feels oily and unwholesome.

I sit back down again and peruse Betsy's notes. The outline is in the sort of curlicue cursive writing surprisingly still typical of liberated women. It's just hard to read. My gaze keeps falling from the page. There's nothing useful here—at least, nothing that immediately jumps out at me and grabs me by the throat. Lots of diagrams for a class on comparative religion, or whatever it is.

"Focus, Lono." My voice seems stifled in the empty room. "You can do this. It's no worse than the Rubén Salazar debacle, and you came through that okay . . . well, comparatively speaking. Those were strange days, and there were strange rumblings in Aztlán, but you've learned a thing or two since then, eh?"

I gird myself, clench the cigarette between my teeth, and try again. From the beginning. I have a sudden urge to read over my own notes instead, then the newspapers again. I reach for my back pocket, expecting to find them rolled up back there, but then I remember that I set them on fire earlier. What time exactly is that spaghetti dinner? They weren't running that stupid comic strip on the funny pages, were they? I never bothered to check, so afraid was I that I'd encounter the cartoon version of myself. Then, my fingers brush the leftover shroom and I realize that I must take it. It will show me what I need to know. I pop it in my mouth, salivate heavily to swallow it, and it hits my stomach like an ineffectual punch. But it's anything but . . . Suddenly the notes make sense, and I'm once again praising those mysterious mushroom farmers in far-flung Yuggoth. I fully intend to visit there one day and sample the rest of their produce. The notes, damn it! Focus on the notes. There's a pantheon of ancient gods who are themselves only dark reflections of dimensions beyond understanding. Indeed, to truly understand them in their entirety would drive a man insane. The Old Ones aren't even so much beings as they are locations, locations such as . . . America. But what will manifest? I flash back to Smitty, drooling blood and gripped with seizures, screaming to me that R'lyeh was rising. Is that what is on the way? Will Cthulhu arrive?

Well, I don't know about Cthulhu manifesting, but Professor Haringa sure does a moment later, and he's got Betsy in tow, along with what looks like a phalanx of Nixon Youth. This isn't the shrooms. This isn't some hallucination. They are here. I can smell their cologne. Most of them are blond, and maybe one could be said to have sandy hair—there's no football at Miskatonic, but intramural men's rugby, clearly that activity is popular enough. Their footsteps ring out sharply in the empty coffeehouse. Haringa is wearing the same clothes that he had on when I first met him, or maybe it's just an identical suit. He meets my eyes and for a moment, he looks shocked. Then he nods, businesslike, as though I were a cocktail waitress who just confirmed his order—dry martini, with a toothpick jammed through a baby's eye for aroma. I snuff my cigarette out on the table.

"Hello, professor. I was in the neighborhood."

"So, you understand, do you?" Haringa says. "What we're trying to accomplish?"

"Some of it." One thing a reporter learns, on one's first day, is that people like to talk. They want to tell their story; they rehearse. The average city-desk editor knows how to break a cub in—send him out to go interview the survivors of the local corpse for the afternoon edition's obituaries. You never say, "Tell me about your husband, miss." You dig up one fact—the late Mr. Bernard was an eagle scout, or a naturist, or the lay speaker at the local church on Sunday—and then you're off to the races. "This is about the remaking of America. A remaking in *His* image. The election: it's more important than any presidential election this century."

The Nixon Youth snicker as one. It's an ugly sound, and I wish I hadn't left my handgun in my kit bag, which is currently stuffed under the seat of the rental car, because a few well-placed rounds at their center of mass would surely prevent further snickers from occurring. Betsy steps forward and volunteers information. "It's amazing, really, when you think about it. Shouldn't there be one America, after all? I mean, all the Yippies on campus say that there's no difference between the Republicans and the Democrats. But—" I see Haringa sharing a conspiratorial look with me, of all people, and rolling his eyes. Deep down, he doesn't like these rich assholes

KEENE AND MAMATAS 101

any more than I do, any more than they like themselves. But what does he want of me, then? What *really*?

"Oh, come on," I say. "Nixon needs to be beaten to death with a pillowcase full of doorknobs for his foreign policy alone. That swine is a blight upon everything that is decent and just. I mean—"

"You mean what?" Haringa says. "Think about it. Who are your real allies, Lono? You're a firearms enthusiast; they're an abiding passion of yours. Don't try to deny it. You've admitted as much in interviews with the press. Indeed, you're a member of the National Rifle Association. Guns make you feel manly, just as your drinking does. And yet, which party is going to take away your guns? The Republicans . . . or the Democrats?" He punches most of the last syllable, *rats*, and it hangs in the air.

"Not just take them away, Mr. Lono," one of the young fellows offers. "They'll take the guns away from the white people, and redistribute them to the black people! And once the blacks enlist the Jews and the browns and all the other mongr—"

Haringa throws a hand up to silence him and thank sweet baby Jesus it works. There's only so much paranoid rambling one can take from a man in a sweater. Had he not fallen silent, I would have been forced to ram the Erich Zann flier down his throat until he'd choked on it.

The professor's eyes remind me of flint. "Fine, let's talk about foreign policy, then. The war in Vietnam? A Democrat war! And it was Nixon who went to China just a few months ago. Do you know *why* Nixon went to China, Mr. Lono?"

"Sideways vaginas on the concubines?" I glance at Betsy, who isn't blushing. One of the boys is though. Mormon or homosexual—it's so hard to tell sometimes. My money is on Mormon. I make a mental note to fuck with him later, if I get the chance.

"Because he *had* to," Haringa explains, a bit testy. "And not for geopolitical reasons or to check the Reds, either. Not at all. He went to China, and Kennedy never did, nor did Johnson, for a simple reason—the Democrats are already in constant psychic communication with their opposite numbers across the iron curtain!"

I laugh aloud at that. It's not even one of those awful psychedelic laughs one occasionally lets rip due to cosmic coincidence; it's just a good old-fashioned belly laugh. I feel a strange sense of gratitude towards the man. It's been a long time since anyone made me laugh like that. It feels good.

"Haringa, you're dreaming," I say. "Either that, or you're just a natural fool."

"You know I'm right, Lono. I can see it in your expression."

"That's the shrooms. Listen here. I've met a fair share of paranoids in my time. Hell, I'm one of them, but you are utterly off the wall. Did you get tenure with that attitude? Does the alumni association know? If not, I certainly think someone should inform them."

He ignores the threat and goes on with his speech; he must have practiced it. Perhaps he is anxious to use it on someone. "Think of it, Lono. Communism. You chafe under the very reasonable demands of your editor, local traffic regulations, the requests of airline stewardesses, zoning laws . . . Do you think you'd thrive under the watchful eyes of commissars, of a State Writers' Union? Do you think you could shoot and bluff your way out of the gulag, because that is what this election boils down to. We"—he gestures expansively with his chin, like Hubert Humphrey might in midgibberish—"are the only people between men like you and the concentration camp. We are your saviors. Do you believe me?"

"No, of course I don't believe you. I don't believe anything I hear anymore."

"Good answer—so you don't believe that people like me are between men like you and the concentration camp. But Starry Wisdom *is* all that's keeping the world on course. So what you must not believe is that you are a man."

"And if I'm not a man . . . it's okay to kill me, is it? Is that the nature of this visit? Is that the agenda for today?" I ramble, stalling for time so that I can calculate my next move. It's five against one. Haringa has a paunch on him, but the quartet of College Republicans look like they run down milk cows and eat them for breakfast. And then there's Betsy. She's feisty and obviously devoted to the cause. I'll need to depend on something other than fisticuffs to see my way out of this predicament.

"Men are but the dreams of gods, Mr. Lono," Haringa says. "Nothing more. It has always been this way. And when the gods stop dreaming, what then of men? *Ph'nglui mglw'nafh Cthulhu R'lyeh wgah'nagl fhtagn.* That is a very old language, Lono, and I don't expect you to understand it. I'll translate for you. *In his house at R'lyeh dead Cthulhu waits dreaming.* What happens when he wakes up?"

Betsy steps back immediately—she's a well-trained girl. The Nixon Youth have manacles in their hands, and in one frantic moment I'm no longer at the table, but on it. I wonder how this has happened, and curse the mushrooms and their land of origin. Yuggoth's fungi have betrayed me. My limbs feel far away, and not just because they're stretched across the surface of the table, the chains somehow meeting underneath. Three of the rugby boys are surrounding me, so the fourth must be down below, tying knots in the chains with his meaty hands. I hope his fraternity ring gets caught in the links, and I tell him as much. If he hears me, he doesn't respond. Like Betsy, Haringa has trained him right.

The professor leans over me, smiling. His teeth seem too big, just like Mac's did in that diner halfway across the country. That seems so long ago now, but time is funny that way, especially if you are under the influence of psychedelics. Then I notice the knife in Haringa's hand. It catches the light just so, and I see myself reflected in the blade. Two things occur to me as I stare at myself in the blade.

One: I need a shave.

Two: I am in deep shit.

At that moment, I feel my old friends fear and loathing. They grip my heart and rape my soul. I think about my wife and son. I don't talk or write about them much, for they are rarely part of the story and some things should be kept private. But I miss them now. Why, oh why did I send them back to Washington, DC? Perhaps if they had stayed in Woody Creek with me, living amongst the fan mail and peacock guts, I'd have never gone on this journey in the first place. I wonder if I will ever see them again? It's not looking good.

"And what is Lono," Haringa continues, "but the god of fertility? Indeed, one of the few gods who existed before the world itself was created. Then there was Captain Cook, whose arrival on Kealakekua under a white sail was taken as a sign. Are you a god, Mr. Lono, a dead god who lies dreaming? Did you take the name, when you decided to go undercover . . . *or did the name take you?*"

My head is swimming as he goes on and on, and the shrooms are playing my synapses like a harp. My nervous system snakes out of my skin in every direction, growing like twisted ivy, seeking something, anything. The knife is so big, the kind I'd use to hack open a pineapple back in Puerto Rico, the sort I'd sometimes find myself waving overhead, screaming as I tore down one hallway or other, in pursuit of a story or a source or a criminal or just good, clean fun. The ceiling disappears and the moon is in the coffeehouse, even though it was daylight outside. Jack Kirby's disembodied head comes flying toward me, originating from somewhere beyond my point of vision. He has bird wings where his ears should be, and his teeth are clamped down on a massive cigar. Kirby's flying head flutters around me, darting down and then soaring back up again. I try to speak, try to ask it where Nixon and Kissinger are, and why I'm not back beneath the White House again, but I've forgotten how to talk and my tongue doesn't feel like it belongs to me anymore. The head flies away, back to whatever subconscious depths it spawned from. I hear waves crashing on some unseen shore. I hear screams. I hear a whisper in the darkness and rats in the walls. Something is calling my name. I see a sign overhead for yet another Odd Fellows club, except that I am still in the Miskatonic coffeehouse. I smell fish and incense, feces and barley. Then those smells give way to the stench of motor oil and brine. My fingers scrape asphalt, dip into the sea. And the ground begins to shake. Something wicked slouches toward Arkham to be born. I gird myself, expecting great and terrible violence as the bowl of wrath is dumped upon us.

"You'll have to forgive me," Haringa says. He doesn't notice the rumbling, or the strange smells, or Jack Kirby's head, or my limbs extending off to the horizon in the four directions, or if he does, then he's too full of the sort of hubris generally only found in movie villains to comment on them or look out the fucking window to see for himself what's approaching. "Well, I'm speaking figuratively. Forgiveness really doesn't play into this. What I'm doing is beyond forgiveness, beyond good and evil. Academics like myself aren't much for practical endeavors, but you know that already, I am sure. I meant it when I said that I was an admirer of your work. I hope there are no hard feelings. In truth, I'm reasonably sure this won't even work, but when an opportunity like this presents itself, one must get one's hands dirty. You're just a man, almost certainly, but the cosmic resonances should count for something, just as they did for Cook, for Cortés, whom the Aztecs believed to be Quetzalcoatl, for—"

And then a huge white sail bursts through the wall. Bricks and mortar erupt like a volcano. I'm on my side, and the table is splintering against my back. The moon is gone and it is daylight again. Betsy trips right over me and I end up under her skirt. White cotton panties, another sail. I can see her outline beneath them, the petals of an exotic yet poisonous flower. Someone steps on my palm, back where it belongs at the end of my ordinary mortal left arm. And . . . ho, ho! The chains are gone. Free at last, free at last. Thank God Almighty, I am free at last! The visions cease, dissipating the way a dream does shortly after you wake up. I pull myself to my feet and there, in the scattered remains of the little campus coffeehouse, I see the cab of a black tractor-trailer that has been driven through the wall. The engine idles like a dragon, and behind the wheel sits Smitty, his eyes as wide as twin moons.

"I'm here for you!" he bellows. He raises his palms like a supplicant, and I notice something wrong with his hands. "Lono, I am here for you! Don't be afraid!"

"Sweet Jesus . . ." I cough, and it hurts my chest to do so. When I gasp for breath, I inhale dust and smoke.

Betsy takes my throbbing hand. I confirm that she has five fingers instead of six, and then I allow the gesture, wondering to myself if she changes sides every time someone new enters the room. She's American, so probably—a dandelion seed on the wind. Cheering for and whoring herself out to whoever is the winning team this week. A light fixture creaks overhead, swinging back and forth, dangling from its wire. Dust swirls in the air. Haringa and the Nixon Youth have fled amidst the carnage. I didn't even see them leave, but when I check beneath the rubble, hoping to find their mangled remains, there's not even a bloodstain. I do, however, find some cast-off newspapers amidst the wreckage. One of each, this morning's editions, just like the ones I threw away and then burned. Fate is smiling down upon me once again. I roll them up and stick them in my back pocket. Then I pull out a crumpled cigarette pack. To my dismay, it is empty. I turn to Betsy and say, "You got a cigarette?"

"No, Mr. Lono. I don't smoke."

"We'll fix that. There is trouble ahead, and probably bloodshed, and if you're going to be my assistant, you'll need to carry a pack on you at all times."

She nods, and then asks, "What do we do now?"

"Are you hungry? I'm hungry. Eating mushrooms and saving the world helps one work up quite an appetite."

"Um . . . I know where some good restaurants are."

"No need. I am in the mood for spaghetti."

Smitty's ability to drive is something deeper than a skill; the fungus from Yuggoth has written it into his veins. I'm next to him, checking the newspapers and pointing. Betsy sits next to me, but she doesn't spend any time off campus, so has no idea where the firehouse is, or what sort of people will be at the spaghetti dinner. I notice a nub on the blade of Smitty's right hand as he makes a hard right up a hill. The truck is way too large for Arkham's tight corners and seventeenth-century streets, but somehow Smitty does it. I try not to think of what I see: that he's growing a sixth finger on at least one of his hands, and that his body is already adjusting by giving him the dexterity to navigate the doglegs and dead ends of this witch-cursed town. Either I'm still hallucinating, and at least half of this isn't really happening—a possibility that is entirely possible, and sort of comforting—or Smitty is turning into a Cannock, the poor bastard.

"You're really taking this in stride," I say to Smitty. It takes me a moment to realize that he just said the same exact words, at the same exact time, to me. The shrooms, of course. Has to be. There's no other explanation.

Smitty says that he didn't know where he was . . . No, scratch that, that he didn't know where anything else in the universe was except for himself, and for me, when he woke up and I was gone. "So I came looking for you. I reckoned you'd be an easy man to find, provided I looked in the right place, and sure enough, here you are! Ain't it grand? We're linked now, you and me. We've shared communion. You were right about those mushrooms, Lono. You really opened my eyes to things. I'm here to help, if I can."

"I appreciate it," I say, and I really do. "I owe you one, and that is a rare thing."

Time has slipped sideways on us once again—another side effect of the psychedelic mushrooms. There is no possible way Smitty could have driven the distance in the short amount of time since I've last seen him, and yet here he is, and who am I to argue with the space-time continuum? My right hand still throbs; I hope it's because Haringa stepped on it when he ran off and not because I'm budding a new appendage. The shrooms could be the source of Smitty's new finger. Ingesting them could be what's turning him into a Cannock. I think of the vagrant back at the bus station in Denver. Was that what had happened to him? Could he have partaken of a fungus from a Yuggoth junkie and grown his tentacle as a result? I try to remember how many fingers he had on each hand, but I can't. Jack Kirby has eaten that time away from me. Sweet fucking Jesus, don't let me turn into one. There are enough people in this world, editors included, who already think I'm a brain-damaged geek without me having six fingers on each hand or sprouting tentacles from my face. Although it does occur to me that an extra penis might be fun . . .

Betsy's quiet but even as I think that she begins to speak again. "I'm sorry, Mr. Lono, I—"

"Please, call me *Uncle* Lono. And no, I understand. I read your notes, remember? It must be hard for a young woman, so far away from home for the first time, encountering a strong, charismatic fellow who claims to have all the answers, and who smells like a fine, peaty Scotch. I almost fell in love with Professor Haringa myself. He's a charming bastard."

She buys it and smiles. That takes care of that, for the time being at least. Now, what other business do I need to attend to? What else needs sorting out? Dare I start thinking about how to dump Smitty, who was kind enough to roar across a quarter of the country, breaking the laws of physics to save my life and my soul from some bloody pagan sacrifice, especially given that the trucker can most likely read my mind, and is almost certainly at this moment figuring out a way to separate Betsy from me so that he can sneak a roofie or two into *her* spaghetti dinner when we find the fire station and take her back to the Midwest—next thing she knows she's popping out six-fingered Cannock children and living in a depressing, rundown industrial town that doesn't happen to have a college in it. This is the future of America. I know. I can see it. I have special powers. Nightmare found, the New Normal perceived and tangled with, mission accomplished. But no, Smitty wouldn't do that, would he? Just because he's about to have an extra finger on each hand, that doesn't mean he'd betray me. We are linked, as he said. These damned drugs have made me paranoid. I need to focus.

"So," I ask, turning to Betsy once again. "What's the real deal here? Tell Uncle Lono a story."

"The plan is this," Betsy says. "Infiltrate the Democratic Party with secret Republicans. Maybe it's too late for 1972, but it won't be in 1976. If a Democrat wins, it'll be a Southern conservative. To the people, he'll appear different, but he won't be, really. And then we keep up the illusion of the two-party system, and all the while, it's really just us. If, in time, we eventually end up electing a black president, or a Hispanic, or a woman, they'll be conservatives too. But to sell it to the masses, they'll *look* liberal; they'll smell the way liberals smell."

"How do liberals smell? Like marijuana, maybe?" I ask, but it's Smitty who answers. Our mental connection must not be complete, as his answer surprises me. "Liberals smell like the perfumes you can't afford, and that queasy nauseated feeling you get when you realize that you did something wrong, but trying to fix it won't help."

He's talking differently now. Whatever changes are occurring inside of him are altering more than just his body chemistry. His language centers have been impacted, too. There wasn't an *ain't* or a *reckon* in that entire speech. He sails over a ridge and the truck rumbles hard. Smitty hits the air horn and shouts, "Gooks! Gooks! Gooks!" Then he howls like a wounded beast, a once brave and muscled bull whose leg has gone lame and whose calves have been torn to shreds by waiting hyenas in the bad distance just too long to reach. "There, I said it and I like saying it and I don't like having to pretend that everyone around me is a human being because the plain and simple fact of the matter is that most of them aren't!"

There it is again. Smitty says *aren't* instead of *ain't*. I wonder how long the change will take, and which is the real him—are the shrooms a gateway or a metamorphosis, or an apocalypse in that most literal of ways: the rending of the veil and a revelation of what squirms beneath it? Then I lay down the newspapers and examine my own hands, turning them back and forth, looking for any knobs or growths, even a suspect mole or freckle that wasn't there the day before, but so far, I seem unscathed. Whatever is happening to him is apparently not happening to me. So maybe it's not the mushrooms? Maybe this is the result of something else? I don't know. It is very hard to tell fantasy from reality at this point. I think back to how this whole trip started, me sitting in my fortified bunker back in Woody Creek just a few days after the New Year's celebrations, with dead peacocks everywhere and something dark and vaguely sinister prowling around outside my door. I wish I were back there right now, and who knows? Maybe I am. The thought makes me smile. Maybe I am still sitting there feeling burned out and pissed off, and this whole thing has been nothing more than a bizarre and vivid dream I had while in the depths of a whiskey binge. It's nice to think this might be so, but I know that it isn't.

"Turn left," I tell Smitty after consulting the newspapers once again for the address of the firehouse. He does as he is told, which means that he is still useful and I shouldn't kill him yet. The big rig bounces up over the curb, nearly crushing a pay-phone booth. On the radio, the Nitty Gritty Dirt Band are singing about Uncle Charlie and his dog, Teddy, and the song gives me a start. "What's this? What are you listening to?"

"The Nitty Gritty Dirt Band," Smitty says. "It's country rock."

"I know what it is," I snap. "I was there when Gram Parsons invented the genre! But why are you listening to it? Don't you listen to Hank Williams and Charley Pride and Merle Haggard?"

Smitty shrugs, and the truck lurches off the curb and back into the street. "I don't know. I don't know anything anymore. I'm just tired."

At the spaghetti dinner I realize that Smitty is right. Not about being tired, or the joys of country-rock music, or about the so-called gooks, but about the fact that most of the human beings I've been encountering lately are only crude mockeries of the sort of person that, say, an Aristotle would recognize as human. The pasta is terrible and starchy and clearly under-boiled, but the sauce—red with lots of meat, so Betsy demurs and munches on bread—is pretty good. Smitty eats with two forks and I keep an eye on the huge garage door, waiting for Haringa and his crew to make an appearance. All the fire trucks are parked out in the lot; Smitty's tractor-trailer is artfully placed on the lawn. If there are any police in Arkham, they must be owned lock, stock, and barrel by either the college or the mill, as they've not made an appearance despite the nine tons of evidence on display outside the firehouse.

A union representative—a big fire hydrant of a man who looks as though he eats other fire hydrants for breakfast—is speaking, half-ignored over the hubbub of quotidian family gossip and outright gawking and hissing at me. Apparently, there are some readers in Arkham after all, and the jury is still out on whether or not they are fans of my work. If I were a betting man, which I am, I'd bet they aren't. The union representative waits until the room has quieted down some and he has everyone's attention. Then he launches into a story. "One day all the parts of the body held a debate over who should be in charge of all the organs and systems of the body." My journalistic antennae start waggling. Thank God the shrooms don't affect those. "The stomach says it should be in charge because it digests the food and provides the limbs with energy. The legs say that they should be in charge because they carry the body where it needs to go. The brain says it should be in charge because it makes all the plans. Then the rectum says—get this, you all; this is the important part." He licks his lips. "*I* should be in charge. I'm responsible for waste removal. You know, like the Genovese family, here in town." That gets a few yawps and giggles. "All the other body parts laugh at the poor anus, so, in a bad mood, he decides to just clamp shut and not talk to anyone. Soon enough the stomach is always upset, the legs start getting all wobbly, and the brain can't even think anymore, all because the waste keeps backing up into all of the body's various parts and systems. Finally, all the parts decide that the rectum *should* be in charge of the body after all, and forgiving them, the rectum loosens up and lets go. And the moral of the story," the fire hydrant says, his smile now wide enough to eat a manhole cover, "is that somebody is always in charge . . ." He waits a beat. "And it's usually an *asshole!*" He erupts in peals of laughter, and the spaghetti chompers do likewise. Some of them don't even bother waiting to swallow. They laugh with pasta and red sauce hanging off their mouths, obscuring their jaws and chins, shaking in their seats at the utter cretin who ruined the perfectly wonderful anecdote by my old friend the Cretan. Suddenly, something inside me breaks.

"That's it! That's it! All hands on deck, now! This is not a fucking drill!" I rush to the buffet table and snatch up a pair of bread knives with serrated edges. Not the best tool for the operations I might need to carry out, but they'll do. "Are you ridiculous bumpkins deaf? Put down the forks, and slap your palms on the tables, now. It's time for a finger inspection!"

"Hey now, mister," the man at the podium says, "You won't be finding any Cannocks here. This is Arkham, I'll have you know."

"I know all I need to know about this town, you pestilent fist-fuck!" I rush the stage like a wave. That's the best thing to do when you find yourself drastically outnumbered. Forget going for the biggest and toughest guy; he'll cream your ass each and every time. Instead, hit the *loudest* one first, especially if he's by the door, which this particular doofus happens to be. I knock him right down, and he falls like a sack of potatoes. "We've got ourselves a new asshole in charge. Show of hands!" Everyone's confused. "Come on. We're not voting on anything in particular; just show me your hands!" And the hands go up, lefts and rights. Like automata these old workers are, recently displaced by the long waves of capital and the gambits of global chess masters, but still ready to do whatever they are told, and in unison too. It's no wonder my editor sent me here. The hands look clean, but the ward boss won't stay down. As he tries—unsuccessfully—to sit up, he bellows, "What do you people think you're doing? He's insulting us all! He's the one who came in here with an Innsmouthian!" And he points at Smitty, the moron, with his hands up and budding digits emergent on the sides of his hands. The silence becomes a murmur, and the murmur boils over. I drop the knives, rush to the door, and slam into it . . . only to then join the fire hydrant–shaped man on the floor.

Delirious. Dizzy. "That's a fire hazard! A locked emergency exit. If my attorney were still alive, I'd have him sue each and every one of you stump fuckers!" There are stars swirling before my eyes, billions and billions of them. My voice is disembodied, long dead, howling from light-years away. I wonder how much of it is from the hallucinogen and how much is concussion.

"We're at the fire station, you jerk," some woman calls out. "The trucks are right outside, the garage doors wide open. What could possibly happen?" They laugh at me. "We hadda lock somethin'!" someone else says in a little kiddie-television voice. Then the door opens. Haringa enters, cross and determined.

"I thought we might find you here, Lono. Should I still call you that? Or have you dispensed with the pseudonym?"

"Listen, pal . . ." I begin but don't get to finish, because now Haringa is ignoring me. I hate being ignored, unless of course I wish to go undetected. He steps over me, as though to confirm the suspicion that I no longer exist, but the Nixon Youth shuffle in behind him, their clothing torn and dusty from Smitty's prior dramatic entrance. They don't ignore me. They jerk me to my feet, each one on a limb now, chains and tables not to be trusted, for I am filled with the spirit of Yuggoth. Haringa picks up one of the serrated knives and makes his intentions clear. He's going to pick up where he left off from before we were interrupted last time. It occurs to me that I don't know any other truckers, and that the doors to the fire station are wide open, so there's hardly any wall left to ram through, even if I did have another fungus-addled teamster on my side. Never have I needed lawyers, guns, and money more than I need them now.

Haringa helps up the squat little ward boss and then helps himself to the podium. He clears his throat professorially and, without even starting with a joke ("usually an asshole!"), he launches into his prepared remarks. At least, I imagine they are prepared. He has no index cards to read from, no notes to shuffle through, but the speech sounds practiced and rehearsed. It's not like the normal election-year speech, either. Oh, no. There will be none of that today. Haringa doesn't stop to reflect on the greatness that is America, makes no promises of prosperity, does not hold out the memory of historical excellence or the hope of future superiority for today's mediocrities to lash themselves to. Hell, the speech doesn't even reference Nixon. Instead, the professor just proposes a swap—the blue-collar union men and women will all become Republicans. The middle-class intellectuals will all become Democrats. It sounds good, on the surface, and I have to admit that I'm begrudgingly impressed. Haringa could have been a journalist, as he knows the secret to persuasive rhetoric: use the simplest possible words but aim your message for the most intelligent person in the room. That person, of course, just happens to be myself, but what Haringa doesn't know is that in a battle of wits, I am the A-bomb, and it's time for me to explode over his Hiroshima.

The two major parties "realigned" before, of course. Haringa tells them this, and he is right. Black Americans used to vote religiously for the Republicans as the Republicans were the party of Lincoln, and it was the Democrats under the white hoods of the Ku Klux Klan. The civil-rights movement of the last decade and Lyndon Johnson's Great Society put an end to that, although there are still a few skunks lurking about. Robert Byrd of West Virginia comes to mind. But Nixon was explicitly appealing to racism in his own election campaign, even as he shook hands with Chairman

Mao ("Gook! Gook! Gook!" I hear Smitty's voice in my head again. We're still connected, if by interstellar distances. Damn it all, the mushrooms are still in my system. I thought their effects had passed. The galaxies swim in my eyes. There's just me, the strong hands of the Nixon Youth gripping my arms and legs, Haringa's buttery voice, and Smitty, him nothing but that long sigh at the end of the universe.) The problem with Nixon's switching, of course, is that intelligent people such as Haringa are far too intelligent to believe in racial difference or white supremacy.

"In fact," Haringa says, "I know that our days are numbered. We're all being watched, manipulated. There is a secret player at work in this election, a force older than history itself, pushing and prodding us toward our destruction. But we can stop it; we can thwart it." He goes on to explain how. Democrats and Republicans all have to unite, as one, while maintaining the impression of warring partisanship and ideological schism. Unite under Nixon, is what he obviously means, and thus, under the even greater evils waiting in the shadows, but Haringa stops short of coming to this logical conclusion. That might be a bit too much for the marks in the room to process. Better for him to appeal to them on more solid ground, speaking to their own hopes and fears.

Finally, he acknowledges my presence. "This fellow, for instance, is an example of what we face. He is a drug abuser, a writer for counterculture and music magazines such as *Rolling Stone*, a braggart who is casually incompetent with his firearms to the point of criminality, a man who cannot hold his liquor, a seeker of sensation and depravity of both the flesh and the spirit. And, worst of all, he's a *storyteller*." The crowd gasps at this, dismayed. "Plato warned us about the poets, how they warp reality for their own despicable ends, rather than keeping their eyes and minds on reality. That's what this man, whose real name is most certainly not Uncle Lono, is doing. He's here on assignment. He told me so himself. He's been snooping around, asking questions and poking his nose where it shouldn't be, all in an attempt to make us look bad. You know his type. New York and California are full of them; they think they're too good for the rest of us. They think they need to make our decisions for us and tell us what to do, and how to behave, because it is in our best interest. Well, I say no more! We won't let this storyteller succeed, will we? It's his story of the election, his story of America itself, that threatens to overwhelm and erase all the hard work that each of you do every day of your lives. Please, please, hear what I am saying. This must be done. For your party, yes, but also, more importantly, for your families, your community, and your country."

Then Haringa makes his mistake. He repeats "your country" once, softly, like the end of a sad prayer. And when he does, I get the giggles. You would too, I'm sure. So would anyone with half a brain between their ears. I get the giggles. I snort and chuckle. I even say it myself. "Your country. Oh, your country. Is it the United States, Maddy? May I call you Maddy, or do you prefer Madison? Or is it Professor Haringa? I bet that's what you want the little girls like Betsy to call you, eh? But never mind that right now. Is it *your* country, Haringa, or is it these United States of America? Oh, why not just 'the Republic.' How about that? Has a nice sound to it, don't you think? It has a good beat and our forefathers could dance to it. I'm a storyteller, you say? You're wrong on that count, too, my friend. Bob Dylan is a storyteller, and he's very good at it. I am something else. Something different. I am a writer, by God, and I make my living with words. I use them like magic, but so do you. You do know how to spin shit into gold, don't you? Is that why you make almost forty thousand dollars a year and get to live in Swampscott instead of Arkham like the rest of these working stiffs? No, shut your mouth. Don't bother to answer because I have special powers granted to me by the high priests of Yuggoth, and I know what you'll say next. You'll pretend to be just like them, like the rest of us, and then you'll declare, 'Anyone who opposes me is a rapist and a racist, a terrorist and an elitist, a communist and a socialist, a blue blood and a lowlife, a baby killer and the enemy of man.' That's the story, isn't it? Don't bother to deny it, Maddy. I am on to you and your kind. Here's the real deal . . . You need a fifty-state victory, or despite Nixon's power and wrath, your nefarious plans just won't come to fruition. Tell me I'm wrong."

Haringa doesn't speak. His jaw tightens and the side of his face begins to twitch as he grips the knife.

"Now what's this?" I say. "Pure pulp fiction, baby. Like something out of *Weird Tales*. Your enemy is helpless before you, held fast by a band of nameless stooges—" One of the Nixon Youth pipes up to introduce himself as Jason, and I say, "Oh, shut the hell up, son," to him and then, to the room, "and you're going to complete a human sacrifice right here and now. Cut open my chest with a kitchen knife, right here in the fire hall—because that won't take twenty minutes and it'll make Betsy cry and strong men turn their heads—and hold my heart aloft and expect cheers and stiff-armed salutes? I told you before that you were dreaming, you brain-dead baboon, but now I know what dream you have. It's the dead dream of a fascist America. You and the rest of your kind. You're nothing more than this generation's fascists, dressed up as something else. Well, forget it, pal—real proud Americans are too cantankerous, ornery, and, frankly, dumb-ass donkey stubborn to be taken in by a silk-briefs-wearing lowlife water head like you."

Haringa looks over at the crowd, and my eyes follow him. With a terrible, cold, sinking feeling in my gut, I suddenly realize that I am wrong. The local Democratic Party establishment—union shop stewards, ward bosses, dues-paying Irish-American patriarchs with beet-red noses and beer guts and enough adult kids to swing an entire voting district with just a word at the dinner table, shell-shocked Vietnam veterans with the DTs and haunted eyes, the sprinkling of black, Asian, and other racial minorities in this little New England city—is wanting a show. Smitty's head is in his hands. I can hear him sobbing. It's Betsy who stands up on the table like a Wobbly firebrand and shouts, "What's wrong with all of you numb nuts?"

I suspect that *numb nuts* is not a phrase she would have used before coming into my vector. She shakes her fist at them. "Don't you people see? Wake up. The whole two-party system is a joke! A trap for the working class!" She jabs her finger at Haringa. "What that man is suggesting is that you all betray yourselves and your own interests for his sake and the sake of his extradimensional masters!"

"Yeah, where is . . . *Moloch* in all of this?" I ask. Betsy blinks, confused. She must have been absent from class that day. "Are you lot," I ask the crowd, "really ready to risk the wrath of Moloch, to tie yourselves to some new master you've never seen, one you can't even conceive of properly? Is that what you're doing here?" Murmurs erupt from the crowd, as if in a film. My old friend, Professor Haringa, looks like he's just going to stick me and fling my entrails to the crowd, caring less about sacrifice than spectacle, but he decides he can still win this and turns back to the microphone on the podium. He clears his throat, and the room falls silent again.

"Good question; even a stopped clock is right twice a day. Where *is* Moloch in all this? Did you know that Allen Ginsberg once wrote a poem about Moloch?" If Haringa expects the name Ginsberg to mean all that much to this crowd—maybe he thinks America has shifted that much to the left, thanks to Red Chinese telepathy and hippie sex magic right out of the *Kama Sutra*, or maybe he really doesn't even know a blue-collar worker when he sees one—he has miscalculated. You can see it in their eyes and in their expressions. They pass right over "Beat poet" and even "homosexual" and "pederast" and alight instead on "Jew," which the collective mind of Arkham could tell just from his name. Oh, don't get me wrong. They certainly know better than to fly right into an anti-Semitic rage in public—these are Democrats we're talking about, after all, and they are in the Northeast. But the discomfort is there all the same, an almost tangible presence hovering over them and filling the hall. The professor is seemingly oblivious to the change in the air. "And he wrote, among other things, that Moloch was a cocksucker!" Haringa says with a thump of his fist.

"Take off your shoe," I tell him. "Smack the podium with it. The echo will last longer! Trust me. I've spoken on campus a time or two."

"And please . . . please pardon my coarse language," he tells the crowd, ignoring me. "But I have no problem saying that, even in mixed company, because, you know what, my friends? I speak the truth. It's absolutely true. This *storyteller*"—he says the word like one says *phlegm*—"is right about that much. Where is Moloch in all this? Didn't you give your souls and lives to Moloch, and the souls and lives of your children to Moloch, just for some safety and security? Wasn't the mill his church, the great steaming vats of dye his altar? But how many mills are still in operation in Arkham, or in Innsmouth, or in North Adams, or in Salem, or anywhere else in this great state? Few or none, my friends. Few or none. And I'll tell you something else. The same poet wrote that Moloch's eyes were a thousand blind windows. Well, the smashed-out windows of the mills along the river are certainly blind now, aren't they? Think about that for a moment, because the truth is this: *Moloch has abandoned you.* That might be unpalatable to hear, but it is true nevertheless. The sacrifice of your children no longer sustains him. He has taken his appetites elsewhere."

The worst part of Haringa's speech is that he's right, in his own way. That's the unbelievable truth about Nixon and his acolytes—they're right, or at least not any more wrong than the Democrats, who are spending all sorts of furious energy making sure that they lose the election while their children are sacrificed in the jungles of Vietnam and campuses like Kent State. But no politician and certainly no academic or cult leader has ever gotten anywhere in America, in *the Republic*, by being so transparently right. The same holds true here in the fire hall, because everyone's confused now.

"No!" A shout from the crowd. Spaghetti hits the floor. A plate explodes into a hundred porcelain shards. "Moloch lives! You lie, professor! *Moloch lives still!*"

The crowd surges, and Betsy falls into it. I lose track of Smitty. Our mental link is at least temporarily severed. Haringa grabs the ward boss and puts the knife to his neck. He hisses something at the ward boss through clenched teeth, but I can't hear what it is. The Democrats surge toward the podium, but not in a rage. They're upset, weeping, like a bunch of spoiled children who have just been told that there ain't no such thing as Santa Claus after having spent an hour in line to get their pictures taken at the shopping center with the old cotton-bearded saint. They want an official denial, a careful hug, and a sprinkle of pixie dust, but all kids in that situation ever see is the undeniable truth of an old drunk in a stained suit, with an obvious erection and bad breath and a pair of cotton balls Scotch taped to his eyebrows for effect. But to Republicans, common workingmen and women in a group, riled in action, is threat enough, even if all they want is to be lied to again and put back to sleep.

The college boys holding me fast go pale, their hands ice cold on my skin; I can even feel the confidence leave the bodies of the two holding my legs through my pants. The last vestiges of the mushroom are leaving my body now, and despite the chaos around me, the realization leaves me a little sad. Man, I need to find some Cannocks tonight, if just for more fungus. The Nazi sophomore who calls himself Jason loosens his grip just enough for me to sweep my leg free and send him tumbling. He squawks like a pelican in heat and crashes into a folding table, sending cheap silverware and plates of half-eaten spaghetti to the floor. I twist out of the grips of the others and snag the other serrated knife that Haringa left lying on the table. He's a murderer, but he's no fighter. Hands up, he drops his knife, releases the ward boss, and backs off. The ward boss runs to the back door, which is just as locked as it was when I tried it. Sadly, his attempt doesn't send him falling to the tiles like it did me. I wave the knife around and shout, making sure I can be heard above the cries and protests of the crowd. "Okay, boys and girls. Which one of you melon heads wants to be opened up first? Let's see the homunculi inside you all, pulling the levers and twisting dials! Nobody, eh? Smitty!"

He's wrestling with a particularly large Teamster member. He pops the man in the mouth with his misshapen hand and turns to me. "Yes, Lono?"

"Get us out of here, pronto!"

"Sure thing, boss!"

I still don't know if I can trust him or not, but right now, I can't afford to be choosy. It's Smitty or the gallows, I'm afraid. Smitty runs to get the truck while his opponent totters back and forth on his heels, wiping blood from his mouth and staring at it as if disbelieving it belongs to him. A few of the man's harder union brothers finally show their teeth, armed with three-tined forks and blunt butter knives. Nothing's worse than a disillusioned believer, a bitter romantic, except for a bunch of them who've had their dinner interrupted as well. At that moment, I am filled with longing for my little canister of CS gas. Wonderful thing, CS gas. Most people know it as tear gas, but I've become something of an expert on it over time, as it's gotten me out of more than one hairy situation, and I know facts about it that the common man doesn't. I'm a big believer, you could say. I know that CS stands for Corson and Stoughton, the two American scientists who developed the chemical compound while at Middlebury College in Vermont. It occurs to me that Middlebury isn't that far from where I am now. Perhaps when this entire cursed escapade is over, and I've made all the bastards pay, I'll take a trip to the Middlebury campus—make a CS pilgrimage of sorts. I wonder if they have a memorial garden erected in Corson and Stoughton's honor. If not, they should.

Ah, CS gas, my best friend, why did I leave you behind in the kit bag? Journalistic ethics, perhaps? The editorial demand for disinterested objectivity? What horrifying mind rot. The plain truth is that the Kissingers of the world should be strapped down and dosed, over and over, with questions about Vietnam and the bombing of Cambodia and the Bilderberg Group and Soviet Jews, and Mamie Van Doren machine-guns at him until he confesses between big, froggy sobs. It doesn't even need to be me manning the gas canister; I could train Frank McGee and Barbara Walters to do it in five minutes. That's how easy it is. And McGee would do it, too. He's a born sadomasochist. Ask anyone in our line of work. But I digress, and as one of the apelike Democrats feints at me with a fork, I poke at him with Haringa's knife, and then run out into the night, gibbering like a loon. Smitty has undone his tractor from its trailer and is ready, cab doors hanging open. I hop in and without a word, we roar off into the dusk as the Arkham branch of the county committee pours out of the fire station after us.

"I hope that cargo you were hauling wasn't too precious," I say.

"It's fine," Smitty says, "the trailer was just full of Innsmouthians." He nods toward the rear-view mirror on the passenger side and I look into it to see a massacre on. The Innsmouthians, squat and hunchbacked, and resembling bloated human frogs, have pushed into the Arkhamite swarm in a perfect V formation, outnumbered but never outmuscled.

"Sweet Jesus . . ." I want to say more, but this is one of those rare moments when I am confronted with something that leaves me speechless.

"That was the worst dinner I ever had, Lono," Smitty says. "I get invited to a lot of them, you see. People in this country, they like truckers. They think we're the salt of the earth. The Essential Saltes from which some proletarian Golden Age can be resurrected—"

"What?"

"Huh?"

"Do you often use words you don't understand?"

"Just started recently, Mr. Lono, since I met you. I think you're a good influence on me."

"Me . . . or the fungi?"

"Oh, you, Mr. Lono. Definitely you." He licks his lips. "I wish I'd stayed in college instead of going to Nam. That Betsy was a piece of . . . She was something, don't you think?"

"She can fill out a sweater," I say. "That seems to be an Arkham trait." Now that the adrenaline dump has worn off, my arms and legs are trailed with bruises, most of them resembling more the marks left behind by a squid's suckers than fingers and palms.

"It sure ain't an Innsmouth trait," Smitty says. "And that's where we're headed."

"Oh, are we?" I glance down at the knife. The trucker is a good guy, and he's in this mess only because I slipped him a mickey and blew open the doors of consciousness as payment for giving me a lift, but I could still do him. Somewhere deep down inside of me, I'm sure I have it in my heart to grab the clutch, slam my foot on the brake, and gut another human being without flipping over the truck I don't know how to drive and don't have the stamina for. I know I can do it because I know I'm still human, and humans can do anything they put their minds to, the poor fucking bastards. *Now I ride with the mocking and friendly ghouls on the night wind, and play by day amongst the catacombs of Nephren-Ka in the sealed and unknown valley of Hadoth by the Nile. I know that light is not for me, save that of the moon over the rock tombs of Neb, nor any gaiety save the unnamed feasts of Nitokris beneath the Great Pyramid; yet in my new wildness and freedom I almost welcome the bitterness of alienage.*

"What?" Smitty barks.

"Huh?" I say.

"You just said a whole bunch of things about Egypt and whatnot. Mocking and friendly ghouls?"

"Oh," I say. "Never mind that. What is going on with you, Smitty?"

"What do you mean, Lono?"

"I mean . . . I don't know what I mean, damn it, and that's the frustrating part. These shrooms. They're aggravating, aren't they? I can't tell fantasy from reality anymore, and that's not a good state for someone like me to be in all the time. I need my wits about me, for there is dirty work ahead. Everything keeps changing. *You're* changing . . ."

"I'd hoped you wouldn't notice," he mutters.

"Not notice! How could I not notice, Smitty? You're turning into a Cannock. What sparked the change? Was it the fungi I gave you? Because if so, then I am sincerely sorry." And I was, and I meant it.

"No," he says. "It's not the shrooms."

It occurs to me that I probably shouldn't kill Smitty after all. I'm far too on edge to be trusted sufficiently enough to find where I put my rental car and file the story before the deadline without his big dumb hands to lead me. So I instruct him to take me to the car, and he complies. We don't say anything else. My head still hurts from running into the fire door, and I am in no mood for small talk, or any other kind of talk, either. But when we get to my car and to my stuff, Smitty has a surprise for me. I collect my kit bag and turn to say goodbye and there is a bright orange snub-nosed flare gun, pointed right at me.

"I'm sorry," Smitty says, and by his tone, I can tell that he genuinely is. "But I can't let you leave."

"What happens if I do, eh? What happens if I just get in this car and drive off and type up my story from a motel sixty miles down the road? I can do that, you know! I have an expense account."

"Get back in," Smitty says, "or I'll light you up like a god-damned gook."

"Sure!" I smile wide, so he can see all my teeth. Damn, my Mojo Wire feels heavy, and Smitty is so far away. I could chuck it at him, but he'd surely get off a shot with that flare gun first. It probably wouldn't kill me, but it could certainly break my ribs, and I'd be a blackened and blinded lipless freak scrabbling around the shoulder of Arkham's main drag till someone in a Chevrolet took me out like an aging squirrel.

"Innsmouth. Where I'm from."

For the second time in an hour, Smitty leaves me speechless.

"Innsmouth . . ." I shake my head. "But your accent. You sounded like a hillbilly, and then like a . . . but anyway, never like—"

"I worked hard to lose it. There was a time when I didn't want people to know where I was from. I guess you could say I got above my raising. But that's where we're going now, Lono. I've got to go back, and I'm bringing you with me. I'm sorry. You've got to meet my people. Let me tell you about me and Innsmouth on the way. Fair enough?"

I shrug and smile, because there is nothing else I can do. Smitty smiles back at me, a wide-lipped, fat-cheeked gesture. We drive on.

SEVEN

The cold January wind buffets the cab as dusk turns to darkness, and for a brief moment, I'm convinced Smitty and I are still in the Midwest, heading for the airport. But no, that's the fungi talking. We're here in the now, rocketing toward Innsmouth while Arkham fades in the rear-view mirror like a bad dream. I'm almost out of tapes. I make a mental note to pick up more. Then I set my tape recorder on the dashboard and let Smitty speak. He's happy to tell me his story. *People want to talk*; never forget that. Remembering that little nugget of wisdom, and carrying a weapon with you at all times, will pretty much get you through anything life throws your way.

"Go ahead," I say, lighting a cigarette.

What he says is shocking:

I woke up one morning. I ate a banana and some toast. I like jam on my toast. No butter. I turned on the TV and watched the news from Boston. It was going to be cloudy. A store was robbed. The sanitation department was on strike. Someone had a book out about carbohydrates. There was a lot of traffic. I felt good to be home, away from all the commuters and the highways. I almost never leave town. I ate another banana and then a peanut-butter sandwich because I was still hungry. I stopped being hungry. The mail came early because I live near the post office. It was all junk mail and coupons. Sometimes, I use coupons. Nothing good today though. I go to Ipswich to shop. I take the bus. It comes only six times all morning and afternoon.

Sometimes, people come here and say that the waterfront smells. I don't smell the waterfront. I never smell the waterfront.

I felt cold. The bus is by the waterfront. The waterfront isn't very busy anymore. Just some guys fishing. Lobster traps stacked high. A few birds. A couple of years ago, one dock crumbled into the bay after a big storm. Sometimes, people come here and say that the waterfront smells. I don't smell the waterfront. I never smell the waterfront. When you've lived here a long time, you can't smell what things smell like to outsiders. It's the same everywhere. I went to Salem State College for a semester and then dropped out. I'd go to Nam. It would be okay. I had a girl friend there, in Salem. Not a girlfriend, but a girl friend. She had three black cats, sort of as a joke. Her apartment smelled like cats. She said she couldn't smell the cats. Innsmouth is like this. The bus smells sometimes.

Today, the bus smells like a bus. I go to Ipswich. I buy some fruit. I buy some pork chops. The pork chops are on sale because they're about to go bad. They have fish for sale too in Ipswich, but nobody from my town needs to buy fish because we live on the water. Sometimes, I buy fish right off the boat. Sometimes, I go fishing myself, with a reel. Sometimes, I fish with a net. Sometimes, I take a boat with Marsh and we go out to the reef. I like to row the boat, but I get tired. Marsh rows better than I do. I buy Pop-Tarts. The kind that are apple currant. I only ever find that kind in Ipswich. I run out of money. Thinking about fishing before makes me decide to go fishing. I like to fish in the evenings anyway. In the morning, too many people try to fish. Some people think this is because the fish bite better in the morning. No, it is really because people who want to fish early want to get there before everyone else. Everyone ends up fishing just as the sun comes up. I'm in bed when the sun comes up. I wait till the morning news to get up. When I go fishing in the evening, I am almost always alone.

I go home and put the grocery bags on the counter. I take the stuff that needs to be refrigerated out of the bags and put it in the Frigidaire. Everything else I leave in the bags on the counter and on the range. I see that I have plenty of room in the Frigidaire for some fish if I catch any. I get my reel and go fishing. I don't use live bait. At the waterfront, I meet Marsh. Marsh says Hello. I say Hello. He says Fancy Meeting You Here. I laugh and say Yeah. We cast.

Marsh uses tiny eels. He talks to one as he puts it on the hook. I look out to sea. I like the white caps. I like to see how long it takes for the Devil's Reef to disappear from sight as the sun sinks down and the water turns wine dark. I read that in college. Wine dark. I brought a banana with me. I start eating it. Marsh says something, but I don't hear him because I think he's talking to the eel on his hook. The last bus comes and the door opens, but nobody steps out. Marsh repeats himself, but I don't answer because I have a lot of banana in my mouth. Then he asks a third time.

How Old Are You?

Twenty-One Now I say.

Would You Like To Join A Secret Society? Marsh asks me. I ask him What Do You Mean, A Secret Society? He says Everyone Around Here Is In It. I say Then How Come I Haven't Heard Of It? Then we both say Because It's A Secret and we both laugh. Then I say Is It Communism? Because I Am Not Into That. In My One Semester Of College, I Learned That Communism Is Perfect Except For Human Nature. Marsh says Oh, You Don't Have To Worry About Human Nature. It's Not Really Communism. I say That Sounds Fine, Then. He says Great. We Should Get Going.

I haven't caught anything. Marsh says he'll give me one of his. He recommends eel for bluefish. We go to the main drag. We go to the Odd Fellows club. Marsh tells me that the secret society is not an Odd Fellows branch. Nobody bothers to take down the sign because everyone is in the secret society. We walk in. The Odd Fellows club smells like brine and salt water. It smells like the waterfront smelled to my old girl friend when she came that one time to visit after I left school. Marsh says Take Off All Your Clothes. Then he takes off all his clothes. He has a belly on him; the rolls look a little like gills on his flanks. I take off all my clothes and leave them in a heap.

We walk down a hall. I hear chanting and burbling. There is a big double door like from a castle in a movie. It opens without Marsh or me touching it. Two people I've seen around town, a man and a woman, both naked, have opened the door. Marsh says Well, Here It Is. The room is huge and full of naked people. I see the mayor. I see my mailman, who is a lady. I see my cousin Freddy, who I don't see much even though we're cousins. There is a big pool in the middle of the room. There's light coming from the water, like there was another sun, a white-wine sun, way down deep. Marsh says In You Go and in I do.

I swim down toward the watery sun. It's awesome. There's a thing down there and she loves me. I never want to leave her. I don't need to breathe down here. Then I hear splashing and see feet and hands bubbling up the water and everyone is with me. Thank You, Thank You, Thank You I think to myself. I'm glad to be from here.

It takes me a moment to realize that Smitty is finished. He shifts in the seat. The springs creak beneath him. Then he just stares straight ahead, eyes on the road. I notice a rash on his neck; it looks like scales, almost. Or the world's worst case of razor burn. The knobs on his hands have grown longer. I switch off the tape recorder, stow it in my kit bag, and pull out the Mojo Wire. If Smitty notices, he doesn't say so. I watch the trees roll past in the dark. A sign tells me that we're entering Innsmouth, and my stomach roils. I can smell it already. I wonder if Smitty is taking me to the Odd Fellows club, and if the stink permeates the entire town.

Is anyone from this part of Massachusetts *not* in an Unspeakable Cult? I thought that nothing could be more insane than the Democratic Party primary process, with its even dozen hopefuls, most of them utter slime. Wallace, the raging racist fueled by nothing more than nigger hate and his desire to out-Nixon Nixon himself, was surely the worst. Most of them were nonentities—Indiana's Vance Hartke was surprisingly progressive, but the sort of wall-eyed policy wonk who could never connect with the masses. Especially not these masses. Wilbur Mills was pushed forward as a joke, and Mayor Lindsay lost any chance of escaping New York two years ago, when AFL-CIO hardhats did the cops' work for them and beat the living shit out of student protesters, and right on Wall Street as a favor to corporate masters that would never be repaid. When old Dutch New York money man from the silk-stocking district gets decried as a Red and a homosexual by organized labor, there's no chance. None of the candidates seemed well positioned to win even their own states, much less the presidency. Yes, Professor Madison Haringa and so many of the others I've met on my travels thus far appear to be dedicated to nothing short of a fifty-state victory.

"You're pissed at me, aren't ya, Lono?" Smitty asks, breaking the silence. "I wouldna brought ya here if I had any other choice. Maybe I shoulda told you everythin' from the beginning, but I couldn't. You see that, right?" *Now* I hear traces of Innsmouth cant.

"I'm too busy thinking to be pissed off at you right now, Smitty. I may decide to be angry with you later, but at this moment, I'm just trying to get to the nut of things. I think we need to get back to Miskatonic U. I have a book I want to check out of the library. A rare tome, a folio in human-skin leather that I've heard about in my travels."

"Yeah, which one?"

"Uh . . . *Unspeakable Cults?*"

"No problem. We got that one at the public library at Innsmouth," Smitty says, casual. The shrooms didn't add anything to his personality, his visions and whatnot aside. Rather, they *revealed* whatever he had been running from. Smitty was an Innsmouth boy, a six-fingered Cannock deep into what used to be recessive genes, now finding expression through pharmacological magic straight out of *The Tibetan Book of the Dead*. The raw "is-ness," Leary called it after experimenting with LSD at . . . where . . . Harvard, in Cambridge, Mass, just forty miles away. Smitty is devolving before my eyes. Becoming what he was always meant to be. Forget the prematurely old veteran proud of his service, bitter over his old girl, and worried about the racial-political freight that words like "gook" carry even when used between two white men, even when used while the war still shreds Vietnamese and Americans alike a world away; as Smitty approaches Innsmouth he becomes like a child again, complete with budding extra digits and a new manner of speech. And whatever that rash is on his neck.

"Look," he points to some vacant lot on which the remains of a clapboard house—not more than half a crumbling wall and elements of a chimney—still stand. "My auntie's house." Then he points out the lights on the cape, which he insists are fishing boats though it is past nine p.m. on this frigid winter evening. His old school, another decaying building, and the mayor's house, a gutted two-story home in the federal style. Innsmouth looks like a classic Norman Rockwell New England town, if the Watts and Newark rioters decided to hold a Superbowl there, but Smitty only sees the sites of the halcyon days of his childhood. He even drives his truck like a boy pretending to be a man, his hands at three and nine on the wheel, every acceleration and shifted gear an expansive gesture saying, *Look at me, Papa! Aren't I a big boy now?*

"So, do you think this public library is still standing? With books on the shelves and shelves on the walls, the way I'm used to back in civilized exurban Colorado?" I ask Smitty, and Smitty nods and says, "Yes, sir," with an Innsmouthian accent: *Yeaah-suhr.* Being home after so long can do that to a body, and indeed something is happening to Smitty's body. It couldn't have been a coincidence that he was the one to pick me up on that road outside the airport, couldn't have been a coincidence that Haringa was in the area, on my flight, so expansively willing to tell me about secret societies. But then again, that's the secret to secret societies—we know all about the Masons and Bilderbergers and the Skulls and Bones; what we *don't* normally know is what they do behind closed doors. Except that Smitty had just told me what his particular organization did, and sure enough, now we were pulling up to the Odd Fellows hall.

"I think I might want to stay at a hotel," I say. Smitty's a nice guy who has helped me out, saved my life, and clearly been through a lot in his own years, but the Mojo Wire in my hands sings like a hammer of the gods. I'll brain him if I have to and hit the road in his stolen truck rather than come face to face with a Deep One. I've watched him drive it enough that I think I can fumble my way through the gears. By the time the tires have eaten all of I-85 and I'm down in Alabama to check out the Wallace campaign, I'll have mastered the intricacies of the Mack truck, I'm sure. And the Ku Klux Klan won't be half as frightening in its wall-eyed backwardness as the northern alternatives. At least with the Klan, you know where you stand.

"This's the 'otel," Smitty says. It's right off the shore, the calm water of the bay lapping the edge of the parking lot.

"And what is it that you had to show me? What's so goddamned important that you had to pull a flare gun on me? More importantly, what's stopping me from going to my room and calling the cops?"

Smitty fiddled around with the flare gun and then stepped out of the truck. "Innsmouth cops or Arkham cops?" he asks. "Y'think either one would help you? Anyway, I'm not going to shoot you,

Lono. I only have one flare an' I'm 'bouta use it. Stand back. Ya don't wanna get this on ya." He holds his arm high and fires off the flare. It streaks up into the inky sky, illuminating the crumbling exterior of the Odd Fellows hall as it does. "You'sa wanna see this," Smitty says. He's grinning, and the expression is obscene. His lips are more fishlike than human now, and I wonder if he's even aware of it. He walks to the lip of the parking lot, to the edge of the sea, and waits. When the going gets weird, the weird turn pro, and I'm after a big story, but it's despite my better judgment that I stay. That and the fact that running off to hitchhike to freedom is what got me into this goddamn mess in the first place.

"Smitty, is there a pay phone around here?" I call out. "I want . . . nay . . . I *need* to call my editor." I feel foolish shouting, but it's not like anyone actually seems to live in Innsmouth after all. It's radically depopulated. If Arkham and Miskatonic were desolate, then Innsmouth is absolutely barren. The rotting buildings are the epitome of silence and neglect. Innsmouth is nothing more than a giant, cancerous tumor, living and beating after the rest of the body has long since passed on. I tell Smitty none of this. I don't think he'd appreciate it. Instead, I say, "You don't understand how editors can be. They're vile, despicable creatures, but this one will pay me money and I'm a big fan of that. I have a deadline, after all."

Smitty waves an arm and shouts back at me to not go too far. I don't tell him that I have no intention of doing so, simply because there's nowhere else to go, judging by the look of things. There is a pay phone at the end of the block, one of the older kind that still takes nickels and dimes but not quarters. I dig through my kit bag for change, take a half second to once again lament the end of the shrooms—my bag is still redolent of the damp, papery smell—and slip all the coins I can find in the slot. It's not a lot of money but it's also after business hours. I call the bar that my editor usually shuts down on weeknights and at first, I have some difficulty reaching him. It sounds like a noisy place, full of confusion and desperation, and the bartender doesn't understand who I'm asking for. I have to go through three other drunken editors before I find mine. I tell him the whole story. I'm off the campaign trail, trapped in Massachusetts as part of a supernatural cult war, and I've had drugs from another planet. My editor keeps thinking I'm saying *Yiddish* rather than *Yuggoth*, and I can tell he's getting offended. To a New York Jew any American with a firearm and a WASP surname is essentially a Nazi waiting for a führer to tell him what to do, and I can't blame him after what I've seen from strong Aryan New England stock this past day.

He tells me to get *something* in by my deadline, *anything* of *any* length, and hangs up. A huge wave kicks up somewhere in the night. As a raging narcissist, I should be happy. What every writer wants is not fame, not fortune, not large and unexpected royalty checks, not even the scoop that could bring down dynasties and destroy presidential ambitions. All we really want is a desperate editor who'll run anything we file and pay us for it relatively on time. But I'm not happy. I'm so terrified that my testicles have formed an escape committee, are even now plotting to steal a small dinghy and row for Boston Harbor. And I'm a fool—I should have used my change to call my lawyer. Now I need to call collect.

A word about my lawyer. So far, throughout this series of hazardous and madcap misadventures, I've said repeatedly that he is dead, and indeed, to the rest of the world, he is dead. The rumors vary. Some heard he'd been shot in Mexico and dumped in a fifty-five-gallon drum of lye. Others were told that he'd run afoul of Colombian drug runners and had ended up being chopped into fish bait onboard a boat loaded with cocaine. Some said he over-dosed on amphetamines and whores in a dingy hotel room in Miami. And who knows? Perhaps one day soon, any one of these rumors may be right. But not now and not yet. The truth is that my attorney has made some powerful enemies since our last trip together, and he's gone into hiding, preferring for the world at large to think him dead. I play along with the charade because I owe him that, but I'm in a situation now that requires his special brand of services. I hate to call him off the bench, because he really has done a remarkable job of dropping off the grid. I think a fake death suits him. He's a good lawyer and a good street preacher, but amphetamines and LSD have rotted away his once-powerful mind, and these days, the big brown buffalo feels that he's doomed to martyrdom and destined to be a messiah. Both of those types always end up dead, so it's a self-fulfilling prophecy.

But never mind that. Desperate times call for equally desperate measures. I am a fan of big guns, and it's time to bring in the biggest gun of all. I make a collect call to a phone number that no one else knows, and after a moment's pause, he accepts the charges. His voice is groggy and he sounds confused.

"Counselor!" I find that barking at him is the best possible response when he's in this state of mind. Drive the crazed brown buffalo into panic mode and let him mow everything down. "Remember the Manson family? Helter Skelter and the race wars and all those Frank Frazetta paperback covers that you love so much? Well, it's all going down. Get the next flight to Logan now and damn the cost. My editor will cover it. That's right, you bastard! Money! Your billable hours start now! Hurry, man. We have no time to mess around. We're going to save the world."

"Hot damn!" he shouts, waking up now and ready to stumble back into the world.

"And one more thing," I say. "When you get here, call me Lono."

I can't tell whether it's my lawyer roaring like a lion or the newly restive ocean. Something slams hard against the glass of the phone booth. A white, six-fingered palm.

Which candidate will earn the Innsmouth vote? I doubt Haringa's propaganda would go over very well here, but the fishy mien of the town, and of its citizens, does suggest a tendency toward Cthulhoid Republicanism. Innsmouth isn't a mill town, but a fishing burg with a few struggling canneries on the shore. Not quite

Moloch territory either. Innsmouth is a swing district, but one plagued with chronic economic depression, FBI infiltration, and explosive race riots between the fisher folk and the inlanders. And the riots have been about race in a way that no race riot in the history of the United States has ever been—the fisher folk aren't all human, not quite factory-model *Homo sapiens sapiens*.

Smitty can pass, or at least can pass for now, as long as he doesn't stick around too long, but some of the members of the older families look like they were birthed right into a vice—narrow heads, bulging eyes, Mongoloid noses. Six fingers is a pretty common, but not universal, trait. They all shamble except for Smitty and some of the young men. They'd shambled right up to me, some of them with obvious gills running down their necks like wayward double and triple chins and . . . showed me to a musty hotel room in the building shared by the Odd Fellows. Here I sit, writing this out longhand in my most careful print, waiting for my lawyer, waiting for salvation. It is cold out here, and the pages in my notebook grow damp. The ink runs like black blood . . . or perhaps ichor.

Smitty called something up from the waters, something not native to this hemisphere and likely not even native to this Earth. I'd been informed of Moloch, had heard rumors and whispers about Cthulhu, but I was *introduced* to a Deep One. He was a huge, fish-headed being, white bellied with webbed hands. Sort of like Hubert Humphrey, actually, but more kindly and charismatic than our thirty-eighth vice president ever was or will be. And the Deep Ones are aggrieved. It seems that back in the 1920s, their underwater city of Y'ha-nthlei, hidden under Devil's Reef right offshore here in Innsmouth, was torpedoed by the federal government. Neither Y'ha-nthlei nor Innsmouth ever recovered financially. This is one of the reasons why Smitty has brought me here. It is his belief that given my countercultural leanings, I might like to write about what happened here, exposing the cover-up and showing people the truth.

With a deep bass voice that would occasionally break into a high whistle, not dissimilar to a whale's song, the Deep One gave his own version of Nixon's famous gaffe, *"North Vietnam cannot defeat or humiliate the United States. Only Americans can do that."*

"We brought fish and gold in exchange for a few human lives, but when the humans killed us, they gave us nothing in exchange at all." He went on to explain that the local ritual of bearing or siring Deep One hybrids more than makes up for the numbers lost in our "slow mammalian reproduction protocols." Smitty and a few of the locals who saw the flare and came running took it all in with the sort of enthusiasm and purely uncynical belief that McGovern would rape children for. The Deep One was something to behold, all right, a Disneyland robot that smelled like sewage, but the Innsmouthians must have been truly desperate to obey it, to worship it, to spread for it on command. And for nothing but the same catches of fish nearby Gloucester hauled in for free, and some golden trinkets too grotesque to sell on the open markets.

I don't know what Smitty was trying to prove with what he called forth. I wasn't awestruck by the being, not after it opened its mouth and spoke in everyday English from a set of prepared talking points. Terrified? For a moment. Impressed? I still am. But not awestruck. In the end I simply felt pity for these monsters of Innsmouth, both the ones who lived under the waves, soggy in their immortality and desperate for human companionship, and the citizens of the shell-shocked and moldering city. If they war against Arkham it's likely out of jealousy and raw hunger, not any political or metaphysical chess game.

I almost regret calling for my lawyer now. He's a ruiner of reputations, a despoiler of economic systems. Who knows what he'll pack—knives, subpoenas, methadrine, a rocket-propelled grenade launcher courtesy of some of his old friends in the Red Army Faction . . . that last would probably have to be checked as baggage. Fraudulent deeds to all the residential, commercial, and municipal property of Ipswich, just so he'd have a town to eat and then shit out all over downtown Innsmouth. He is surely on his way now. The first cab that roars down the main drag will be him. I'm only glad he is on my side, and not Nixon's.

Half-frozen, I spend a few hours in the library. They open it for me, despite the fact that the sun isn't even up yet. I smoke cigarettes and drink hot, black coffee laced with generous helpings of whiskey, and read through old newspaper clippings and town history books. Founded in 1643, Innsmouth was renowned for shipbuilding before the American Revolution. It prospered throughout the early nineteenth century, but the War of 1812 and the loss of a number of sailors in a series of shipwrecks left it floundering economically. By 1828, the only fleet still sailing to the South Seas for trade was one that belonged to Captain Obed Marsh, the patriarch of the town's leading family. Desperate to save his town, Marsh started a cult in 1840 called the Esoteric Order of Dagon in the building now ever-so-casually marked *Odd Fellows*. Although Marsh learned of Dagon from a group of Polynesian islanders he met during his travels, Dagon really seemed to get around, and was worshiped by other cultures, as well. He started out as a fertility god, but then the Hebrews got their hands on him and made him a god of fishing. The Amorites and the Philistines worshiped the old bugger, too. However the Polynesians learned of him, it was Marsh who brought Dagon to America, and when he did, Innsmouth's fishing industry exploded, becoming more profitable than ever before. The townspeople loved Marsh—and Dagon—as a result, but what Marsh didn't tell them was that he had entered into a pact with the Deep Ones. Ever the businessman and capitalist, that Obed Marsh. The deal was this: the Deep Ones brought the town plenty of fish and gold (which they kept at the bottom of the sea) in exchange for Marsh keeping Dagon in human sacrifices. It didn't end well. These things never do. Marsh had trouble keeping up with his new god's appetite, and Innsmouth ran scarce on living inhabitants, so they had to start preying on travelers and residents of other towns, especially nearby Ipswich and Rowley. Marsh and his followers were arrested in 1846, and with them went the sacrifices. Dagon and the Deep Ones were unhappy with this turn of events, and the Deep Ones retaliated, putting the fear of Dagon into the townspeople's souls. Soon enough, the sacrifices started up again, and the cult grew strong once more. Maybe there weren't enough eligible bachelors left or maybe the Innsmouthians were just depraved, but whatever the reason, they began interbreeding with the Deep Ones, which led to obvious deformities and mutations. After that, anybody with half a brain went out of their way to avoid Innsmouth, until 1927, when the town came under investigation by the federal government for bootlegging.

Now here is where it gets good. The department in charge of the investigation was the Bureau of Investigation, the precursor to the FBI—specifically, the General Intelligence Division, which was headed up by good old J. Edgar Hoover himself. Calvin Coolidge had appointed Hoover as the director of the Bureau of Investigation three years before, after the previous director, William Burns, fell under suspicion for his involvement in the Teapot Dome scandal. Even back then, Hoover had it in for radicals, subversives, freaks, and other ne'er-do-wells. His first order of business upon accepting the job of director was to fire agents who he thought "looked stupid like truck drivers." Ah, the irony, eh? Of course, that type of behavior is typical of Hoover even today. How many times over the years has he overstepped his bounds, both in his role at the FBI and during his time with its predecessor? The German and Japanese scares, the Verona Project, his complete and total bungling of the investigation into the assassination of John F. Kennedy, and his plan during the Korean War to suspend habeas corpus and round up twelve thousand American "dissidents" suspected of disloyalty. Hell, just last year, we learned about the abomination that was COINTELPRO, which came about because of Hoover's frenzied certainty that communists lurked behind every door, especially if those doors were in Hollywood or the print district. Why, then, would it come as a shock that Hoover, prior to his position with the FBI, was in charge of an operation in 1927 in which the government blew up Devil's Reef and the Deep Ones' abode, and then arrested most of the locals? That's par for the course for Hoover. Business as usual. Hey ho!

J. Edgar Hoover is a rotten, perverse beast. Paranoia and corruption leak from his diseased pores, and yet he stays in power. Truman, Kennedy, and Johnson all considered dismissing him, but ultimately let him remain in power. He's been investigated, castigated, or censured by several House select committees and civil-rights groups, yet he always comes through unscathed. I'd admire the bastard's tenacity if not for him being such an obvious pig fucker. A man like that only stays in power if he has power to begin with. I have no doubt that Hoover's powers are great and vast and terrible, and now Smitty and his friends are asking me to rattle that cage and expose the truth? The offer is tempting, and the potential for fun and high jinks can't be denied, but it would also be dangerous. Only a fool would undertake such a risk, and I am such a fool. But to do so, I will need lawyers, guns, and money. And I also need to figure out how it all tied into Cthulhu, Moloch, Nixon, and the rest of the Happy-Fun Club.

The sun is up by the time I'm done, which means it's time for me to go to bed. Smitty puts me up in a ramshackle boarding house with a leaking roof and a porch that looks like it's about to collapse. The wallpaper is peeling, and there are veins of black mold spider webbing the plaster beneath. As far as I can tell, I am the only occupant, other than the bulbous-eyed clerk at the desk downstairs. I finish off the last of the whiskey and then lie down on the bed. I don't bother to undress, but I do kick my shoes off and throw them at Smitty, one at a time. The first toss misses, knocking over a broken lamp, but the second shoe hits him in the shoulder. Smitty tells me not to run off, and I've no doubt they'll post a guard of some kind, but I assure him that they don't have to fear. I am intrigued enough to stick around and poke my nose into things, and I am also expecting company. A California earthquake is about to hit Innsmouth. Where were you when the fun started?

There's a fat knock on the door and before I can even find a blunt object with which to brain whoever is outside, it opens and he is here. Five hundred pounds in an aging Nehru jacket, hair like a dead and burnt oak tree, wearing his standard-issue loud tie, elephant-trunk arms wide, reaching from one end of the room to another, for a hug. "Lono," he bellows as he scoops me up like a child. "You're alive! You're fucking alive!"

"I'm not the one who's been faking my death, you fat bastard. Put me down!"

I get a kiss on each cheek before he puts me back on my feet, but his arms are still around me. "What are we doing in Innsmouth, man? This is a bad scene. As your attorney, I advise you to leave immediately and fly to Acapulco with me."

"We can't go to Acapulco. The story is here."

He picks his flowered attaché case with the Chicano Power sticker on it up from the floor and strides into the room, shutting the door behind him. "Don't you know what they do to outsiders out here? They filet 'em and use 'em as chum."

"Where'd you hear that?"

"The fucking cabbie. I had to pay double the meter just to get him in the city limits. He didn't want to come. He said that everyone here has extra chromosomes, and brother, from the man behind the desk downstairs, I gotta believe him. There's bad karma all around here, man. What the hell are you doing in a place like this? These people don't even qualify as voting citizens, do they? Aw hell, don't answer that. I'll write my senator later. Let's get down to more important matters. Where can someone get a drink around here?"

"An excellent question. Let's hope this wasn't one of those awful Puritan beachheads back in the olden times," I say.

My counselor snorts and mutters something about sailors and fucking the freshwater manatees. "This place should be swimming in grog."

We head downstairs and find the front desk deserted. The counter is damp and the place reeks of seaweed and brine and mildew. My attorney sniffs, but it has nothing to do with the stench and everything to do with the small vial of cocaine he tucks back in his shirt pocket. "You bastard," I screech. "Give me some of that. Don't hog it all."

"As your attorney, I advise you to have a drink first."

We wander out onto the empty street. I see no sign of Smitty or his truck and wonder where he could have gotten to. Sleeping with the fishes, perhaps, in the literal sense? Maybe his change is complete. If so, I wish him luck. He'll need it should Hoover come back and decide to finish the job he started here all those years ago. There is a small bar down on the first floor of the Odd Fellows lodge, open to the public and full despite the early hour. Apparently, this is where the inhabitants have all been hiding. We're issued drinks in the form of raw eggs cracked into icy beers. " 'T's all we serve," the bartender says. My request for my usual breakfast of coffee, whiskey, Heineken, and grapefruit juice is met with consternation, as if instead of ordering, I'd asked the barkeep if he'd like to sodomize Ray Coniff with Neil Diamond's hand. My lawyer pushes his stein back and orders a triple.

"Triple what?" the bartender says.

"Triple eggs, what the hell else!" the counselor bellows. What few tête-à-têtes were being held in the corner booths stop and a room full of bulging eyes and slurping, twitching lips turn our way, but my attorney gets his three eggs with haste.

"So," I wonder aloud, "what candidate does the average Innsmouthian support, eh?" The locals aren't shy about answering the question for me. The sloped brows and haddock-white faces would suggest they are Nixon supporters, but I am surprised—McCloskey.

The former marine turned peacenik Republican and Earth Day supporter? "That's t' one," an old-timer, still mostly human, tells us.

"Well, he's not going to get the nod from the Republican bigwigs, so ultimately you're all for Nixon," I say.

"Nope," the old-timer says. His friends agree with him. Slow shakes of the head all around, and a few slobbering grins.

"Well then, who the hell are you going to vote for? Are you going to stay home? Shirk your civic duty! Do you know how many gooks I killed overseas so that people like you could roll out of your salt-encrusted waterbeds and vote!" My lawyer is already on his feet, his head nearly brushing the low ceiling of the bar. He may have been on the bench for a while, but he eases back into the job like a fish . . . or a Deep One . . . into water. "Dozens," I moan. "Oh, those motherfuckers still haunt me. Their heads exploded, man! It was like a greasy teenager popping his goddamned pimples. That's how *easy* it was, and now you fish-stick suckers aren't going to vote?"

"We're votin'," the old-timer says, not impressed, "for McCloskey."

"Why? Because you still have a hard-on for Hoover after what he did to your town? Wake up, man! That's no reason. Hoover stays in power no matter which party is in office."

"Ain't got nuthin' t'do with him . . . much. Here in Innsmouth we don't vote for what we don't want."

"Then you're not going to win!" As happens whenever my lawyer gets this way, I start casing the joint for blunt instruments, unclean steak knives, fire alarms, emergency exits, forgotten handguns, loose change, undercover cops, John Birchers who might be holing up for a drink, loaded for bear, and ready to legally shoot a brown person—even a brown person the size of my attorney.

"Aw, we'll win, all right. It'll be a wicked-close election," the bartender says. "But we'll win. So why don't you settle down a fair bit, sir."

"Close!" the lawyer spits all over the place, a rabid dog. "Bullshit! It's not going to be a close election. This country is going down one path or another—more and bloodier war, institutional paranoia, the triumph of cretinism! Or . . ." and then something happens that I'm not used to. He's stuck. "Or . . ."

"Or?" the old-timer says.

My attorney makes quick work of another triple-egg-and-beer shooter. That seems to help grease his wheels. "Or, if a Democrat wins, then we have a chance to end this war. We have a chance to really remake this country into—"

"A Great Society?" the bartender offers. Fishy, blubbering laughs percolate up from the floor.

"I know, I know." He licks his lips. It's a game he likes, an argument he's had a thousand times before, with AK-47s pointed at him, over mounds of coke, in frantic precoital tumbling with those wool-stocking-wearing girls who still read *The Militant*. "But look at it this way. We're a two-party system and both the parties are capitalist parties, that's for sure. But one is the party of finance capital—that's the Republicans—and one is the party of industrial capital: the Democrats. So, think about your own interests. Are you a Wall Street bigwig?"

"Cain't say I um," says the old-timer.

"But you probably depend on industry."

"I depend on my god," he says.

"You've got to see this god, by the way," I tell my attorney. "I met him last night in the parking lot."

"You got any more of that stuff, Lono?"

"I'm telling you, it happened, you swine! I wasn't on fungi from Yuggoth at the time. I had control of my senses."

"Fun guy from where?"

"Never mind that."

Then my attorney turns his attention back to the old-timer and the bartender and, with his voice loud enough for the rest of the bar to hear, says, "The point is this. You don't have to fight for the pigs that claim to be on your side, but you have to make sure that the other side doesn't win. The guy you're voting for, what's he going to do if he gets a delegate or two at the Republican National Convention? Nothing. He can't take that one delegate and transform Nixon's policy planks, and he certainly can't give that basset-hound bastard a personality, or a lobotomy. So what are you gonna do about it?"

"We're all votin' McCloskey," someone says in the back. "We had some a them Arkhamites comes around here telling us different too, 'cept'n they were tellin' us to vote *for* Nixon. Say he's gonna win, but he needs to win it all to bring about the new age. Needs to win all a fifty states for it ta happen. Sumpin' ta do with numberology and such. Says fifty is a powerful number. Fifty brings 'bout the new age. Well, maybe we don't want no new age, and maybe we don't want no Moloch either." At the word *Moloch* a general murmur rises up and the clientele stand as one and approach us.

"Why don't you all come outside with us," says the bartender as he rounds to the front. He has a Louisville Slugger he picked up from under the bar, just in case we had other plans for the afternoon.

My attorney deadpans, "We're gonna play a little Cape Cod summertime ball, are we?"

"Now listen," I say, jumping to my feet. "I'm here as an invited guest, and this man is my attorney. And even so, I'm more of a football fan than a baseball fan."

"We'll make you one," the bartender promises. "Got no need for yer kind round here."

My attorney straightens up. He's a big man, but there's only one of him. "Stand down, Chesty," I tell him. "These are a peaceful bunch, except for the occasional ritual murder." He's not convinced, but we are surrounded, so we're back out to the parking lot and not by choice. The locals follow us through the door. The old-timer has three dozen eggs with him, taken from the bar. Unceremoniously, he dumps them off the edge of the parking lot and into the water, where they sink. Despite the season, the water hasn't frozen over. Gulls circle overhead, shrieking as they dive-bomb the offering like Japanese kamikaze pilots.

"Holy shit," my lawyer says, "those eggs just sank! Eggs don't fucking sink."

"Yes, they do," I say. The circle of Innsmouthians around us all agree. Yes, yes, of course they sink. Haven't you ever boiled an egg? If eggs didn't sink, ducks wouldn't come ashore to lay them. All that folksy garbage. Having met a Deep One yesterday, I'm pretty calm, despite the fact that all I have to level myself off—now that the shrooms are out of my system—is half a beer and most of a raw egg, and the whiskey I drank last night. But I'm not ready for what happens next.

The water begins to boil and churn and steam, and from it emerges a huge webbed hand, one larger than the hands of the Deep One I saw the night before. It moves away from the edge of the parking lot, but then a massive, fleshy dome emerges. For a moment I fear losing control of my bowels; is it the top of a giant head? No, a huge, distended belly. Then the rest of her—yes, her—with two pendulous and fleshy tits—no, four of them—emerges. A Deep One, gigantic, the size of a tugboat, floats on her back, her four engorged breasts flopping, her arms wide and extended like an infant reaching for a hug from the sun and sky.

"Mother Hydra," the locals say, not quite in unison. They're religious but still have minds of their own. Once again, I am overcome with a sense of kinship, the same as I felt for Smitty, even after the bastard kidnapped me with a flare gun. I could get to like these Innsmouthians; maybe because they're not all that human after all. And my lawyer, he's entranced, as well. I haven't seen the bastard like this since he fell in love with the girl behind the counter at the taco stand in Vegas. That didn't end well, and I don't think this will either. He steps forward.

"Oscar!"

"Holy mama," he says. "This is why you called me here, Lono."

"Huh?"

"I'm gonna do this lady right," he says. "I'm gonna show her a good time."

He takes another step, then a third, then flings out his own arms wide and lets himself fall off the lip of the parking-lot jetty and down into the slimy embrace of Mother Hydra. He lands softly on her stomach like it's a California king–sized bed in an expense-account hotel room, and together they sink back into the briny waters of the shore.

"Shit!" I rush to the water's edge. My cigarette tumbles from my gaping mouth. The Great Brown Buffalo has just been dragged under by the Great Green Fish Bitch. Willingly, maybe even lovingly. I always knew the bastard would die horribly, but I never imagined he would go out like this.

"He'll be back," the old-timer tells me. He's hugging his empty cardboard crate of eggs tightly to his chest. "When Mother Hydra comes out, ittsfer to claim an audience, not to hold court up here. It'll be fine. You'll see."

"Are you crazy? He'll drown, if hypothermia doesn't kill him first!"

"Nah, he won't. She'll keep 'im warm and such." The crowd of men laugh at *keep 'im warm*. "She'll breathe for him down there, too. She can do that; she can bring a body down there. Even a full-blown, full-grown, human body. That's why you called him here, after all, no?"

"No!" I shout. "I called him to . . ." To what? Wreck the town? Bring the pain to ground zero of the American Nightmare, to a bunch of old bastards who don't deserve it and who likely wouldn't even notice. Or was I . . . moved somehow to bring my lawyer to this sweaty armpit of a town, to mate him with Mother Hydra? An intriguing theological question, but really I just want to get back to the bar.

"So we just wait here for his head to break the surface of the water again and pull him out?" I finally ask.

"You c'n," says one of the others. "I think we'd all just as soon go back to the bar and finish our breakfast. There's a ladder on the far end of the pier; he can climb on back up out of the water." And with that, they walk off, leaving me standing there. For a minute or so I stay in the cold winter air, on the border of a small town that should be waking up for its puny version of rush hour, but there's no trade here, no commerce. Not even Loch Ness–style tourism. That flummery only works when there isn't a monster down below.

Back in the bar, I find out that beer isn't just for breakfast; it's for lunch as well. Nothing else is on the menu, though I'm told I could order out for sandwiches if I want to. Instead I head back to my room and fetch the Mojo Wire and the rest of my kit bag. With nothing else to do, and with all the fun over for the moment, I am left to write. The Mojo Wire earns me some taciturn nods and raised eyebrows—to the extent that the Innsmouth look even includes eyebrows—as I begin jotting my story down by hand and then feeding each sheet of paper through the machine.

"What's that, then?" the bartender asks. "Tellin' the truth about things?"

"I always do. I like to stand out in an otherwise-crowded marketplace."

"Think it might affect the election?"

"Doubt it. The only people who read my stuff are already dedicated McGovern voters, for the most part. If he makes it to Miami Beach, maybe that'll be because I spiked the Muskie campaign, but . . . it's just . . . Nixon. I don't know his plans. And he has them, plans within plans. Dossiers on everyone, even himself. He records his own rants and then plays them back to himself in bed, just to see if he can remember what it was he was feeling during the day. He doesn't even cheat on his wife, and he's the president! You know what kind of iron will the man must have to keep himself out of Hollywood B-list bush?"

The bartender starts to answer, but his gaze is drawn over my head and behind me. The door thumps open like a piece of cheap scenery in a Hollywood western. It's my lawyer, dripping a puddle in the doorway, his hair plastered to his forehead and cheeks and coated with ice. Icicles are forming on his nose and eyebrows, too. Despite this, he has a smile on his face, one I've seen once before, in Las Vegas, when we took a little vacation to talk about the Chicano social movement and the plans to create a new Aztlán, but we ended up . . . distracted.

"Where the hell have you been?" I shout.

"Up the Manuxet River, beneath the ice. And out to the sea. I need several drinks."

The bartender sets him up with three triple-egg sliders, while I feed another sheet into the Mojo Wire and ask, "Do you want to change clothes? You'll freeze to death."

"No need," my attorney says. "Time enough for that later." He walks up to me, shoes squishing and squeaking, and takes the stool next to mine. His teeth are chattering. "What a woman! She told me things, man. Secret things, things only the sea could know, the story of a thousand shipwrecks and ten thousand drowned souls."

"Go," I say. "Just let her rip. Tell me what she said, unexpurgated."

"It's not like that." He digs a cigarette out of the breast pocket of his suit jacket and doesn't even seem to realize that it can't light. I offer him one of mine instead and remind myself to deduct it from the bill for his services, but he waves it away and continues clutching his. "I mean . . ." he sighs. "There's too much for you to write down. It would take the rest of my life to speak, and the rest of yours to transcribe, and I don't have much time left, you know."

"I do?"

"You do now."

"You're faking it again when we're done?"

"No, this is the real thing, man. She told me when I was going to die, and I'm telling you. It will be soon. And you know what? I'm at peace with it, because I'll go out the way I always wanted to, you know? Anyway, it's like . . . how the world works? Who's right? Karl Marx? George Fucking Washington? The *Popol Vuh*? Even she doesn't know, man." He slides off the stool, waves his crumpled, half-frozen cigarette around, looking uselessly for a light from one of the patrons. "Well, it's, there's the Cannocks, see, and Cthulhu. Mother Hydra is even on Cthulhu's side, but the stars aren't right. That's what Nixon's up to. If he can win it all, not just the election, but all fifty states, then . . ."

My lawyer wobbles where he stands and looks at me, his eyes brimming with tears. "Or? What *or*? Oh Christ, these fucking monsters. God." He sinks to his knees and begins to sob, loudly.

"Who is that man?" one of the lunch shifters asks. "I saw you last night, son, but that fellow's new to me. I think he's got a drinkin' problem or sumpin'."

"This man is a famed civil-rights lawyer. The American Indian movement, the Brown Berets, the Black Panthers. He's represented all of them! He ran for the sheriff of the city of Los Angeles on the platform that he'd eliminate the whole department if he won."

"But he din't win, eh?"

"See for yourself." I nod.

"Nixon!" my lawyer suddenly says. He's staring into those giant hands of his, those gargantuan meat hooks that have crushed men's skulls like overripe watermelons. His fingers are white from the cold. "We gotta kill Nixon; that's the only way." He looks up at me, his eyes wild like flaming movie screens. "Let's go! By God, we'll give him what for! Pull him out by the roots like the evil skunkweed that he is! It's the only way to save the fucking world! The whole motherfucking world . . ."

"Calm down," I say. "Ye Gods, man, get a grip on yourself. The first thing you need to do is drink." I draw his attention to the three raw-egg-and-beer sliders that the bartender has so thoughtfully arranged for him. My attorney lurches to his feet and grabs one with both hands. He gulps it feverishly, smacks his lips, and sighs.

"Got anything warm?" I ask the bartender. "Tea or coffee or maybe some mescal?"

"This's it. I tol' ya that afore."

"This is okay," my attorney gasps, and then starts in on the second mug. While he recovers, I turn off the Mojo Wire and stow it in my kit bag. I'm considering running the equipment back up to my room and finding him some dry clothes when he spins on his stool and grabs my face in his hands. My cigarette falls onto the bar. His fingers are like blocks of ice. Jesus, I think. This is it. He's finally snapped!

"We've got to go," he says, his tone more urgent than I've ever heard it before. "You don't understand, man. Once Nixon wins all fifty states, the game is over. He can give the whole fucking world to Cthulhu with a fifty-state win. The stars are almost right. See, this Cthulhu, he's sort of dead but not really. Everyone just *thinks* he's dead." My attorney pauses then, clearly delighted at the irony. "What he's really doing is sleeping. He's asleep down there in the sunken city of R'lyeh. But the stars are right, and if Nixon wins all the states, then Cthulhu will wake up and R'lyeh will rise again. We've got to put a stop to that shit. We've got to kill the bastard for good this time!"

"Calm down," I shout. The locals stare up from their mugs and I lean close, lowering my voice. "Get a grip on yourself, man. You've just been swimming with something that makes Jeane Kirkpatrick look positively lovely . . ."

"Who? The lady running Henry Jackson's campaign? He doesn't stand a chance."

"Never mind that! Will you shut up and listen to me? You're half-frozen—not nearly drunk enough—your cigarettes and your vial of coke are ruined, and you're sitting here in a bar announcing at the top of your diseased lungs your intentions to assassinate

Richard Milhous Nixon. Clearly, you have experienced a great shock and have taken leave of your wits. As your doctor, I advise you to drink heavily. Then we'll sort this whole mess out, eh?"

He nods. "That is good advice."

"Well, of course it is. I never give bad advice. Now finish your final egg shooter. I've had enough of this swill. I believe there is another bottle of whiskey in my room, along with some dry clothes. They won't fit you, but at least you'll be out of the cold. Now stand up, thank the nice man behind the bar, be friendly, and for God's sake don't attract any more attention. I'm becoming attached to these Innsmouthians and I don't want you embarrassing me any more than you already have. I should have never called you in on this job."

He starts sobbing then, succeeding only in drawing even more stares. I throw some money on the bar, nod to the old-timers, and then hustle him out of the Odd Fellows lodge and back to the boarding house. The bulbous-eyed clerk is back behind the front counter again, and he smiles as we walk in, revealing gums lined with bony nubs of gristle rather than teeth.

"Went swimmin' with Mother Hydra, did 'e?" he asks, indicating my attorney. I nod and grin and shove the Samoan in the direction of the stairs. " 'E'll be okay," the counterman assures me. "They're always like that afta' first communion. Let 'im get some sleep and 'e'll be good as new."

I lean Oscar against the wall and walk over to the clerk. "Listen, is there anything to drink in this town besides seawater, eggs and beer, or Deep One spunk?"

"Ah-yuh. I've got bourbon and—"

"Whiskey! Have some sent up to the room, right away. And food too, if you have it. I need brain food, gasoline for my mind! Grapefruits and mushrooms. Do you know where you can get me mushrooms? This is serious business."

"You ain't talkin' 'bout the kind ya put on yer pizza?"

"Of course not, man! I said brain food."

"Ain't nuthin' like that round here, least nottin' that I know of."

"Well, send up whatever you can find. And make sure we're not disturbed by anyone . . . Wait, scratch that. Make sure we're not disturbed by anyone except for Smitty, the guy who brought me in this morning. Do you know who I mean?"

The clerk smiles and I squash the urge to wince and turn away. "A'yuh, I know him. We're sure glad t' have him back home. He's a good boy."

"If he shows up, tell him I need to see him right away. Anyone else, they leave a message. And if a guy from Arkham comes around looking for me—and you'll know him if you see him: pompous, collegiate, patches-on-the-elbows-of-his-corduroy-smoking-jacket type—tell him you've never heard of me before, and that we're not here. This is important. Do it, and there's a nice tip in it for you. I'll have my editor take care of things."

He nods, his expression enthusiastic. He is happy to be a part of things. Something exciting is happening, and although he doesn't know what it is, he's ecstatic to be involved in some small way. In a town where subhuman fish people breed with the local homecoming queens and mold and mildew are the interior-decorator colors of choice, I am something bold and different and fresh and new, and this guy can't wait to see what I do for my next trick. And neither can I, because as of right now, I don't have a fucking clue what that next trick is going to be, or how I'm going to fix this mess and set things right again.

"It has to be this election," my attorney warbles as I help him up the stairs. "If they miss this chance, the stars aren't right again until 2012. It's a long, involved process, and a lot of bad shit has to happen in order to prime the ether. That's what's happening now; Manson and Vietnam and the Starkweather kid and Kent State, they're all a part of it. Those things occurred so that the ether would be primed. And as the stars line up, Nixon can make his move. If he blows this shot, then they have to start the whole process over again. If that happens, they can't really start cooking until 2001 or so. Oh, they'll still have their people in office. They'll have a succession of presidents and elected officials who will make sure things stay on track, but they can't ramp up the negative energy until 2001, and then it has to simmer, like a kettle on the stove. It has to boil over at the same time as the alignment."

"And that's in 2012?" He confirms for me that it is, as I unlock the door and shove him into the room. That's why Nixon and his cronies are so desperate to succeed. Many of them will be dead by the next time the stars are aligned right. This is their one and only chance. If they fumble the football, the next generation will have to take over. That certainly can't sit well with old Tricky Dick.

My attorney is so weak and numb from cold that he can't undress himself. I have to do it for him. Nothing smells worse than a five-hundred-pound Samoan lawyer who's been traveling on an airplane and is exuding alcohol and cocaine from his pores after swimming in seawater with a Deep One, all without the benefit of soap or shampoo. I get him cleaned up as best I can, and then I stick him under the covers. He babbles contentedly to himself while I get out my tablet and work. I write:

1. The Cthulhu-worshiping Republicans, led by Nixon, need to win all fifty states, thus handing the world over to Cthulhu and issuing in a new dark age.

2. The Moloch-worshiping Democrats are no fucking better, but I'll deal with them another day.

3. Haringa and his cronies want to sacrifice me as part of some bizarre, pagan ritual to help cement Nixon's election victory, and thus, Cthulhu's reign on Earth.

4. My attorney wants to kill Nixon, and thus, stop them before they succeed.

5. I'm along for the ride, because this is where the story is taking me, and also because it beats sitting at home and wading through more fan mail and dead peacocks.

6. How the hell does J. Edgar Hoover figure into this, and how

does his attack on the people of Innsmouth and Dagon's spawn tie in? Ah, that's the rub, isn't it? The million-dollar question. Whose side is he on, really? Moloch's? Cthulhu's? Or is he playing both sides against each other in pursuit of his own demented endgame? After all, he's served both Republicans and Democrats in his time, as well as other masters. So the question is, who gave Hoover the order to dynamite the Deep One's city? One of the political parties, or maybe one of the shadowy groups working within those parties? And for what purpose? My instincts are no good on this one. Part of me wants to find out who would have benefited most from the federal government's raid on Innsmouth, but another part of me suspects Hoover might be a dead end, and not connected to this in any way. A red herring, perhaps, but if so, then an intentional one, or simply happenstance? What's your story, J. Edgar?

"He doesn't matter," my attorney says, and I don't realize that I've been speaking aloud until he does.

"What's that?"

"Hoover. He doesn't matter. She told me."

"Who told you?" I ask, but I already know the answer. I just want to keep him awake and talking until the whiskey arrives and I can get it down his throat.

"Mother Hydra," he says. "She told me while we were swimming. Did you know he's a fruit?"

There had been rumors that Hoover was homosexual dating all the way back to the forties, and like all good journalists, I'd heard those rumors, and I said so.

"He likes to dress up like a woman," my attorney says. "High heels, stockings, frilly dresses with lots of lace. He's not just a queer . . . Hoover goes whole hog. He's a thirty-third-degree Mason, too."

"So what's your point?" I stub my cigarette butt out in the ashtray and light two more. I give one of them to my attorney and smoke the other. "What are you suggesting? That we blackmail Hoover with this information in the hopes that he helps us expose the cultists?"

He inhales a lungful of smoke, coughs, and then inhales again. His color is returning, and the ice in his hair is beginning to melt. He no longer resembles a frozen buffalo, instead looking more like a drowned wharf rat with each passing moment. "No," he wheezes. "I'm saying that Hoover doesn't matter. He's a dead lead. Literally. She told me that he'll die later on this year."

"Assassination? Serves the bastard right!"

"No . . ." My attorney shakes his head. "Heart attack, brought on by high blood pressure. It happens this May."

"Do you believe her?"

"She told me when and how I was gonna die, too, man. You don't understand. It's like I told you before. She knows everything and she told me all of it. There's no way I can repeat it all to you. We don't have enough time. One hundred years wouldn't be enough time. And we don't have a hundred years. We have until election day, and that's why we need to kill that fucker now. What are we waiting for?"

There is a timid knock at the door. I grab my CS gas canister from my kit bag and creep across the room. Then I fling the door open and scream, trying to startle my opponent so that the element of surprise is on my side, but it is only the clerk from downstairs, and he has a bottle of bourbon for us and some dry clothes for my attorney. I smile and nod, assuring him that I greet all visitors this way, and then stow the tear gas and take the proffered items, telling him to put them on my bill. After his footsteps have shuffled down the hall, I hand the bottle and the clothes to my lawyer.

"Here. This is what we were waiting for. Medicine. As your doctor, I advise you to start drinking heavily."

He doesn't protest. Instead, he upends the bottle and takes a long guzzle. Whiskey dribbles down his chin and pools in his chest hair. The rest of his color returns, and I am confident we've passed the danger of frostbite. I take the bottle from him and pour myself a glass—five fingers. I wonder if Cannocks ever ask their bartenders to pour them six fingers? But that way lies madness. I cannot ponder

Cannock culture right now, no matter how fond I'm becoming of the Innsmouthians. I hand the bottle back to my attorney and he resumes drinking.

"You need to harden the fuck up," he says, and I tell him that's a great slogan and he should put it on a cock ring. He scowls at me and then spits a mouthful of bourbon in an arc across the bed. "Fuck you, man. I'm serious. We need a goddamned plan. You don't want to kill him. Then come up with something else! All you ever do is write, write, write. Fuck that. Writing won't fix things this time. We need action! How are we gonna stop him from taking all fifty states?"

"I . . ." My gorge rises and I grit my teeth to keep it down. This is one of those situations I loathe . . . admitting that I have no clue what to do next, no plan, no ideas. It's a terrible and desolate feeling when your wits and powers have abandoned you, and all you are left with is the looming prospect of total and absolute failure, barreling straight toward you like a swarm of buckshot from the business end of a sixteen-gauge shotgun. "I don't know," I admit. "I'm working on it. I'm writing notes."

"Writing ain't gonna do shit for us right now! Don't you understand what's at stake here?"

"Of course I understand, you bloated hyena!" I thunder across the room again and fling my notebook at him. It lands on his prodigious gut with a sort of squelching sound. My attorney picks the notebook up and frowns, staring at my list dumbly. "This is how I work, and I'll be damned if I'll let a half-crazed brute like yourself push me into some action before I'm ready. That's how people get killed. I'm no fan of getting killed, at least at the hands of others. The fish-woman told you when you're going to die? Well, bully for you, shit eyes! I'm not ready to die yet, and since I'm betting she didn't reveal the details of my death to you, I plan on sticking around a little while longer. And I'll tell you something else . . . I am not going to die at the hands of Nixon and Kissinger or their little cronies like Haringa. I'll eat a bullet first.

I'm prepared, you know! If you doubt me, then you're a fool. I prepared for that eventuality a long time ago. I even had Ralph draw up a diagram of what I want for my memorial—a giant fist, two hundred feet high. Death doesn't scare me. Well, maybe a bad death scares me, but so what? I just don't want to die yet. Not until this is finished."

"She didn't know," my attorney murmurs, so softly that at first I can't understand him. He has to repeat it two more times before I do. "She didn't know when or how you'd die. Think about that, man. She knew everything. She told me there used to be people living on Mars. She knew about Atlantis and Lemuria and who drew those lines out in the desert of Peru. She taught me about demons and angels, the Old Ones and the Elder Gods, and all the things in between. She told me about the secret language of plants, and the secret names of people, and what really happened to the dinosaurs, and how Moses and Jesus and Muhammad and Buddha and Krishna and John Lennon are all just reincarnations of the same thing, a spirit, and how that spirit is always—always—destined to be sacrificed or martyred in some way. She knew how big the universe is. I mean in a mathematical, definable fucking way, man. She told me about the Plateau of Leng and the unknown cold wastes of Kadath and the fucking dreamlands. Yeah, that's right . . . dimensions that we go to when we dream or trip. And she told me about this guy named Carter who used to travel back and forth between them, and how on certain nights—"

"Get a grip on yourself, goddamn it! You're babbling like a madman. What's your point?"

"Man, don't you see? She knew all of that shit, but she didn't know how or when you were gonna die. She said you are the Variable."

"The Variable? What the hell does that mean?"

He shrugs and says, "I don't know, but as your attorney, I advise you to start taking this shit seriously and come up with a plan. And I don't mean just writing."

"Well, I've been a little distracted trying to keep your toes and fingers and pecker from falling off."

My lawyer tilts the bottle to his lips again and polishes half of it off. Then he sighs, a big, loud groan of satisfaction, and smacks his wet lips together. "I still think we should go to Acapulco."

"How is going to Acapulco going to help us right now?"

"Kissinger is in Acapulco. Didn't I tell you, man?"

"You may have. I don't know. I've been a little distracted by Deep Ones and high-priest professors and other high jinks."

"Kissinger always goes to Acapulco this time of year. He's got a little love nest down there. I say we go to Acapulco, kidnap Kissinger, and hold him hostage until they give in to our demands. We'll exchange him for Nixon, but then we'll pull a double-cross and kill them both."

"I think your swim with Mother Hydra turned that once-fine legal mind of yours into a popsicle."

This time, we hear the footsteps coming down the hall before the new arrival knocks. They are different footsteps, not the shuffling, limping gait of the boarding house's counterman, but of someone different. Haringa has tracked us down, of course, and I'll have that fucking clerk's fish eyes for telling him where we are. I grab my gun from the kit bag and toss the canister of CS gas to my attorney. He may be drunk, half-frozen, and out of his mind, but his motor skills and reflexes are still sharp. He catches it with one hand and slides out of bed effortlessly. The knock comes a second later, strong and sure. This is not a timid knock. This knock is not fucking around. It lets us know that it has purpose and meaning. It is self-assured, and it occurs to me only as I grab the door handle that Haringa would most likely not knock on the door, and if he did, it wouldn't be like that. He would just have Jason and the rest of the Nixon Youth break the door down, and then barge in and say hello. Well, I can say hello, too. I open the door, and before the figure outside can react, I grab him by his shirt and yank him into the room. He squawks, so I kick him. Then, I kick the door shut and jam the handgun under his chin, and say, "Got you, shit eyes!"

"Mr. Lono . . . ?"

It takes me a moment to recognize Smitty. The poor bastard's metamorphosis is accelerating at an alarming rate. It can't just be his proximity to his hometown that's responsible for this. Maybe it's the combined reaction of the shrooms and being in Innsmouth? Maybe the fungus has sped up the natural process? Whatever the case, things look grim for my favorite truck driver. His skin is pale white now, and I imagine Smitty won't be spending much time in the sun anymore; he is beyond albino. The rash on his neck is now clearly a set of reddish-pink gills, and his eyes have grown larger since I last saw him. The nubs on his hands are now clearly fingers, but he's also sprouted webbed skin between each digit. His nose has flattened, more nostril than flesh at this point, and when he opens his mouth again to speak, I see that he's begun to lose his teeth.

"Smitty!" I pull the gun away and flash him a sheepish grin. "We were just talking about you. This man is Oscar. He's my attorney. Oscar, say hello to Smitty. He's been helping me out with the story."

"Jesus," my lawyer gasps, "the fuck happened to you? Did you fall into a vat of chemicals or something?"

I rap my lawyer on the knee with the pistol's handle and bark, "Manners! Smitty is our guest. He's going to help us, because it's partly his fault that I'm in this mess. Isn't that right, chum?"

Nodding, Smitty takes a seat on the edge of the bed. The springs creak, but not as loudly as they do a second later when my lawyer scampers away from him.

"Any sign of our friend the professor?" I ask, crossing the room and parting the yellowed, dusty blinds with my finger. I peer outside, but the streets are deserted—status quo for Innsmouth. Everybody must still be at the Odd Fellows hall, drinking eggs and beer for dinner. Eggs and beer, it does a body good! Puts hair on your chest, as the old-timers back in Kentucky would say when I was younger. Except that in Innsmouth, hair on the chest is probably the last thing growing boys want. Sweet Jesus, can you imagine going through puberty in this town, knowing that when the time comes, instead of your first whisker or wet dream, you'll turn into a goddamned fish and spend your time swimming up the Manuxet River or frolicking out past those rotting wharves, the sand-choked harbor, and the long black line far beyond the breakwater that is the ruined remains of Devil's Reef? No wonder the town is deserted! If I had grown up here, I would have run away the first chance I got, seeing as how my options were getting sacrificed to Dagon, having sex with a Deep One, or turning into a Deep One myself. No thanks, Mom and Dad. I'll take my chances out on the road. Which, in a way, was what Smitty had done. But blood always calls to blood, and here he is again, the returning hero, fucked.

"I'm gonna open a window," my attorney says and moves to my side. He pulls the blinds up and tries the window, but it's nailed shut. "It's rotten enough that I can probably push it right out," he says. I tell him don't bother, because we're not going to be here long enough for it to matter.

"Why?" He turns to me, eyes focused again. The whiskey has cured him, and once again I was right. Always listen to your doctor. That's the moral of this story.

"Wha's t' plan, Lono?" Smitty asks from the bed, as the room begins to stink like fish.

"Yeah," my attorney echoes. "Enough of this sitting-around bullshit. We've got work to do. What's the plan? What's our next step?"

"I'll tell you," I say, and then I do.

EIGHT

At the Innsmouth Public Library, we check out a copy of *Unspeakable Cults*. It's a cheap Photostat of the real grimoire, with that cheap, plastic-leather library binding that you find on so many books these days. Ye Gods, I hate that sort of shit. The library is deserted, except for a geriatric librarian behind the front desk, who stares at us balefully with enormous fish eyes magnified by her equally enormous eyeglasses. She doesn't say a word to us. She simply stares.

"I don't like this," my attorney whispers. "This place has a real negative vibe, man. There is bad karma here."

"Never mind that. Stand in front of me and block the librarian's view."

"Why?"

"Because I'm borrowing this book, and I don't have a library card."

"As your attorney, I have to advise you not to steal that book. Time is running short and we've got a lot to do. We can't do it from jail." Nevertheless, he moves in front of me, blocking the aisle and hiding me from the librarian's watchful eyes.

"We won't go to jail. First of all, we're not going to get caught. Second of all, they don't put you in the slammer for stealing a book.

Especially not this book and especially not in Innsmouth. This fucking thing doesn't even have an ISBN, or a Dewey decimal number." I slip the book into my kit bag, nestling it between the Mojo Wire and an empty whiskey bottle. "Plus, I don't think there are too many readers left in town. They won't miss it. We just need two more things now, and one of them should be along any moment. We'll pick up the third on the road. By the way, are you carrying?"

My lawyer hoists up his attaché case and pats it twice. "Of course."

"Good," I say. "Now listen to me very carefully, because this applies to your billable hours. If you see me growing gills or a sixth finger on either hand, or my eyes suddenly bulge out even when I'm not doing coke, I want you to shoot me. I'm serious. I am not fucking around here. Shoot me in the head, and make sure that does the trick. I'll sign a waiver, but we can't get it notarized, not around here."

I begin to close the kit bag, when a thought occurs to me. "Sweet Jesus, you're right. We don't have to steal this book."

"Would you make up your mind, man? I thought you weren't fucking around?"

"I'm not, and Smitty better not be either. I told him to find us a ride." I glance around, making sure we're still not being observed, and then I pull both the book and my Leatherman utility tool from my kit. I flense the spine from the book with a few flicks of the knife, and then set up the Mojo Wire. The librarian, deep in the throes of the Innsmouth look, her mouth full of needlelike fangs, her eyes spilling out from their lids, her breathing the horrid gasp of a pregnant scud flopping around on the deck of a fishing trawler, says nothing to us, not even when I unplug the phone on her desk and start feeding pages of her blasphemous tome to my editor in New York. Here is wisdom, and I shall share it with you because I am feeling generous: the trick with libraries is not to break the rules, and there can be no rule against mutilating and infringing the copyright of a book that does not exist. (You know, much like this one, dear reader . . .)

"No problemo," my lawyer finally says, not even bothering to look up from flipping through a ratty paperback of his own biography, which the library inexplicably has on the stacks. "And how about me? I saw things down there while I was with Mother Hydra . . . things that called to me, like the twisted snake gods of my ancestors, piles of waterlogged hearts on Cyclopean staircases, slabs overgrown with lichen fed by the blood of men. And I think I liked it. If I start, you know, turning into one of these Innsmouth people, will you shoot me, too?"

"No, but I can put you on retainer to shoot yourself. My editor has given me carte blanche. There is nothing more dangerous or desperate than a writer with carte blanche."

I finish transmitting the book, and then I pack up the Mojo Wire and we head for the door. I nod at the librarian, thanking her for her time, and she stares at us as we leave. Outside, it is snowing.

"Ah, here's our ride." And it's Smitty in his half-ruined black tractor-trailer cab. He honks the horn. Shave and a haircut. Two bits. My attorney eyes the truck the same way the librarian eyed us.

"We're riding in that thing?"

"Of course! It'll be a tight squeeze, the four of us, but we'll make do."

"Four of us?"

"Yes, indeed. We'll pick up the fourth on the road, I'm sure of it."

"Who the hell else are we bringing along down the yellow-brick road?"

I shrug. "Dorothy? Toto? A dozen flying monkeys?"

"I guess that's better than bats," my lawyer mutters.

"Oh, ho," I say, clapping him on the back. "You have no reason to fear. We're not going anywhere near bat country."

We clamber into the cab, and Smitty smiles a disconcerting catfish smile at us. Our connection is even less than tentative now; it's a fond memory, but it works. Smitty has fond memories of the Nam too; he's itching for another war, and we're bringing the war to the steps of the White House in the way the Weather Underground could only dream of. Ho ho! I feel a tingling in my journalistic loins. My lawyer grunts a greeting and Smitty burbles in return. I sit between them like an awkward child stuck in the middle of fuming parents. Smitty's white as cod, and my lawyer has the natural animosity an oppressed brown person would have toward a big Anglo Teamster, all his jive about the international working class and the Revolution aside. And in truth, I think he just might be a little . . . envious? Jealous? After all, Smitty was my sidekick on this journey long before my lawyer came along. Smitty has been fulfilling a role that my attorney sees as his. The same sort of quiet animosity used to exist between Ralph and my attorney, until Ralph began coming up with excuses as to why he couldn't make the trek across the pond. That poor bastard. He was never the same after the Kentucky Derby, but I warned him it was decadent and depraved. That's what made him the perfect person to capture it with illustrations.

"It's going to be a long, strange trip to DC, fellows, so let's try to keep it civil, eh? And keep the perspiration to a minimum; we can't afford to have our windows steam up." I see her, wandering with a one-shoed limp on the shoulder of the highway. "Ah, there she is." Miskatonic University's favorite sorority girl, Betsy. "There's our Dorothy."

Smitty blows the air horn, and Betsy nearly leaps into the grass. My lawyer rolls down the window and shouts, "Hey, *chica*! Come for a ride with us!" She's stunned, as women often are in his presence. "Your country needs you!" I add. Impatient, my lawyer rolls out of the truck, lumbers toward Betsy, and unceremoniously grabs her and flings her over his shoulder. "Come on, darlin'. The doctor's waitin'!" he says.

"He's a forward type, innit he?" Smitty asks.

"Listen, man. That's exactly the sort of attitude you want in a civil-rights attorney. Look! See there? He doesn't even notice her little fists beating against his back. It's like his cousin's *quinceañera* all over again." Smitty frowns. "I'm just kidding," I tell him. "He's not usually like this. It's just . . ." I wave my hands about the cab, at a loss for words I want to use.

Betsy calms down when she sees me, which is pretty peculiar since she did just participate in a conspiracy to commit deicide— that is, to kill *me*—the other day. But then I remember how she changed teams quickly when it looked like I had the upper hand over Haringa.

"Get in," I say. "We're going to visit J. Edgar Hoover, and we need your help."

My lawyer shoves her onto my lap; I awkwardly hand her the book as we both get shoved into Smitty. He seems happy with the arrangement. I notice that his clothes are damp and his skin feels clammy.

"Gentlemen," I say. "Meet Dorothy. Dorothy, I think you know the Scarecrow and the Cowardly Lion? And I, of course, am the Tin Man."

"What the hell, Mr. Lono?" she demands. "What kind of crazy, wacked-out trip are you *on*?"

Smitty has us back on the road in a second, and we're tearing up the highway now. The radio is playing a weather report. They're calling for six inches of snow, and the roads are rumored to grow treacherous. My excitement builds. Nothing can stop us now, as long as I can keep my attorney from pawing Betsy before we get to our destination. He is eyeing her bosom like a starved hyena. His dalliance with Mother Hydra has made him so hungry.

"What kind of trip am I on?" I ask her. "The same trip we've all been on for years now, sweet child. But this trip has a terminus, even if it doesn't have an ending. We're going to see Hoover, and we're going to demand reparations for his attack on Innsmouth. We're going to show him this book, see, and tell him that my editor is ready to publish one chapter a month, every month—"

"With color photos," Smitty ad-libs.

"Unless he cooperates," my lawyer finishes. He cracks his knuckles like a bowl of walnuts.

"J. Edgar Hoover? Are you all insane?" Betsy says. "Don't you know how powerful he is?"

"More powerful than Nixon, maybe. How many administrations has he outlived, after all? More powerful, but also, in the end, mortal. Can we say the same thing about Nixon?" I riffle through the leaves in my bag. "Look! Did you even *do* your reading in Haringa's class before you signed up for extracurricular activities?" I show her the page I'd been looking for, one whose contents are so mind raping that I dare not even allude to them here except to suggest that in the text it describes another orgy, one in which Nixon was a satyr rather than a wallflower. And there's a line drawing. Listen. There are books out there, and the things written in those books will drive a man insane. This was one of them. Better to describe the horror within by telling you that I can't describe it. But I do show it to Betsy, and only because I have no choice. We've already abducted her, and we have very little time to fuck around. Better to make her a willing participant in this misadventure than to risk blowing it all if she decides to jump from the truck. She's a brave girl, Betsy, as she stares at the horrific page and barely blinks and bites her lips hard enough to start blood dribbling down her chin.

"Hey now, put that away," Smitty says, scratching his crotch, "or I'll want to look at it too."

"That was just on the recommended-reading list," Betsy says softly. "And on reserve in the library. But whenever I went there, one of the boys already had it out. You met them yesterday." She jerks suddenly, and I see a flash of brown leave her thigh.

"Easy, big man," I tell my lawyer. "You can have what's left after Hoover's done with her." I expect him to laugh, but she does instead.

"Oh boy, Mr. Lono—"

"Doctor. I was Uncle Lono, but now I'm feeling more like my old self. Call me doctor. I am, among other things, a doctor of journalism."

"*Dr.* Lono, then." She smiles, flashing perfect teeth. "Don't you know anything? If you're looking to bargain with J. Edgar Hoover, then you've chosen the wrong person for a sacrifice. Doesn't a with-it journalist like you know that Hoover is . . ." Suddenly sotto voce, as if her mother is in the cab with us, "a homosexualist."

"Of course I know that! I was not born yesterday, sweetheart. I know Hoover is a homosexual. That's why we've got Smitty here," I say. "Just in case."

Smitty yawps and slams on the brakes, sending all of us headfirst into the dashboard.

Four years ago, the streets of Paris were filled with revolutionaries. Columbia University, home to the best and brightest and very much the wealthiest of New York City, was aflame. Suicide squads rose up from the bush and showed the leader of the free world that it did not own, and indeed, would *never* own Saigon. The Soviets rolled tanks into Czechoslovakia, while here at home, dark forces killed Bobby Kennedy and assassinated Dr. Martin Luther King Jr. And in the midst of this madness and mayhem, Nixon won the presidency, but only by the slimmest of margins. Only because it seemed that the barbarians were at the gate, that the children of Levittown had eaten drugs and gone mad for anarchy and Negro music and wanton fornication. Nixon had beaten us all back with a coalition of cornpone racists and alcoholic insurance adjusters, the John Birch crowd and the "silent majority." The silent majority, a term coined by Aristotle himself, though he was a happy old sodomite and his use of the term was meant to describe the dead. And who knows? Maybe that is true. Perhaps the dead really are the silent majority. If so, the dead won America back. Dead Cthulhu lies dreaming, but he won't be for much longer because of

Nixon's Machiavellian schemes and Faustian bargains, with all the ruthlessness implied by the former and supernatural traffic hinted at by the latter. But it wasn't just Nixon, who is in the end just another monster in a flannel suit that brought America to the brink of oblivion; it was us too. The hardhats betrayed the hippies, the hippies betrayed their women, everyone betrayed the Negro and the Chicano. The world fell not into the wild and liberating chaos of Freak Power, but into the bloody confusion of division and conquest. In four years, a lot can change.

In four seconds, even more can change. Following Smitty sending us all into the dashboard, we spin wildly, and the world is full of stars. Pages of *Unspeakable Cults* fly from the open window of the truck, escaping on evil wings like four-and-twenty demonic blackbirds baked into a pie. How long, oh Lord? How long? Is this how it's all to end? No great and terrible plan, no showdown with the forces of evil, no frantic hope, no McGovern surging ahead on the hopes of millions and setting the world aright for another generation?

If this road trip to DC is any indication, then the answer is no. We're all on edge after the near crash, all counting coup and looking to settle scores of our own. Smitty mutters about eyes in the bushes and then hunches over the wheel. He apologizes, a little bit, and says that he doesn't need a "cherry daddy on this mission." Something like a man, but with giant moth wings, had run out into the road. He says that's what made him lose control of the truck. It wasn't at all my remark about him and federal arch-fag J. Edgar Hoover that got him all worked up—no, sir. My lawyer, meanwhile, is picking on his teeth, working a thick thumbnail between them and sucking hard. He is deep in thought about whatever it is his kind think about when they have idle time on their hands. Betsy, sitting beside me, has her hand on my knee. We bonded a bit after we stopped the truck and spilled out, woozy and dizzy, to gather up the pages of *Unspeakable Cults*. The last thing America needed was for a wind to pick up and one of the blasphemous pages to slap against some poor slob's windshield at the wrong moment. Imagine the chaos that could ensue. Where were you when the fun stopped, eh? And poor Betsy . . . poor, darling girl. She doesn't know that I know she is COINTELPRO, but it's obvious. At least, it's obvious to me. I am a professional.

By the time we pull into Washington, DC, it is morning. May Day morning, the counselor tells us. A holiday with an American origin, but we can't tell from the Monday-morning traffic snaking into the city. My lawyer is hanging out the window, by turns waving my Leatherman and beating on the passenger-side door with his cinderblock of a fist. "Hey, pigs! You're all shitting yourself because of those Russky missiles on the news this morning? Well, you all fucking better be! *Viva la revolución!* We're here to hang your asses!"

Betsy snaps, "Hey, you'd better relax, mister. The DC cops don't mess around, and we already look suspicious."

"Well then, I'll give 'em something to look at!" he says, and I put my hands up to the ceiling. This is not our first trip together, and I know what he's going for. Betsy foolishly thinks it's her and throws her forearms over her chest, protecting her breasts and drawing further attention to them. Ignoring her, my lawyer reaches for the bag and grabs two great handfuls of sheets from *Unspeakable Cults*, then flings them out the window. "Go on, here are some incendiary leaflets for you! Read 'em and weep, you bloodsucking leeches!"

Betsy screams and tries to dig her nails into my lawyer's arm. "Hey, that's assault and battery," I say. "That's a crime, and a tort! Don't liberal-arts colleges teach basic survival skills?" I grab her wrists and upset the bag. Even Smitty takes a few pages and dumps them out the window. "We were taught this book like catechism in school. Never hurt me a'tall," he says.

As I said, can you imagine the chaos that would ensue? Where were you when the fun stopped?

The traffic ahead of us remains slow, but behind us it snarls into impossible gridlock. Some commuters leave their cars to gather up the pages, others just rev their engines and grind ever forward, rear-ending the vehicles ahead and keeping their feet on the pedals to push and push and push some more. There are curses, some crunching, a few screams, the sound of grapes slowly crushed on the hot concrete, and suddenly the off ramp is ours alone.

"Save a few of those pages," I say. "It's our way into the Department of Justice and Hoover's office."

"You're just going to waltz up to Hoover," Betsy says, "and expect no resistance, no obstacles, and—"

"And hand you over to him, yes. By God, you have been paying attention. I knew there was a reason I made you my assistant!"

Smitty mutters next to me, but at least this time he doesn't jerk the clutch hard enough to give us all concussions.

"Hoover's a freemason, you know," my lawyer says. "On the square." He shuffles through a few of the *Unspeakable Cults* pages. "He'll fucking love this stuff. If he doesn't already stuff his bra with pages from his own collection of occult tomes, that is. Hey, look at this." He holds up one featuring peculiar geometric designs—a five-pointed star, the shape of a compass, a triangle. "A map of the city."

"Of this city?" Smitty asks suddenly.

"Yeah," my lawyer tells him. "Of Washington, DC, man!" Smitty seems nervous. "Is this Moloch territory . . . or Cthulhu?"

Betsy sniffs. "You mean you don't know, fish face?"

"Man, Betsy girl, you're not a very good travel companion," my lawyer says. "This is what this election is all about, let me tell you," he tells Smitty. "That's what I learned down below, on Devil's Reef. Nineteen seventy-two is *it*. Moloch or Cthulhu? That's the million-dollar fucking question, isn't it? That's the question burrowing away like a rat in the back of everyone's brain, and most of these poor bastards we're freaking out don't even know what's causing their damn migraines. They probably just blame saccharin." He snorts, filling the whole cab with steam.

"Never mind that right now," I say, "because here come the police." And then we are surrounded by black-and-whites, and a handful of cops in riot helmets snake between the cars with their long, antibeatnik truncheons held high, and there, trotting toward us in the distance, are a trio of officers on horseback. And this is the American Nightmare in the end, isn't it? Two horrifying choices, and the only people with even an inkling of how to stop it are surrounding by well-ironed fascists with licenses to kill. I open my mouth to say something poignant and meaningful, but the air brakes protest like drunken banshees as Smitty grinds us to an abrupt halt, and for the second time on this leg of the journey, we meet the dashboard.

As has often happened to me in my life as a journalist, I am dragged from where I've been sitting, separated from my possessions, and then the shit is beaten out of me by some hoods—law-enforcement officers are nearly always hoods themselves, given purpose and clarity in their violence by the state. It reminds me of Chicago, and what a fun time that was, eh? My lawyer bellows and screams, and a cop goes flying. Smitty falls under the hooves. The horse whinnies and does a little two-step on him. Betsy, as I'd predicted, slips past the makeshift cordon of police cars and watches the chaos. The last thing I see is my lawyer swinging a wild haymaker at one of the cop's horses. The beast falls flat and loses consciousness, and then, a second later, so do I.

I awake on a hard slab in what appears to be a dusty warehouse—another fairly common occurrence in my working life—but this time the woman standing over me isn't a sensitive and starving young Puerto Rican whore, all hips and breasts and tongue, but Betsy, wan as usual and wringing her hands nervously. Just as she did the other day, in fact, the last time I was in this predicament.

My hands and ankles are strapped to the slab. There's something on my head, some sort of hat or other bizarre contraption that brings to mind Ken Kesey's novel. All in all, I think the plan is going pretty well, and that makes me smile. I wish I had a cigarette, or some more fungi. No, scratch that. Last thing I need right now is to go tripping. I'll save that for the victory celebration.

"Thank you," I say. And then she understands. Her face falls into utter despair, and it is a wonderful thing to see. Betsy has never been more beautiful than she is at that moment. At least not to me. I decide to push further. "You know, Lenin never worried about spies. He wasn't concerned with COINTELPRO or anything like that. Paranoia never consumed the Bolsheviks. Nope, not Lenin. That old Commie just assumed that the Party was full of czarist agents, and he put them all to work. Whatever intel they gathered or traps they laid or plots they hatched didn't matter, because just to keep themselves busy so they could remain members in good standing took up all their free time."

"How did you know who I worked for . . ."

"It was easy, sweetheart," I tell her. "First of all, and most obviously, your politics made no fucking sense whatsoever. Even a deaf and dumb wombat would have seen through that nonsense. You just flapped your lips about unity, or the People, or the Republicans, as though you had memorized from *Cliffs Notes for Radicals* . . . well, skimmed, more likely. And your skirt never once wandered even an inch above your knee. You also didn't go mad when exposed to the pages of *Unspeakable Cults.*"

"*You* didn't go mad either. Neither did that bag of human garbage you call an attorney." I smile at her again, showing off every one of my teeth, until she gets it. "Look, it doesn't matter," Betsy says. "Mr. Hoover will be here soon to explain what we want with you."

"Is he currently powdering his nose? Or putting on his bra? Perhaps a nice, lacy little strapless number?"

"No," Hoover's distinctive voice comes from somewhere. "I'm here and ready for you." *Rheadah foh yaw.* "Thank you, Miss Betsy; you may leave."

"Yes, Betsy, you've served your purpose well. Hooray for you! Well done, lass. Be sure to sashay out of here and into a loveless marriage with a water-headed Goldwater supporter. He'll knock you up good, and keep you in Valium and martinis until skin cancer or an in-ground pool accident takes you in your forties. Have a nice life!"

She leaves without another word, without even a victorious saunter, and I turn my attention on the man of the hour. He's much shorter in person than you might expect.

"So, Mr. Hoover, am I to be sacrificed in order to ensure a fifty-state sweep for Nixon?" I ask.

"Oh, that won't be necessary," he says casually. Always a clever little bulldog of a man—does he mean that he doesn't care about the fifty-state election result that Nixon needs to complete his diabolical plot, or that his forces have already guaranteed the result he wants the old-fashioned way through crooked voting machines, agents in every ward, mass hypnosis, intimidation, LSD in the reservoirs, subliminal messages buried in the headlines of the major newspapers and scratched into the grooves of Perry Como and Pat Boone albums, and last-minute censorship of Negro music?

"You seem in fine fettle. No particular brain damage from various injuries and abuse of illicit substances anyway. That's good," he says, appraising me like a side of beef.

"Well, I am a doctor, after all," I remind him.

"Yes, yes. Doctor. Journalist. Local god of the indigenous Hawaiian population."

"Yes. All of those and more."

"Sportsman, reprobate," he continues. "Degenerate."

"Be nice now," I say.

"Inspiration for a comic-strip character," he adds.

"You goddamned swine," I say. "You really know how to hurt a guy."

"I do." Finally, Hoover stands over me. He's not looking well. Gray, like his own photo in the newspaper, and extra jowly, which is quite an achievement in Washington, DC. In his hands he holds a pair of metal canisters, thinner than a Thermos but about as long.

"So what's the story here, eh? What do you have there? I think you'd better buy me dinner first, Josephine, before we get down to business."

"Your juvenile scatology doesn't suit your reputation as a wordsmith, Lono," he says. He says my false name slowly, enunciating every syllable. Hoover's a true pig, through and through. I can tell because he doesn't sweat, he doesn't lick his lips, he doesn't frown or react at all to mere human words, outside of what seem to be programmed responses. He doesn't even blink. And then he surprises me. "And your reputation is what I need. I need you, Lono. Your country needs you."

After I finish laughing, he strikes one of the canisters against the other, setting off a hollow-feeling tone. "You can get close to Nixon. You've done it before. And even if you can't, then *I* can get you close to Nixon. Do you know what these are?"

"Are they . . ." I think back to the few seconds I spent flipping through the original *Unspeakable Cults* manuscript back at the library as I fed those blasphemous pages into the Mojo Wire. "Mi-Go brain canisters?"

"Correct," he says. He sits on the corner of the slab, his buttocks spreading conversationally.

And what ugly bastards the Mi-Go were. The woodcutting of them in the *Unspeakable Cults* manuscript showed a giant, pink, crablike thing with wings. Instead of skin, the creature was made out of fungus, and instead of a head, it had a series of fleshy rings shaped like a pyramid, complete with antennae on top. According to what I read, the Mi-Go could transport humans—and other creatures—from Earth to outer space and back again by removing their victim's brain and placing it in a brain canister like the one Hoover held. They could then hook the canisters up to a machine that allowed the brain to see, hear, and even speak. Hideous, monstrous things, the Mi-Go, but I'd still rather take my chances with them than be caught on the street after dark in Cleveland on a Saturday night. But I digress.

"Mi-Go," I say to Hoover. "Sounds like a cheaply made foreign car, doesn't it?"

"Indeed it does. What do you know of my career, Dr. Lono?"

"Well, I know that you've outlived eight presidents—"

"Please," Hoover says, "Eight *administrations*. A significant difference." He peers down at the objects in his hands, as if admiring them for the first time. I shiver then, and it has nothing to do with the temperature in the room. "I entered public service during the Great War. I was head of the Enemy Aliens Registration Section. This was before the FBI was founded, of course. And there were aliens among us then, Dr. Lono. Not just Reds from Russia and Germany either." He moves his gaze up toward the ceiling. "We found these canisters in Brattleboro, Vermont. It's taken us decades to figure out their use and how to reverse engineer them. Amazing things, really. They allow their user to remove and store a healthy human brain without killing it."

"Must be pretty handy in the spook game, eh? Tell me, Josephine. You ever trade brains with Huey P. Newton?"

"We're not *spooks* at the FBI. And believe me, I—" He puts the canisters on his lap to raise his hands and flick his fingers to mimic quotation marks. "*Get* your attempt to pun using racial humor. I would have thought such a thing beneath you, but then again, I'm familiar with some of your columns. And no. We did try to get close to Nixon . . . I tried to get close to—"

"Mamie Van Doren! By God, that's it! Ho, ho . . . I fucking see it now! You goddamned ol' queen, you *were* Mamie Van Doren, weren't you? You switched minds with her yourself to get close to Nixon. *And* to Kissinger, too." I howl like a mad ape. If only I could reach my knee to slap it—or, hell, even the old queer's back. "Was it a dream come true?"

"President Nixon has many flaws, but unfortunately infidelity is not one of them. But like most great tragic figures, his greatest flaw is hubris," Hoover says. "He wants . . . the counterculture vote."

"The Freak Power vote?" I try to say more, but another round of laughter leaves me breathless. My stomach muscles hurt, I'm laughing so hard.

"It's true. Nixon wants to be—" His hands hit the air again. "*Cool.* It drives him absolutely mad that McGovern, a little man from a nowhere state, a man who spent much of his childhood in Calgary, Alberta, Canada, would capture the imagination of the youth, of the Negroes, of . . . women. Even our Betsy will probably end up voting for McGovern, despite her oaths, despite the signs and tokens we have shared with her and the ceremonies she has participated in. It's a way for people to assert their independence, this fascination with the Democrat McGovern."

"You don't think Nixon being a blood-soaked maniac has anything to do with it?"

"Blood-soaked mania rarely has anything to do with achievement or success in politics, doctor. It's a null trait, such as on which side one might choose to part one's hair," Hoover says. "The best way to determine the ultimate victor of the presidential race is to count the number of balloons dropped immediately after the acceptance speech at the parties' respective national conventions. Have you ever done that, Dr. Lono?"

"Well . . . no. I can't say that I have." Those canisters. Suddenly they begin to feel real. This is all real. Perhaps it was the last of the shrooms finally sweating out of my body, but the cool is suddenly gone. I'm going to die. No more self-mythologizing, no last-minute rescue from twitty Teamsters, and my lawyer sure as hell isn't going to bust in here with a copy of the Constitution on the tip of a flagpole and run this revenant monster through to save my rum-soaked skin.

I'm going to die before this job is finished, and the story will never get written, and I will never get my memorial Gonzo fist tower back in the mountains of Woody Creek or have my ashes shot from the cannon on top of it, because my ashes won't be found. They, like the rest of my body, will be made to disappear.

"I'm surprised," Hoover says, and judging by his tone, I believe him. "At any rate, I have people count the balloons as they fall immediately after the acceptance speeches at the party conventions, and without fail the party with the most balloons wins. It makes sense; the party who can afford more balloons has a greater war chest with which to buy the balloons. They have space in their convention hall for the balloons, and don't need quite so many snipers in the rafters in the case of rogue delegates. Do you follow? Good. The Republicans have so many balloons on order, Dr. Lono. The rain forests of the Amazon are actually shrinking, did you know that? Because of the insatiable demand for . . . *rubber*." With that, Hoover touches his own chest with his palms and caresses himself.

"What do you care? Are you telling me that you're not voting for Nixon?"

"I'm voting for Hoover. I'm old, Dr. Lono. Too old for this job, too old to run for president myself. But I can be president without running. I can be president without going through the bother of campaigning and the electoral process. I can be president without worrying about my age. I can be president for life, for a million lives if I want to. It's simple. You and I will exchange brains. You will die here, in this room, in this body seated here before you. I will interview President Nixon, and while we are alone—and I have already taken the necessary measure of arranging for you and he to be alone and without Secret Service personnel—I will switch brains with him. Nixon will surely go insane and try to kill me, once he finds himself trapped forever in your depraved, despoiled, and venereal-disease-ridden body."

"That's a lie," I shout. "I never had the dreaded herpes!"

Hoover goes on, ignoring me. "And I will then kill him in self-defense, using a particular item Nixon always keeps nearby. And then, *Dr. Lono*, I will become president of the United States of America. I will make sure that I, as Nixon, only win forty-nine states, rather than the fifty they need. There are still enough Irish mobsters to throw Boston to whoever the Democrat is, and enough small towns full of eccentrics and schismatics happy to throw their votes away for a higher power. I'll save the United States from Cthulhu, and from Nixon's own more pedestrian ambitions. I'll save this country, and you'll help me do it. You are many things, doctor, and most of them are deplorable, but the one thing about you that can't be denied is that you are a true patriot. You love this country as much as I do."

It's an odd feeling. For the first time in my adult life, I have absolutely nothing to say. I feel like I've just been told by my general practitioner that he has good news for me, and some bad news to go along with it. Hey, hey! No prostate cancer, Lono, despite your disgusting habits in American Samoa. The bad news . . . well, you have testicular cancer instead. Win some, lose some. Something occurs to me then, something beyond death. I do love my country. I love all the agony, all the nonsense, every pile of twisted limbs. I love the oppression and the rebellion, the open road and filthy alleys. It just doesn't get any better than this.

"And then," I say, "after Nixon serves his term, let me guess. You swap brains again, with whoever might win in 1980."

"Ronald Reagan, yes."

"*What?*" I jerk up and nearly snap my wrists against my bonds. "Are you utterly insane? I've heard some absolute gibberish on this latest road trip, but that beats all! Ronald Reagan? He can't be president!"

"Of course he can. And he will. He's a very handsome man. Virile," Hoover says. "And after that, George H. W. Bush will be president. You know him, I'm sure. He's a gormless fellow. We have also prepared a clone for the term of the millennium. Yes,

cloning has been perfected. Has been since the end of World War
II. Some of Germany's best scientists gave us the technology. The
clone is a real cutie. George Bush Jr., we've taken to calling him.
Perhaps in the 1990s I'll play a Democrat, if just to throw off suspicion and forestall revolution. The Negroes will vote for a nice,
southern-cracker type." *Crakah*, he says. "They will, even as he
undoes the Great Society and replaces it with indentured servitude
and a radically expanded prison infrastructure. Imagine a George
Wallace, but with a warm smile and the appearance of human
dignity. A charismatic fellow, the type who will sell you a used
car while fornicating with your wife, and you'll smile and thank
him for it."

"Such a thing, sir," I say, "is beyond my imagination."

"But not mine!" Hoover says. He leaps to his feet and holds
the canisters high. "There are no limits to my imagination, or to
my ambition! And I have a weakness too. I admit it." He turns to
me, leans over me, intimate, almost ready for a kiss. "And this is
it. For so many years I've toiled, an *appointee*, biding my time, col-
lecting my secrets, perfecting my methods. Sharing the scope of
my planning with nobody. Conspiracies within conspiracies I've
discovered, some older than man itself, but none cleverer than
mine. *Checkmate!*" He stands erect, huffing like an aged house.
"And I've never had anyone to share my vision with. Nobody save
you. Rather like a pulp-fiction villain, don't you think, doctor? I
used to read all the detective and crime magazines. I always wanted
to give a speech, sir, and now I have. It is done. Now I'll transfer
our brains into one another's bodies. Your country thanks you for
your service, Lono."

"My God, man. Don't I get one last cigarette?"

Hoover moves out of my line of sight and says only, "This will
tingle. Quite a bit, actually."

It begins not with a single memory, but instead with a deeper
part of the mind, the autonomic system—I know that my ability
to get an erection has been removed, physically, from my body,

and then the horror surges forth but that too is sucked away, and yes though resignation rises up to replace it (this is the resignation of a young man imagining old age, not the pure resignation of a lifetime of defeat) it is also removed from my cere . . . cere . . . the back of my skull, along with so much trivial information: *What's a transom?* I ask myself as the word remains but the concept is gone except that I know it has something to do with the publication of pulp fiction and the gray snows of New York winters, but all I remember of "pulp fiction" is Hoover's thick lips inches from my face and then his face is gone but he is somewhere, somewhere growing inside of me, colonizing the very synapses of my mind for indeed no brain could live in that little tin canister—it's a *microprocessing computer!* I realize but in Hoover's voice not my own (I'm an eavesdropper in my own metacognitions) and that voice was younger then and it continues *We're fools with our transistors and our childlike daring to reach the moon; the switches in this device are three atoms long; it can contain all the information of a human brain; that is how the Mi-Go do it!* and with that long-ago glee of a young man fresh from rousting some Wobblies from the art deco movie theater on Brattleboro Vermont's main drag did his . . . what's the word, *scheme*, no that isn't quite right but it will have to do as the mental version of that book of words, not a dictionary, the other one used by bad writers the way a drunk uses a lamppost has left me in both word and actual function and Hoover digs deeper burns the candle of my mind on both ends I can no longer blink or inhale except in the shallowest of *hmmps* up my nose and even as my autonomic nervous system is shut down to be rewritten a few feet away in the superannuated body my memories go—goodbye the sultry nights on San Juan, farewell the smoke from my pipe, the hot breath on Groundhog's Day in Colorado the flash of metal against teeth at the bottom of the rancid pork-fat ocean of Hells Angels and then the drugs the mescaline the coke the heroin the uppers Quaaludes all at once so many experiences and memories in contradiction sativa LSD dissolved in Teacher's set aflame and spread on saganaki then consumed in a Volkswagen microbus with a bunch of cackling Romanian gypsies with fewer teeth than cousins the enteric system now it remembers with body wisdom all the things Lono has ingested a stew of elective psychoses and a few feet away where my nerves dance in a new body something begins to happen Hoover is too hungry for this too eager to travel down the damned highway of excess to the flaming wreckage of wisdom all the vice cases the dead Courier letters on hectographed forms nothing compares to experience from innocence to objurgation in the action of one stark fist and then yes yes I know I can win this Lono his white sails unfurled the women running to the black sands breasts swaying as in Eden this is no *Weird Tale* no diaphanous Margaret Brundage oil painting just pure love of a God without repression without the whiff of sulfur and then yes yes I understand and see the pattern beneath the system the roads of the District of Columbia the tentacles reaching across the inky blackness of space and somewhere the lights flicker the eagle its mouth full of liver alights and leaves Prometheus to heal and break free of his chains for no iron can hold a Titan and there is a molecule and the lights flicker and it is an iron not of this earth and something is burning and there is a circuit just six atoms wide made of two switches and my arms fail and my legs fail but they cannot move these atoms but Lono can and he does he does he does and the switch is thrown and Hoover gets it all every bit of it at once every turn of phrase every sizzling spice on the tongue every esterification of $C_5H_{11}OH + HONO \rightarrow C_5H_{11}ONO + H_2O$ and then seven seven seven and Lono triumphs.

Hoover's dead, I know it. I can feel his dead heart in my own chest, a stone superimposed with my own raging, adrenaline-stocked timpani of an organ. The poor old square, the sad, pathetic bastard, despite his many squalid perversions and a lifetime of extracurricular vice investigations, despite his own field trips in the busty body of Mamie Van Doren, just couldn't handle what I have to offer. Somewhere in Washington, DC, a clock chimes twelve. It's still 1972, and Lono has landed on the shores of America. This was my plan all along. First Hoover, the queen who thought he was a pawn who thought he was a king. My lawyer will be along, any moment, with a phalanx of ACLU Jews and a pair of comically oversized bolt cutters to set me free. My old friend Eagleton, warped by electroshock and the forces of CREEP, will torpedo McGovern. Moloch will rage and burn and with one last streak of soot and fire across the middle of America collapse into torpor, only to rise up in Japan, in China, in Indonesia. The six-fingered hand will stiffen and die with its fingers on the neck of the liberal intellectual elite. And I will steal Nixon's brain, just as Hoover tried to steal mine, and save the world from Cthulhu.

Yes, indeed!

Absolutely.

Any minute now. My attorney, the brown buffalo, a sacred symbol as potent as Lono's white sails, will be along any minute now.

Any minute now . . .

NINE

Revolution Number Nine . . . Number Nine . . . Number Nine . . . In the Belly of the Beast,
Eating Hors d'Oeuvres as They Come Rolling down the Chute . . . And We Won't Have
Richard Nixon to Kick Around Anymore . . . Last Call . . .

I have no idea how much time passes before the bald man, not my lawyer, not even Smitty, comes to rescue me. Comes to rescue Hoover, that is. The old eater of dogs, Nixon's dragon himself, stands over me. This is the first time I've ever been this close to him, and it is easy to see why the man has the reputation he does. This is one scary badass, projecting waves of fear before him like a crawling chaos. He looks over at where Hoover's carcass must be, and he says the sign. "McGovern wears little pink girlie panties." The countersign was one of the little bits of Hoover inserted into my gray matter during the procedure, so I know how to respond, and I do. "And Jane Fonda wears boxer shorts."

"Congratulations, Director Hoover," the bald man says. His voice is higher pitched than you might expect, yet melodious. He could possibly have a career in radio, should he ever tire of this game. "So, your body expired during the transfer?"

"And Lono with it, the reprobate."

The bald man smiles and reaches behind his back to withdraw a snub-nosed revolver from his holster. Two taps to Hoover's head. My heart should leap with joy! Finally, the old tyrant got what he so richly deserved, and at the hands of a right-wing enforcer. But

Hoover really did love this country, and our connection was in its own way as intimate as the one the fungus of Yuggoth had granted me back in Arkham, and plus, the man thought he was killing *me*. It is reckless; won't someone talk one day? An FBI corpse caulker or a black-bag man looking to make a publishing deal with Random House? "Yeah, man, they had Hoover all laid out, garters and everything. It wasn't a heart attack, no matter what was on the front page of the *Washington Post*. I know; I was the one with the spackle, the guy who had to mix gray paint and flesh-colored makeup till we got it just right." But I suppose the bald man has a plan, and I am right, because a moment later he tells me what it is.

"Thank you, Director Hoover," he says to me. I hunch my shoulders and stick out my chin in the hope of passing as an alien in my own body, someone awkward with limbs longer than a piglet's. "Now, if you don't mind, I'd like to be alone with you . . . uh, the body." Then another flash of borrowed memory— Hoover was so confident that he had finally mastered the Mi-Go brain canisters that he'd made a bet. The bald man would get to fuck the skulls of any dead bodies the process left behind. Not the first, of course. They say Johnson did the same to Kennedy, while his corpse cooled on the tarmac. Still, I snicker as I collect the canisters. This guy's packing a .38 in his pants, is he? Just the sort of information that might need to be subtly leaked to the press as a psy op against this raving monster.

"I presume a car is waiting for me outside, and that you have made the necessary arrangements?" I ask the bald man, but he has no eyes for me. He's only interested in Hoover's corpse. His hands go to his belt. His breathing grows husky. I take my Mi-Go brain canisters and the little spaghetti-strainer setup, put them into the black bag by Hoover's body, and run.

I don't know everything that Hoover once knew. I don't know the names of State Department Communists or what really happened at Roswell or where in our national parks the Black Power movement conspired with hippies to interbreed marijuana plants with heroin poppies, but I know the basics of the plan, and why the bald man is in on it. The Freemasons are making an end run around the various cults infesting America, unspeakable and otherwise. Baldy was in deep—he sold his soul a dozen times over, and not even always to the highest bidder. When he got over his childhood fear of dogs by tackling one as it charged him and tearing out the dumb beast's throat—losing five of his own teeth in the process, mind you—he did so in the name of Baphomet, the secret god of the Masons. Hoover "rode the goat" long ago and claimed an easement on the bald man, superseding Nixon's claim. The bald man, who did so much of Nixon's dirty work, like taking out Leary on the astral plane and fixing the White House plumbing, is bound by geas and contract to turn against the president. But he isn't happy about it, and is furiously exorcising his frustrations on Hoover's brain box.

Me, I have my own mind in my own body (thanks once again to the massive quantity of psychoactive substances I've consumed over the years), two examples of exquisite alien technology in my hands, and a car waiting for me outside. I can't help but notice that the driver is a broad, flat-faced fellow who, as he waits for me, sits with one hand leaning out the window and five fingers drumming against the Detroit steel of the driver's-side door. Five fingers, while his thumb rests in the trough of the rolled-down window.

"Are there any normal fucking people left in the world?" I demand. I smack one of the brain canisters against the roof of the car.

"You'd know better than I," the driver says. He's a Cannock, of course. It's my old friend Mac. I recognize him from the diner. He still has a bruise on his head. "Wouldn't you, Dr.—"

"Mister. Mr. Hoover."

"Whatever you say, chief," he says as he gets out to open the back door for me.

"Yes, whatever I say as *FBI* chief. You know I'm Hoover, right, in Lono's body? It's very important that you understand that, because we're on a mission extreme in its peril and importance. Not the sort of thing you'd want to be driving a reporter to, not even in this Moloch-fueled monstrosity."

He tips his hat and waves me in, his freakish hand waving like a scuba diver's webbed flipper. As I slide into the back seat of the limo, I notice something else disturbing. The small bar is entirely empty of any alcohol. There is sufficient glassware for a senator's daughter's wedding and even a bucket set into the armrest for champagne, but not a drop of any actual, God-blessed booze. The privacy guard is up, so I bang on it. "Hey, hey! The bar is dry back here!" I shout.

"FBI director's orders," the chauffeur says. There's an intercom system somewhere, but I can't be bothered to figure out which button does what so I keep shouting. "That's madness!"

"Hey, chief, are you 100 percent sure there isn't some vestigial Lono in you?" he says through the intercom.

"As a matter of fact, no. You know what they say; each body part has a will of its own. The brain just thinks it's the boss, and the hand, and the eye, and—"

"And the . . ."

"And the liver. Anyway, this body," I say, touching myself, trying to play up the foreignness of it all, "it has remembered cravings. It's been abused so long its needs are practically hardwired into the nervous system. The vehicle in which I ride needs whiskey, damn it! Now drive me to the nearest and skeeziest early morning bar now, before I crack your head open and eat your pineal gland!"

"Wait, by *vehicle*, do you mean the limo, or do you mean the body—"

"Just drive!" I slam both palms hard against the privacy barrier, and we are off. This being Washington, DC, half a block later we find a decent-enough bar. It's the usual sort of place that at one point probably attracted a better breed of clientele than ten a.m. drunks and doctors of journalism—a dark, oaken bar, clean glasses, a single bartender with sufficient dignity to nod once when I enter, even a jukebox and some taxidermy on the walls. I rush in and demand a Heineken, two Wild Turkeys, and a glass of grapefruit juice—the bartender shrugs and says that they're out of juice. A fish, stuffed and mounted behind the bar, stares at me, begging me to drink quickly for the sake of Innsmouth and the Deep Ones. God, that bastard Hoover. Genocide right off our own shores. The bartender offers me a small bowl of limes instead. This bar has definitely seen better days, I notice, as I give the stool I'm sitting on a spin. I had a fantasy that my lawyer would be pacing this bar or huddled up by the pay phone, shouting demands for my immediate release until he ran out of dimes. But there can be no rage in such a place; this is the pit of the noonday demon, keeping his own chronic buzz on with a steady supply of that basest of sipping liqueurs—the fermented souls of former bureaucrats, unseated civil servants, disgraced lobbyists, and current city-government officials. Is that the mayor of Washington, DC, masturbating in the shadows, so close to power and yet so far? Even the beer is warm and flat, like medicine.

My lawyer is surely in a rage if he's conscious, but he's probably trapped in a piss-stained holding cell fighting for his life to keep his shoes on his feet, bellowing with every haymaker, bobbing and weaving, but he's surrounded, and the other inmates are used to working in concert. They've had to share the single stainless-steel toilet jutting out of the far wall for three days and three nights already. And Smitty, he's long gone, likely half-dead of dehydration, so far from his ancestral waters, or stomped to a fishy pulp by that police horse. And then there's Betsy. Betsy did her work, for Hoover and for me. If the bald man didn't do her before coming to free me, she's probably already been sold to the Saudis for a sex ring. Too bad I'll miss it.

I finish my round and realize that I have no money. There is a pay phone in the corner though, so I take a chance and call my editor, collect. The conversation is extended, one sided, and brutal. I would have thought that his executive assistant would have handled the incoming faxes, but no. With a five-page blank in the feature well, the editor made the error of grabbing what I'd sent right off the top of the tray of his industrial Mojo Wire—those five pages being from *Unspeakable Cults*. Guttural Latin and Aramaic and languages older than human tongues spill out the receiver. Even a shrieking editor usually sounds tinny and far away on a pay phone, but now his voice is within me, reverberating in my very bones, attempting to once again reprogram my brain in direct competition with Hoover, with bourbon, with my own sense of holy mission. I don't so much understand the words—well, except for "deadline" and "kill fee" and "you smegma dump"—as I simply consume them. This is not the season of Lono, the god of peace. Now is the time for work to be done. It is the season of Kü, god of war. I realize I'm not going to be getting any cash from my editor—how does one even say Western Union in the language of the Elder Things, and could those words mean anything other than me, a god coming from the burning mouth of the setting sun, in a union with a once-formidable enemy, to slay a great evil? I'll need a presidential pardon from Nixon to forgive my tab and also the stuffed marlin on the wall. I drop the receiver and run at the bar, vaulting it easily. The editor's howl of *Tekeli-li! Tekeli-li!* drives me on. I wrestle the baseball bat out of the bartender's hands and jam its butt in his throat. Like an ax I hold it over my head and swing. Glasses sing as they shatter and the great mirror behind the bar back crumbles. The marlin atop the bar eats four or five shots before it finally falls from its display panel. Is that the mayor of DC, looking up from his frantic wanking, awed to see a man alive, a god with a great war club whooping and pounding the stuffing from the mighty fish? The head comes off fairly easily. Everything smells of chemicals and blood; my palms are raw and burning from my grip. I drop the bat, and as my editor finally regains the ability to speak English and shrieks, "Lono, you're dead! Dead for what you've done!" I place the marlin head on my own as a war helm, take another Heineken for the road, and leave the bar.

My chauffeur stumbles out of the limo when he sees me and salutes with his crazy, six-fingered hand, then rushes to get the door for me.

"Like the chapeau, junior?" I ask him.

"I have to say it suits you, sir."

'That's a good boy," I say.

In the car he lowers the window between us and asks, "Are you really going to wear that to meet with the president? Won't he . . . suspect something?"

"Doesn't Nixon always suspect something, ace?" I ask. "Isn't he essentially a paranoid schizophrenic along the lines of Joseph Stalin? And don't you know that the only man Stalin ever trusted was Hitler?" I finish my beer and let the bottle drop to the floor. The limo is on the bald man's credit card anyway, or, more likely, the card of some eighteen-year-old Georgetown coed he waylaid the night before. "Well, we all know how well that worked out."

"Huh?"

"We won! America won! The American Dream!"

"Well, all righty then, doctor."

I spy myself in the reflection of the tinted glass. "Maybe I'll leave my new totem in the car. It'll give me something to look forward to when I get back."

The appointment is at the Watergate, right on the river. The complex is monstrous, curvilinear, nearly non-Euclidean, its construction funded by the Vatican and its design the brainchild of Luigi Moretti, formerly patronized by Mussolini. It's a horrifying stack of offices, hotel suites, sprawling luxury penthouses for the power brokers, and leaky efficiencies for first-term representatives from Kentucky and New Mexico. Watergate East is leaky enough to be called the Potomac *Titanic* by wags with a better sense of meter than humor, and that's where I'm meeting Nixon for a sit-down discussion about the American youth movement. Maybe I should wear the marlin after all; I might need the gills. In the parking lot I decide against it.

One of Nixon's secretaries meets me at a bank of elevators. This is usually where I'd get some sour look or a gasp of astonishment, and that's even without my hair all matted from the ichors and preservation fluids, without days of unrest scratched forever into my features, without my usual inability to finish a sentence without descending into cement-truck grumbling, without sudden twitching movements, without the *axis mundi* aligning with my chakras. This one, a young fellow probably only six months out of Princeton or Miskatonic, doesn't even ask me what I'm a doctor *of*. He knows. I decide to let him know something else, once we're in the elevator.

"Hello. I'm here to kill Nixon," I tell him.

"We've been getting that a lot lately," he says. He has one of those reassuring faces, the kind that look good during a comforting nod. *Oh yes, do kill Nixon.* "We had a large brown man make it almost to the parking lot just this morning."

"Oh?" This elevator seems very slow. "Did he . . . give a reason?"

"Oh no, this man was entirely unreasonable. Built like a tank—well, if tanks had beer bellies. He was ranting and screaming about New Aztlán, demanding the president's heart to sacrifice to his winged snake god." He sniffs. "I have to say, despite all this, he smelled a bit better than you, doctor." He glanced up at the top of my head again.

"Secret Service took him out, I presume. Two taps to center mass."

"Oh no, we hired him on," the secretary says. "He was an attorney, came highly recommended. And with his connections with the Chicano community"—and that was odd, hearing a Republican flunky even acknowledge that the word *Chicano* was preferred these days, much less use it—"he'll be a good man to have on our side. Border issues are important to the president. We're worried about drugs in the inner cities, about illegal immigration possibly bringing down the standard of living for American workers, and of course anti-Hispanic sentiment is sure to be a problem going forward. It's crucial that we lay the groundwork for a united country as we enter a New Aeon."

"Uh . . ."

"Sir, do you have a tape recorder with you? A pencil and pad? Would you like me to fetch one for you?" The elevator stops, and the door opens into a reception area. "I have plenty of whatever you might like at my desk." He steps into the room and I follow.

"Do you happen to have any . . . fungus? From Yuggoth?"

"Yes!" he says brightly, and he opens the top right-hand drawer of his desk, where one might keep legal pads or a calculator or a Derringer. He digs though a small pile of brown wax butcher paper, but comes up empty. "Oh. We seem to be, um, fresh out." He opens the drawer on the left side, where there are indeed some legal pads and what looks like a pearl handle of a small firearm, but quickly closes it. "This is unusual. I'm very sorry, Dr. Lono." He glances over his shoulder, to the brief hallway leading to the room where Nixon supposedly is waiting for me. Where Hoover arranged for him to be killed by my hands and his will. Where, somewhere under Foggy Bottom, in the silt of the Potomac, the star spawn of Cthulhu stir in their sleep. In a room hoisted up to the sky on Molochian steel and concrete, its exterior stained with generations of His soot. So close to the Friendship Lodge of the Odd Fellows, on streets drawn with Masonic precision . . . oh Jesus, I'm rambling. Everything is everything. That's the real American Dream. Not the nonsense about success and individual achievement—that's a fantasy, or a daydream at best. An American Dream, the one written in the unconscious mind, that's what Nixon is. He's uncanny—universally loathed, ugly and twisted, yet at the very top of society, on a throne of bones atop a mountain of one billion bodies, thanks to the conflicts between a million nameless horrors, a thousand unspeakable special-interest groups, and a sacrifice in blood and fire of the North Vietnamese. And I digress.

"Lono," the secretary says. "Perhaps you should just see the president now. I'm sure"—his eyes dart back to the drawer where the fungi certainly isn't—"he's expecting you. I'm sorry I didn't have what you requested." He opens the left-side drawer again and pulls out a small pistol, the one with the pearl handle. "Would you like this instead?" He looks up at me, eyes wide like a virgin on her knees before her senior prom date. I would like it, I decide. It's a .32, with a nickel finish, probably S&W, looks well used. "It's from the Spanish-American War," the secretary chirps.

"Great. It should blow up in my fucking hand nicely," I say. I check the cylinder; it's loaded, all right. The bullets look new at least. I'm jittery enough that I decide not to put the gun in my pants. I can see the headlines now: FORMER JOURNALIST SHOOTS SELF IN GROIN. NIXON PLEASED WITH SPECTACLE, SURGES IN POLLS.

I loiter in the hallway, only for a moment. To remember life before this interview. What will the walls look like when I leave the room? What will my brain be like? Hoover, deep in my cerebellum, urges me to kick the door to Nixon's office in and fire at any gray blur I happen to see. Instead I try the knob. It's open. Nixon calls for me to come in.

"Hello, Dr. Lono," Nixon says with the sort of forced cheer one offers one's childhood confessor ten years after the buggery ends. He's at his desk, almost curled up in a chair too large for him. If he notices the gun, his face doesn't betray that fact. It doesn't betray any facts. Nixon's a caricature of himself now, sweating profusely, jowls everywhere, like an editorial cartoonist's rendition of his famous televised debate with Kennedy back in 1960. His eyes roll like marbles from the gun to the bag to my head, then back to the bag. "Black-bag job, is that it? And son, if you're going to meet with the president, even if just to assassinate him, couldn't you at least bathe? Run a comb through your hair? Put on a new shirt, perhaps. Be a mensch." He coughs in his fist and says, "If this is a legitimate interview, will you tell your readers that I used a Jewish word correctly? Or are we going to talk football?"

I point the gun, cock the hammer. "First question—why Cthulhu?"

And then Nixon laughs. Not a rueful laugh or a sardonic chuckle. A real guffaw. "Oh Lord, Lono. You don't start with a softball. You think I chose to bind myself to Cthulhu? Do you think children choose to die of cholera? Didn't Hoover brief you?" He glances at the bag again.

"Hoover's dead. I inherited the bag—"

"And its contents. Have you familiarized yourself with their use?"

"Sort . . . of."

Nixon gets up from behind his desk and walks over to the conversation pit—a loveseat, a small but comfortable chair, and a coffee table—in the corner of the room. "Come, come. Let's have a drink and talk." Nixon opens up a globe of the world and pulls a crystal carafe with a glass stopper from within. He pours two glasses and takes a drink. "It's fine, see. You can drink straight out of the bottle if you'd like." I would like, I like indeed. I take the couch and put my bag on it as well so Nixon can't sit next to me. He takes the chair.

"I was born and raised a Quaker, you know. My flesh trembleth for fear of thee—I stand in awe of thee. I shudder at the conscious-ness of thy presence." He drinks. I drink. "The Psalmist," he says. "The best of the writers of the Bible. I live in fear, Lono. Fear of failure, fear of success. There are two ways out, as I see it. Win it all, or end it all."

"And you want to win it all. A fifty-state sweep of the election. And usher forth a new age. R'lyeh will rise! The stars will fall from the sky, and Cthulhu will reign triumphant."

Nixon peers at me for a long moment. "I'd hoped, my friend, that you would be more perceptive than all that. You're a journal-ist, a trained observer. You're Lono, a god whose existence predates the earth itself. You're a doctor. You have to be a smart fellow to be a doctor. There's no pulp-fiction island going to rise; it doesn't matter to Cthulhu whether I win fifty states or am dragged out of the Oval Office in disgrace and humiliation." He just looks at me. I seriously contemplate shooting him through the head right now. The gun feels good in my hand. Cool. The brandy he poured us is substandard. I suppose there is a war on; costs have to be cut.

"Here's where you are wrong, Lono. Cthulhu's *been* reigning. There is no age of triumph to come, this is as good as it gets!" Nixon flings his arms wide, spilling some of his own brandy. He quickly licks some of the splatter from his fingers. I'm tempted again to shoot him. "What do you think is wrong with the world? Is it us? Human nature? Of course not. Even you, you're a wild man. Wouldn't a Freudian psychoanalyst say that you have an overdeveloped id? Aren't you promiscuous, a drug abuser, a betrayer of women? Don't you wish the world were just a bit less civilized so that you could pull iron and kill whomever you liked?"

"I thought I was here to interview *you*, Mr. President," I say.

"Interview me, kill me, keep me from a sweep. It's all the same, as none of it matters. This is the point, friend. Do you think I'm not aware of my own liabilities, as a statesman, as a person? Regardless, I am the level-best single individual to lead this country. You've seen those antiwar protesters? Those hippies? How many of them are waving around copies of Mao's little red book? How many millions of people has Chairman Mao starved to death, tortured, killed—"

"And you made overtures to Chairman Mao!" I say.

"I did!" Nixon blurts out. "And . . . he's a nice fellow! We smiled and joked with one another. Told a few off-color stories. I'm glad my wife wasn't sitting in on our meeting. He's just as nice as you or I. You're an ethical man, after a fashion. That's why you oppose me. But if you had your hands on the reins of power, you'd slaughter a world, Lono.

"Captain Cook! He was to be Lono too. And now look at Hawaii, look at the people he encountered. And they were the lucky ones; they killed him. They ended up part of the United

States of America. You should see what those frogs did to Tahiti. The explorer and conquistador Cortés was confused with Quetzalcoatl . . . or perhaps he truly was that winged snake god, come to ol' *Mejiko* to deliver a reckoning.

"We're all gods, Lono. If we're not omnipotent, it's just because of the competition. If any one of us really put our mind to it, we could find out all the occult secrets, or rediscover them, and conquer the world . . . destroy it if we like. Isn't that the American Dream in the end: to get whatever you want because you want it more than anyone else?

"We are all Cthulhu," Nixon says as he leans back into his chair. "And we have all always been. If I could convince the RNC to make that my campaign slogan, I would. They're afraid we might lose the Episcopalian vote if I do."

I raise the gun and point it right at Nixon's forehead. I half expect him to take it like a man, to sit calmly and dare me to pull the trigger. But he cringes, hides his face behind his shoulder, raises his knees. "Please don't shoot me! I don't want to die! I—I . . . I'm sorry, Dr. Lono, I truly am, but I am who I am. I don't want to have to kill all those Vietnamese, but I *have* to. I wish I didn't have any enemies, but I have lots of them. I wish the Negroes and the whites and the Jews and the Christians could all get along, but they don't and they won't ever." Finally he straightens out. "Someone has to be in charge! Of everything! No dissent, no sectionalist sentiment, no enemies!"

"You're right," I say. "Now open the bag, you pig-headed bastard." I push the barrel of the gun against his head, a school bully poking at the chess-club geek. But this time, I'm offering the answers to the test, not taking them. "Trust me, I'm a doctor."

The process is painless. Nixon is a different sort of man than Hoover. Nixon is a cringing coward. Nixon is ashamed of his body. Nixon wishes people could get to know him. Nixon lives in fear of revealing himself too much. Nixon began his occult studies in the hope of finding a method of raising the dead. Nixon almost succeeded. Nixon hated Checkers, the dog. Lono hates himself. Nixon seethed with resentment whenever he saw that damn dog. Nixon's alchemical experiments began with that damn dog. Nixon isolated the Essential Saltes of men and animals. Nixon knows where the bodies are buried. Nixon doesn't like getting his hands dirty. Nixon, for a moment, feels an electric charge at the possibility of living life in my body. Lono drinks to stave away the boredom of life. Nixon could fuck willowy young blonds who believe in free love and uninhibited self-caresses if he lived in my shell. Nixon worries about my credit rating. Nixon fears change. Nixon knows that change is inevitable. Nixon smoked opium in China. Nixon met a black dragon that looked at him with eyes of creamy jade. Lono wishes he could publish fiction, but without the patina of experience, the sentences just sit there on the page, lifeless and wilting. Nixon never met a Harvard man he liked. Nixon wishes he could strangle them all. Nixon runs his old election campaigns over and over in his head. Nixon dreams about his losses in California, his loss to Kennedy. Nixon felt no joy in beating Humphrey. Lono taunts death and puts himself in extreme situations to remember how to feel. Nixon wishes someone would strap down Spiro Agnew and torture him. Lono often thinks, *Maybe I should just kill myself.* Nixon doesn't know anyone who disagrees with him on this but can't find anyone to do the job. Lono surrounds himself with weapons in order to kill himself. Nixon's best friend is the bald man, but he's sure the bald man doesn't reciprocate his warm feelings. Lono seethes with every typo, every unpaid bill, every unreturned phone call, every kill fee. Nixon would make his own friends from spirit familiars if he could manage to gather sufficient will to summon one. Lono counts it as a victory whenever he wakes up and knows where he is. Nixon's first encounter with Cthulhu destroyed whatever was good and kind and fair about Nixon. Nixon taught himself how to fake it. Nixon comforts himself by imagining that his mother is still alive, and speaking to her, asking her advice. Nixon's first attempt to reanimate the dead ended poorly—*looming hideously against the spectral moon was a gigantic misshapen thing not to be imagined save in nightmares—a glassy-eyed, ink-black apparition nearly on all fours, covered with bits of mould, leaves, and vines, foul with caked blood, and having between its glistening teeth a snow-white, terrible, cylindrical object terminating in a tiny hand.* Lono is in pain every day and every night because blotter acid is easier to get one's hands on than Thorazine without a prescription. Nixon occasionally fantasizes about killing Hoover. Nixon considers it a rare victory that he is alive and Hoover is dead, but there is still a bittersweet quality to this victory—he wasn't the one to squeeze the life out of the FBI director. Nixon gets erect when he thinks of killing someone. Lono feels jealous of Senator Eagleton, who was strapped down to a table and given electroconvulsive therapy. Nixon credits this psychophysiological peculiarity with his ability to remain faithful to his wife. Nixon is very surprised to hear of Hoover's Mamie Van Doren trick. Lono wishes women liked him better than they do. Lono wishes he were a myth, white sails on the shore, someone important and meaningful. Lono feels that he is always on the sidelines, not quite intelligent enough to do something about world events. Lono thinks he is really going crazy this time. Lono says, ". . . Counselor," and tears the apparatus from his head and runs from the room, leaving Nixon swamped in a daze of memories that aren't his, and emotions that aren't quite human.

That's enough of that, eh? Downstairs, in one of the Watergate's hotel bars, I see my lawyer. I don't know where the gun is, but my lawyer is surrounded by angry busboys, jabbing a folding tray holder at them as they encircle and try to grab at him, so I go to help anyway.

"Oscar!"

"Lono!" I lurch forward at the sound of my own name . . . no, not my name, something else. A momentary identity I wear like a blanket over my head on a witch-haunted, black, and hideous night. But it's me; my lies are as much me as anything else. For a moment, it occurs to me that I am in Washington, DC, and that perhaps I should check in with my wife and son, whom I'd sent here just days before the start of this misadventure. But then I decide that reuniting with them can wait a little bit longer. There are other things I need to attend to. Serious business for serious professionals, and there is no one more serious or professional than my attorney and I. The busboys are more Oompa-Loompa than man. Outflanked, they scatter, and my attorney and I embrace.

"How did you get away from the cops?" I demand.

"I didn't, man. Made some bail. Met some Chicano dudes in the holding cell. They had some friends on the outside front me bail money," he says. "I'm going to have to do some favors for them. Board a boat full of white snow. That's why I'm here. To meet a guy about a guy, but the fucking kitchen is out of fucking grapefruits. Christ, Lono, the country's gone apeshit. Even the fucking busboys are voting for Nixon. Man, you should come south with me. It's not good here anymore."

"You know that the border ain't nothing but a dotted line, you fool. And anyway, it's over."

"Over?" my lawyer asks. He raises his hand to his temple, points a finger, and clicks his thumb. "Like that?"

"No, not like that. Let's just say that the road of excess leads to the palace of wisdom."

"You've got some funny marks on your forehead, Lono. Like little hickeys. What the hell were you doing up there?"

I shrug. "Saving the world. Nixon's not like he used to be. I got some of his mojo, gave him some of mine. He's a five-star fuckup now, a do-gooder doomed to self-destruct."

He grabs me and hisses in my ear, "The shit! He's a goddamned monster!"

"We're all monsters, baby. Gods and monsters." I kiss him on the cheek, like a real man does. Out of words, we go back to the bar, take a corner booth, and close it down at two in the morning.

TEN

The Long, Cold Winter of My Discontent, Redux . . . Heavier Weather . . .
More Strange Rumblings and General Weirdness . . . The Ghost of the American Dream . . .
The Ascendancy of the American Nightmare . . . Football Season Is Over . . .
I've Gotta Get Out of This Place, and It's the Last Thing I'll Ever Do . . .

Winter once again in Woody Creek, Colorado. It is just after midnight on January 5, 2005, and I was here when the fun stopped. They still call this the wee hours, and there is still nothing small about the hours between midnight and dawn. These hours last forever, each one as long and endless as the black gulf between the stars. As I search for the correct keys, the ticking of the clock slows along with the world's heartbeat, and the occasional hunt-and-peck tapping of my typewriter grinds to a lethargic halt. Each ponderous breath feels harder than the previous one. These are not wee hours; these hours are among the last in my life.

They also still call this the witching hour, and they are right. This used to be when I did my best work, under the cover of darkness. This was when I was strongest—when the whiskey and the mescaline and the pills coursed through my body, and my mind burned with a terrible righteousness and sense of indignation. But those days are gone. These days, I write about sports for ESPN's website. Ah yes, the Internet, eh? It made things like my trusty old Mojo Wire an archaic relic of a gentler age. And so am I. But never mind that! When the going gets weird, the weird turn pro, and I have certainly been both in my life. Ask anyone. They know.

They remember. They'll tell you that I was both weird and a pro. And now . . . Now . . . I'm just old. I am no longer Duke or Lono or any of the other pseudonyms I've used in my career. All that I am is a scared old man who lives in a constant state of pain and fear. Hoover and Nixon are always with me, ghosts at the base of my brain, reminding me of evils once so loathsome that now seem quaint. I didn't just find the American Nightmare; I took it home with me. But America kept growing worse.

The world has turned dangerous and strange once again, but these days, I am not dangerous enough or strange enough to save it. No, not this time. That is a job for younger men, but I see no one stepping forward to volunteer for the duty. There is something prowling around outside my front door, and though I have heard it many times in my life, I still don't know what it is. It might be a deer or a coyote or a big bastard of a bear, but then again, maybe not, because the darkness has a way of changing things. Darkness is Mother Nature's LSD, and instead of a wild animal, the thing on my doorstep could be Nixon or Hoover or even my old friend Professor Madison Haringa. Worse, it could be a Betsy. Whatever it is, my heart is filled with fear and loathing. I am unarmed, unarmored, and I feel naked against the cold, stark truth lurking in the dark.

The American Dream is still dead. Its ghost remains only in the minds of people my age. In another generation, not even its memory will remain. I thought we stopped the American Nightmare—me and Smitty and my attorney and everyone else involved in that little caper. I thought we'd prevented it from happening when we stopped Nixon's plan to win all fifty states. But if time is a cruel mistress, then she is also a lying bitch, because the time has come round once again. Signs and portents. Portents and signs. Lines within ley lines. The stars are right once more, and in his city far beneath the ocean, Cthulhu lies sleeping . . . but not for very much longer.

It happened just like Smitty said it would, far back in 1972 when we were racing to the airport and he had a head full of primo fungi from Yuggoth. The Columbine massacre. The attacks on the World Trade Center and the Pentagon on September eleventh. Those things have come to pass, and I know what is coming next. I may be old and bitchy and no more fun for anyone, but I still have great and terrible powers. I can see into the future. I can remember Smitty's visions. New Orleans will be devastated by a hurricane later this year, probably toward the end of summer. After that will come the tsunami, and everything else that Smitty predicted would happen. What was it Haringa said? Or was it Hoover? Or Betsy? I can't remember anymore, for I am old, and the pain medication I take for my hip leaves me groggy and unsure. And never mind that, because I digress. Whoever it was . . . one of those rat bastards told me that the cycle would start all over again. That they'd prime the psychic aether and make another attempt in 2012.

And so they are. It's already started. The American Dream is all but forgotten, a fairy tale we old ones whisper to our grandchildren when they come to visit. And the American Nightmare? Well, that pig fucker is back, bigger than ever and ready for business. And business is very, very good. I am reminded of what is perhaps my favorite passage of my own work, of how the sixties were a wonderful time, when the energy of an entire generation came to a head and we were all riding the crest of a high and beautiful wave. The time was ripe for change, but in the end, like all ripe fruits, things spoiled on the vine and turned rotten. Screw Las Vegas. Go up on a hill anywhere in the goddamned world, and look west, and you can very much see the high-water mark in the distance, that place where the wave finally broke and rolled back, revealing a horrible, tentacle-faced monstrosity called Cthulhu. It is coming. The stars are right, and I no longer need to ask, "How long, oh Lord? How long?" I've gotten my answer. The stars are right again. Welcome to the new dark age. The age of R'lyeh.

I am tired, and I no longer have the strength to fight the bastard. I don't have it in me. I can't reinvent myself anymore. Not after years of talk-show appearances and that Vegas movie that they finally filmed. No, it's too late for all that. Too late for one last misadventure. Now I'm just another member of the No More Fun Club. I have one final task to complete, and it's one I've contemplated since I was a young man. I once told Ralph that I would very much feel trapped if I didn't know I could leave this world by my own hand at any time. At sixty-seven, I still feel that way. I'm not trapped yet, oh no indeed . . . but I see the writing on the wall and the signs up in the heavens, and I fear that pretty soon, I *will* be trapped. And believe me when I tell you . . . I don't want to be here for the end. I've taken that trip once already. I think I'll sit this bus ride out.

Tonight, I began my final preparations. I ventured down into the basement and went through boxes of files until I found these nine missing chapters from my otherwise-exhaustive chronicles of the 1972 election. My publisher and I both agreed not to print them at the time, for fear of what we might unleash. Ye Gods, better to print *Unspeakable Cults* or pages from the *Necronomicon* than to print this stuff. We tried that once before, of course. I'd convinced my editor to publish excerpts from *Unspeakable Cults*, but the pressmen went mad as it was going to print and smashed all of the machines and then killed themselves. After that, Nixon had the pages suppressed. But once I'm gone, it won't matter anymore. So I'm packing up those nine missing chapters, along with this epilogue, and mailing them off to two young speculative-fiction writers, one of whom is an avowed communist and the other of whom is a vicious Libertarian. Mamatas and Keene. Brain-damaged geeks, both of them. Despite their differences, they seem to work well together. I sense in them a kindred spirit, much like my connection to Smitty all those years ago. I will mail them the unpublished chapters, and I think they will know what to do with them. Congratulations, boys. You've just been drafted.

After that, it's just a matter of wrapping things up and bringing them to a close. It shouldn't take me more than a month. Keep in mind, I am a professional, and even in this—especially in this—I will overcome and be triumphant.

My fingers slow again, growing numb above the keys. Outside, the wind howls and the darkness shrieks. I shiver. Why is it so hard for me to stay goddamned warm these days?

I think about my life and my literary estate, and smile as I light a cigarette, safe and secure in the knowledge that the world will know I was here. That it will have heard my roar. I think about the line of broken, beaten, battered, and bloodied editors I've left in my wake. I think about my peers. I think about my family and my friends.

I think about my sidekick. My partner. The one man who always stood shoulder to shoulder with me when the hellhounds were on our trail and the bullets were flying and the bastards came at us with sharp knives.

I think about my attorney.

My lawyer.

I bring my hands to my typewriter and type.


```
Feb 22 05
counselor


I am typing into the future—what little future
there is left. For although this is only Janu-
ary, I think that February twenty-second will
be a good day to do it. There's a certain magic
to that number. 222. It should give the occult
types and the conspiracy theorists something
to nod about.
     I look at it again, the date and that one
word. I think it's a fitting epitaph. I think
it says it all. And yea, though I am about to
enter the valley of the shadow of death, I will
fear no evil, for he will be there with me,
and he is the meanest son of a bitch in the
valley.
     Selah!
```